Sign up to Niel'
and receive a (
Arkship Countd

F

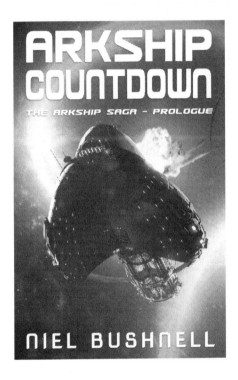

Visit **www.NielBushnell.com/Subscribe**
for more information.

THE ARKSHIP SAGA

Also by Niel Bushnell

THE TIMESMITH CHRONICLES

ARKSHIP OBSIDIAN

THE ARKSHIP SAGA - BOOK ONE

By Niel Bushnell

MAGIC
NUMBER
BOOKS

First published in 2017 by
Magic Number Books
www.magicnumberbooks.co.uk

2 4 6 8 10 9 7 5 3 1

British Library Cataloguing in Publication Data available.

ISBN: 978 1 9997128 3 9

For Diane, with all my love

'We are all reflections of a Fractured God.'

The Changed Time, Chapter 3, Verse 9
from *The Word of The Infinite*, Scribe Barrahaus III Edition

ESCAPE

'Warning, proximity alert.'

The voice was distant, isolated in a fog of echoes, just a single star of noise in a black nothing. He felt cocooned, surrounded and sheltered. Safe. The words repeated, luring him towards them. It was a woman's voice, cool and measured. There was no hint of fear or desperation in the words, yet he sensed the urgency in their message.

'Collision alarm. Collision alarm.'

The voice was louder now, closer, drowning his ears in a muffled claustrophobia. He felt afraid. Adrenaline surged through him, kick-starting his senses. He had to open his eyes.

'Brace! Brace! Brace!'

Light flooded his vision. For an instant, he saw a blurred shape rushing towards him, a giant mass of smoke and fire. Instinctively, he raised his hands to cover his face, just as the flaming object struck. The impact jarred him, ripping him to one side, filling his ears with rage, searing his eyes with white hot light, stinging his face as pin pricks of molten metal danced over him. Something tore at his shoulders, pushing into his skin. Straps? He was pinned down, he realized, held in place, in a chair. He felt as if he was spinning, twisting, falling, and his stomach lurched in response. He couldn't see any more – smoke filled the space in front of him – but he could hear a cascade of sound: twisting metal, churning and grinding, the crisp chatter of flames, a rhythmic beep tapping out an unnecessary warning. And over all the noise was the woman.

' . . . hull rupture. Stabilizing trajectory. Cabin atmosphere compromised. Initiating purge.'

There was a rush of air striking his face. The pressure increased, pushing on his ears until they popped, then he felt the air being dragged away from him, taking the noxious smoke with it. The gas cleared, and he coughed in relief. Blinking, he wiped his stinging eyes, letting them focus.

The first thing he noticed was the window in front of him: a circular dome of glass that was covered in a spider's web of cracks. As he watched a small metal appendage telescoped from somewhere beneath his chair and began to inject a gel onto the fractured glass. The segmented device continued its repair, covering each crack in turn, then disappeared out of sight. Cautiously, he reached out and touched the translucent gel with his fingertips. Already it was hard to the touch and had formed a neat seal with the damaged window.

Then he saw beyond the glass, to the hellish vision outside; a wall of blackness broken by lines of light that streaked past his window in jagged arcs. Something came into view, a giant shape that was dotted with fire. In between were fragments of metal and plastic, a sea of objects that collided with each other, bouncing off the window with frightening regularity. The view turned from the burning object, and fell into a cloud of red gas, smearing the window with ochre ash. Then, as the gas cleared, the rotating vista slowed, and the lines of light became dots, fierce pinpricks of white and blue and yellow against the blackness, and he realized they were stars.

Space! He was in space. He gasped, panic overwhelming him. He pushed back in his chair, his legs scrambling to retreat to safety. But there was nowhere to go. He was in a tiny spherical capsule; not much larger than the chair he was strapped into. The curved walls were lined with a cream-colored padding which had come away in places to reveal the metal structure beneath. In front of the chair was a small display screen with a carousel of numbers and statistics that flashed impatiently. He ignored the screen and focused on the exposed metal skin of his world. He reached out: it was hot to the touch. Something outside banged against the surface, three times in rapid succession.

'Hello?' he said. No one replied. Another bang came, this time from the opposite side.

'Is someone there?'

'Hull collisions.' It was the woman's voice again, louder and clearer, as if she was standing behind him. 'We are passing through a debris field. I am adjusting course to compensate.'

'Who? Who are you?' he asked, startled. 'Where am I?'

'You are in a lifeboat. Please try to remain calm, you may have a concussion.'

'A lifeboat?'

'Lifeboat SA-0709, out of the *Ark Royal Obsidian*. I am the on-board computer system. We have sustained damage during our escape from the battlefield, but life-support remains intact. I am currently searching for a safe harbor to dock with. Once I have a confirmed our flight-plan I will inform you. In the meantime, is there anything you need?'

'N–no,' he said. This was too much to take in.

'How do you feel?'

He stared at the view, not answering. As he watched something fell past the window, something that looked like a person.

'I cannot find your I.D. chip,' the female voice said, it's tone almost conversational. 'I am unable to access your medical records without it. What is your name?'

The question was like a knife to his brain, and a dread realization followed it.

'I . . . I don't know,' he said, feeling terrified. How

could he not know his own name? Then, as he searched his memories, he realized he knew nothing about himself. His family, where he lived, everything up to the moment he'd opened his eyes inside the lifeboat, it was all a sickening empty page. 'Who am I?'

'I have no information,' the computer responded.

'What did you say earlier?' he asked desperately. 'You said something about Ark . . . Ark Royal . . . ' He couldn't remember.

'The *Ark Royal Obsidian*,' the computer said. 'That is where you came from. It is the capital arkship of the royal family of Kenric. It was attacked earlier today by an unknown force.'

He searched his mind for some recollection, but found nothing. 'Show it to me.'

'I do not understand your request.'

'Show me the *Ark Royal Obsidian*,' he demanded.

'I'm sorry, the visual display system has been damaged. I have audio communication available. Would you like that?'

'No. Show me the *Ark Royal*. In the window.'

The computer paused. 'I am trying to preserve our fuel until a safe harbor can be found. I would not recommend unnecessary maneuvers at this time.'

'Please, I need to see it,' he insisted.

There was a hiss beyond the metal skin, and the lifeboat turned, adjusting itself. After a moment, a vast structure inched into view, a beautiful curved body of metal and glass and stone that shone out through the debris field. The head of the ship was a massive structure of docking bays and sensors cut into the polished skin of the ship. Behind, the rounded hull divided and stretched into three elegant arms that housed the ship's engines, all dead, spewing dark smoke into space. Even at this distance he could tell it was vast. Tiny rows of lights marked its contours – windows, he guessed, hinting at the colossal scale of the vessel.

'The *Ark Royal Obsidian*,' the female voice noted.

Along the arkship's graceful body were the scars of impact craters that had torn into the skin of the ship to expose the interior decks to the vacuum of space. Fire dotted its length, eating into the damaged body of the ship. He didn't know why but he felt connected to that dying craft, and its loss filled him with remorse.

'Would it help to listen to the *Ark Royal Obsidian's* command frequency?' the computer offered.

'The command frequency?'

'It is the official channel for communication between the arkship and its support craft. We are unable to communicate on that frequency, but we may listen.'

'Yes, do it.'

The computer obeyed, and a static-ridden channel filled his ears.

' . . . still people in the aft section. I can't get to them.'

'ARO Command, *Demon Star*, are you away?'

' . . . too many of them. I need back-up! Please! Anyo–'

'–emon Star . . . I can see her. She's on fire.'

The voices overlapped, too many conversations to keep track of. He listened, watching this beautiful vessel being torn apart. A smaller craft emerged from the front of the arkship, trailing fire in its wake.

'That is the *Demon Star*,' the computer said.

' . . . Hunter One is on board the *Demon Star*,' the static voice shouted. 'All ships, defend the *Demon Star*, at all costs.'

The little ship cleared the mouth of the arkship and began to gain speed.

'–is *Demon Star* to ARO Command, we are burning up. We need–'

The voice broke off as the distant craft became a silent point of light, flickered, then faded into the background.

'*Demon Star* is down!'

' . . . was he on board?'

'–lost him. We lost–'

'–all remaining fighters, converge on my co-ordinates. Defend the *Ark Royal* at all costs–'

As he watched the battle, he felt a sickening dread fill his stomach. Those tiny points of light were people dying.

'Hunter One was the codename for Prince Halstead,'

the computer noted.

The name meant nothing to him. Frustrated, he tested his memory once more, trying to recall his own name, clawing to know this one tiny piece of information. In a flash, it came to him.

'Wynn,' he said, startling himself. 'My name is Wynn.'

'I have checked the population list for the *Ark Royal Obsidian*: I do not have a record for a Wynn, first or last name. I am sorry, my files may be damaged.'

Wynn settled into the padded chair, satisfied to know something about himself. In front of him the battle waged on. It was hard to see detail at this distance, just the explosions that tore into the *Ark Royal Obsidian's* hull. The static voices continued, increasing in tempo, their tone full of panic. They were losing this battle.

'Who are they fighting?' Wynn asked the computer.

'I do not know. There is another arkship nearby which appears to be giving tactical support to the attackers. The ship is not listed in my directory.'

Wynn thought about this as he scratched at his face. The skin about his left eye and cheek was uncomfortably tight. As his fingers touched it he winced in pain.

'Are you unwell?' the female voice asked.

'My . . . my face.'

'You have suffered severe burns to the left side of your head. Your nose is also broken. I have treated them as well as I can, but you must seek medical attention as soon as possible. I am negotiating with a Ciation medical ship to see if they will treat you.'

'Thank you,' Wynn said, his eyes drifting back toward the battle. The arkship was almost in two, its once-gleaming surface torn by a string of erupting bombs. The vast structure buckled, ripping itself apart as another series of detonations dotted its surface. The rear of the ship disappeared in a giant explosion which pushed the rest of the structure ahead of it. Wynn watched as the giant *Ark Royal Obsidian* crumbled in a cascade of explosions. As the fireballs dissipated all that was left was a tangle of debris. He felt rage build inside him, and with it came a desire, overwhelming and pure: revenge.

'I was on that,' he whispered to himself. 'I was on that ship.' He tried to picture himself there, but no images came to mind. He had no memories to cushion him. Was he glad to be alive? Had he struggled to survive? He didn't know. He was lost in his own mind, he might as well have been one of the bodies adrift in that maelstrom of metal.

'Warning, proximity alert.'

Wynn's eyes widened as he pulled himself out of his reverie. 'What is it?'

'The debris field from the *Ark Royal Obsidian* is expanding,' the computer explained.

'Can't you out-run it?'

'This lifeboat is not equipped with a high velocity thrust system. I have negotiated your passage and treatment on board the Ciation medical ship *Bardolino*, but we will not be able to dock with them before the debris field overtakes us. The *Bardolino* will not wait. I am sorry, Wynn.'

Out of the window Wynn saw the growing dots of metal chasing him. 'There must be something you can do!'

'I am sorry.'

'How long have I got?'

'The debris field will overtake us in eight minutes.'

'There has to be other ships nearby?' Wynn asked, 'some other survivors who might help me?'

The soothing tones of the computer's voice filled the confined space of the lifeboat. 'Only one vessel is in range, Wynn. I'm sorry, but it's not a Kenric aligned ship.'

'So?'

'This is a Kenric lifeboat, from the *Ark Royal Obsidian*, the capital arkship of the royal House of Kenric. You are therefore a citizen of the House of Kenric, so–'

'I realize that!' Wynn interrupted.

' . . . so, a ship this close to the battle that is not in allegiance with the House of Kenric must be in allegiance with the attacking ships.'

Wynn stared out of the window at the approaching wreckage. 'We don't have a choice. Plot a course for the other ship.'

The computer voice hesitated. 'I do not think that is

wise, Wynn.'

'Do it!'

'I have plotted a course . . . stand by . . . stand by . . . '

'What's taking so long?' Wynn asked impatiently after a moment of silence. 'What's happening.'

'I am sorry to say they are powering up their thrusters. They are moving clear of the debris shockwave, away from us.'

'How long till they're out of range?'

'They are already too far away from us. We cannot keep up with them. I am sorry, Wynn. The debris field is now five minutes away.'

Wynn stared at the cracked window. It couldn't withstand another onslaught. 'Turn us around. Turn the window away from the debris field and put us on a perpendicular course to it. I want as much speed as you can manage.'

'Course?'

'It doesn't matter,' Wynn barked. 'We just need to ride out the wave, that's all. Do you understand?'

'Yes, I understand, Wynn,' the computer replied, 'but putting us on a high-speed trajectory without a course will almost certainly leave you adrift without fuel far from any possible rescue.'

'One problem at a time,' Wynn said. 'We have to survive the debris field first.'

'I am uncomfortable with–'

'Do it, please. Turn us around and get us moving, now.'

Wynn heard the familiar hiss of the thrusters turning the lifeboat. The disturbing view changed as the vessel rotated. The oncoming debris field fell away. Ahead he saw a giant silhouette shape, cut out by the stars. 'What about that? Are they in range?'

'No. That is the other arkship I mentioned. It is far away. Its size can confuse the human eye, Wynn.'

'They attacked the *Obsidian*?'

'I believe so.'

Wynn took a moment to study its shape. It was an elongated structure, not as elegant as the *Ark Royal Obsidian*, with a rocky outcrop close to the front. 'It's built out of an asteroid?'

'Many arkships are.'

Above the stony structure was a series of towers, jutting out like claws scratching at space. The peaks of the two highest turrets were crowned by a circle of red light, which gave the impression of a pair of demonic eyes atop some dark insidious creature. Wynn watched it until, as the lifeboat continued to turn, the striking arkship disappeared from view.

'How long?' Wynn asked.

'One minute, thirty-eight seconds.'

'Okay,' he replied, reassuring himself. 'There's always the chance we won't be hit by anything, isn't there?'

'It's a possibility,' the computer admitted. 'Would you like me to run some simulations?'

'No.'

He took a deep breath, calming his mind as the seconds counted down.

Above his head a panel popped open and a face mask lowered into view.

'Please put this on,' the computer asked. 'In case of decompression.'

Wynn pulled the mask over his face. The material expanded, rolling over his aching skin until it had enveloped his entire head. The subtle machine noises of the lifeboat disappeared, leaving only the sound of his own breathing, a rasping wind in his ears, back and forth, back and forth. His heart raced, thumping blood through his veins. It must be time, he thought. As the seconds ticked by in pensive silence Wynn allowed himself a flicker of hope. The shockwave must be almost upon him. Perhaps he might survive this after all. Then an alarm sounded.

'Brace! Brace! Brace!'

LANDFALL

Wynn could taste blood, sickly sweet, coating his teeth. He coughed, trying to breathe. The red spittle coated the air mask over his face, marking his view with circles of crimson. A chorus of alarms sounded in his ears, confusing his senses. In front of him a flicker of brittle lights danced over the small display screen, each one desperate to convey its message of warning: HULL BREACH, PROXIMITY ALERT, LOW FUEL, CABIN PRESSURE FAILURE. The circular window was shattered completely, just shards remained around the perimeter, but instead of the blackness of space Wynn saw a foggy grey. Water dripped through the hole, collecting inside the lifeboat, but it was falling sideways, pooling against the interior padding close to his left arm. That's when he realized it wasn't the water that was sideways: he was.

'Computer,' Wynn said, his voice feeble. 'Where are we?'

No reply came.

He looked about him, trying to make sense of what

had happened. The dripping water gave away the presence of gravity; his lifeboat was too small to have an artificial system built into it. And liquid water meant it wasn't exposed to the freezing vacuum of space. So, he was somewhere else, somewhere inside. It was hard to think straight. He felt slow and dizzy, as if his brain wasn't working quickly enough.

'Warnnnn . . . ing . . .' The computer's voice barely registered, its words broken and labored. 'Air mask . . . deee . . . pleted . . . oxygen level at . . . zero.'

Panic set in as Wynn understood the reason for his fatigue: he wasn't getting enough oxygen into his lungs. He was suffocating. Wynn gazed at the restricted view, at the dripping water, at the new warning icon flashing at him from the display screen, and he realized he had to take a chance. He held his breath and pulled the mask away from his face. After a second's hesitation, he inhaled. The air was crisp, icy against the skin of his nose, but it was breathable. As his lungs expanded he felt light-headed and he closed his eyes, gripping the edge of his seat until the sensation eased.

Wynn blinked quickly, trying to focus as he looked at the display screen and found the hatch release mechanism. His cold fingers pulled on the handle and an explosive charge fired. The side of the lifeboat flew off, letting the collecting water fall out. Wynn looked out of the opening, down at a mountain of junk, half obscured in a blue-grey haze of mist. There was a low groan of metal, followed by a rumble that vibrated through his lifeboat, and the mound of debris began to move. The lifeboat fell with it, tumbling end over end, throwing sharp pieces of broken machinery in through the opening. Wynn closed his eyes, tensing as he rolled over and over, until the lifeboat came to a sudden halt. The collected junk rattled around him, coming to a rest at the base of the lifeboat. Wynn hit the release button for the harness that had kept him secure in his seat, and set himself free. He lifted himself out of the chair, realizing his legs were shaking under the effort, and climbed out of the now-upwards-facing hatch. Exhausted, he fell out of the lifeboat and rolled down a slope made of debris. He rested at the bottom, taking a moment to catch his breath as he stared around him. He was in a vast dimly-lit hanger, it's walls obscured by the icy mist. The space was filled with a sea of junk, heaped into featureless mountains that faded into the background until they were barely discernible in the fog. Was this the remnants of the *Ark Royal Obsidian*? he wondered.

'Hello?' he called, his voice reverberating through the space. The echo dissipated, and a deathly silence took hold. He picked up a length of twisted pipe and threw it over the closest hill of junk. It disappeared out of sight, rattling as it hit some unseen object.

Somewhere far away a low rumble began to grow. He felt it in his stomach before he really heard it, but soon the noise was unavoidable. It seemed to be coming from everywhere at once, as if the entire grand space was shifting. About him the wisps of fog swirled, pushed by the moving air currents as the sound of grinding metal grew. Wynn climbed up the slope, trying to gain height in the hope of seeing what was happening. As he reached the summit, there was a blast of air that knocked him off his feet. He turned to see a giant door had opened in the far wall. It was more than a door, he realized: the entire wall was retracting into the ceiling. With a thunderous grinding of debris, the door shuddered to a stop. An alarm sounded briefly, then Wynn felt an uneasy sensation in his feet. The mounds of wreckage began to tilt as dark voids opened in the sea of junk around him. Wynn stumbled backwards, falling with the collapsing metalwork. He recovered, ignoring the sharp objects pulling at his clothes, and saw the walls of the hanger begin to fall. He felt his stomach lurch, and he intuitively knew what was happening.

Gravity was shifting position.

Wynn hardly had time to react. The banks of rubbish were being pulled into new alignments. It took all his concentration to stay ahead of the churning expanse of dead spaceships. He managed to climb onto a larger panel and run along its length as his world rotated about him. He kept moving, dodging the raining shrapnel until he was almost at the far end of the panel. At that very moment, it began to tip upwards, rising into the air, taking Wynn with it. He clawed to the ragged edge, shifting position until he was resting on its peak. The wasteland of junk was spread out beneath him. It was as if it was boiling, its surface breaking apart, finding new resting places. The upturned panel swayed in the breeze, then it began to fall once more. Wynn twisted, found an exposed beam, and pulled himself on top of the falling shard. The panel landed in the rubble, throwing up a cloud of dust that turned the air brown.

Wynn laid there, gasping as he waited to see if the panel might move again. As the dust cleared he saw the giant door was now above him: the artificial gravity had turned ninety degrees so that the floor was now the wall, and the wall was now the ceiling. With a sickening dread, he understood what was happening: more debris was about to be dropped into the hanger through the open door. There was no time to think. Instinct took hold and Wynn scrambled for cover under the panel. He found a gap in the surrounding wreckage and dug himself under. There was a deathly rush of air and he realized that the new delivery had been dropped into the space. He tensed, waiting for the inevitable crush. Instead, he felt a moment of weightlessness, as if he was about to fall upwards, then the slow return of gravity pulling him down again. Hidden deep under the panel he couldn't see the falling detritus any more, but he pictured it slowing under the adjusted gravity, expertly guided to its resting place. He heard the soft landing of the metal, felt the panel above him groan and shift under the added weight. But it didn't crush him. He waited there for several long minutes, listening to the creaks and sighs of the wreck, then Wynn dug himself out.

He climbed up the newly sculpted hills and took in the vista. About him was more flotsam from the battle: twisted metal, broken plastic, leaking fluids that pushed noxious fumes into his nose. Columns of smoke rose upwards from the junk-field, marking the sites of small fires. He rested on the top of a mound, wondering how long he could survive in here. His mouth was dry, coated with dirt and dust, and he yearned for water but there was nothing to drink here.

The wind whistled over him, making him shudder. He began to explore, and he saw a rag of cloth not far away. Hoping to wipe his mouth, he scrambled towards it and pulled it from the mess. As he lifted the material from the debris a grey hand rose with it. Wynn let go, crying out as he stumbled backwards. He lay in the dirt, watching the scorched fingers. It hadn't crossed his mind that there might be bodies in here with him. He was about to stand and walk away when the fingers twitched. He rushed down to the hand and began to dig at the junk burying the body. An arm came into view, moving slowly, then a shoulder. Finally, a head emerged, a crop of dust-white hair with patches of dried blood on one side. Wynn pulled at the arm, turning the figure over, exposing the face of a woman in her early twenties. As he worked at the rubble around her legs he saw her eyes flicker open, register his presence, then close again. She coughed, clearing her throat, filling her lungs with air, then spoke softly. 'Thanks,' she managed before another fit of coughs took hold.

'I don't have any water,' Wynn explained as she sat up.

The woman pulled at a tube embedded into the tattered overalls she wore and placed it to her lips. Water poured into her mouth, running down her chin, cleaning the dust from her skin. She lifted the tube to her eyes and let the liquid clean them as well. Then, as she wiped her face on her sleeve, she offered the tube to Wynn. Grateful, he took it from her and drank, rejoicing in the relief of the water. The woman let him take a mouthful, then snatched the tube back and returned it to its housing on the chest pocket of her overalls.

'Don't want to waste it,' she explained as she stood, using Wynn's shoulder for support. 'Are there any others?'

'You're the only other person I've seen,' Wynn replied.

'We need to get out before they turn it again.'

'They?'

'Bone-Grubbers,' she replied.

The woman scanned the hanger, her head flicking in different directions. 'There.' She pointed to the distant horizon of the hanger wall.

'What is it?'

'A hatch. Our way out.'

The woman began to limp in the direction she had pointed to.

'Bone-Grubbers?' Wynn asked as he scrambled to catch up.

'Scrap dealers. They don't care much for anyone still alive in the scrap. They don't like claims on their finds.' She glanced at him. 'You haven't heard of them?'

Wynn shook his head. 'What's your name?'

'Bara,' she replied.

'Bara?'

'Sēbarā Delaterre, engineer, second class, but everyone calls me Bara. It's easier.'

'Were you on the *Obsidian*?'

Bara raised her eyebrows. 'Where else would I be from?'

Wynn hesitated. 'Another ship.'

Bara laughed wearily. 'Don't worry, we're on the same side.'

'How do you know I am?'

'It's obvious.'

'Is it?'

'Your accent,' Bara explained. 'Obvious Kenric. And

well-off too. Not one of the workers, are you?'

'I... I don't know,' Wynn confessed.

Bara stopped and studied his face. 'You don't know?'

'I can't remember. I can't remember anything. I don't know who I am.'

Bara laughed.

'I'm serious!' Wynn snapped. 'The first thing I remember is waking up in a lifeboat.'

'What's your name?' Bara asked.

'Wynn... I think.' Frustrated, he kicked at the debris, sending a tower of plastic tumbling down the slope. 'It's like a wall in my mind. There's nothing before it.'

'Do you know what happened to your face?'

Wynn touched his aching scars. 'No.'

'Okay,' Bara said, folding her arms. 'You're a Kenric, educated and well-off from your accent, about eighteen, nineteen?'

'If you say so.'

'Those clothes: a service team overall, but you're not part of the service division, I don't think.'

'Why not?'

'Your tunic underneath, it's far too good to wear for a cleaning shift,' Bara mused.

'I . . . I don't know. I can't remember.'

'It'll be shock from the battle,' Bara suggested. 'It'll come back in time, if we get out of here.' She turned and continued her awkward march towards the door.

'What happened to you?'

Bara shrugged. 'Was on an arkship, arkship exploded, now I'm on a junk barge.'

'A junk barge?'

'You really don't know anything, do you?'

Wynn tensed, staring at Bara. She was almost as tall as him, with an athletic frame hidden under torn overalls. Her hair was dark under the dust, black perhaps, short and unfussy. She was no more than twenty, he guessed, with large trusting eyes and a gentle nose. A small patch of blood marred her soft mouth, spoiling her full lips, but the dirt and grime couldn't hide her natural beauty.

'A junk barge,' Bara said eventually, 'is a scavenger ship. Bone-Grubbers aren't affiliated to any one family, they're go-betweeners. They pick off what they can, sort it, recycle it, sell it on. Anything they can't use they dump. And they can't use us, so, we're not wanted. We need to disappear before the spiders get us.'

Wynn looked at her. 'Spiders?'

At the same moment, he heard a distant clatter echo around the hanger.

'That's a spider,' Bara said, pointing to a sinister silhouette coming over the brow of a hill of garbage. A skeletal body rose over the landscape, supported by six appendages, jabbing at the mounds of metal, probing beneath the surface, searching. At first Wynn thought it was some sort of animal, then he saw the pistons that powered the legs, the cables that ran between the segments, the array of sensors and lights that formed a head atop its dark body, and he knew what it was.

'A bot,' he whispered.

As he spoke the spider turned its head, and the light of a dozen sensors locked onto him.

'Run,' Bara gasped, not waiting for him to respond.

Wynn fell after her, scrambling down the bank and out of sight of the bot. He followed Bara inside the carcass of a small shuttlecraft and hid with his back to the hull. Outside he could hear the synthesized warble of communication, distant at first, but getting closer and closer.

'It's hunting us?' Wynn gasped.

Bara grimaced. 'There'll be more than one of them. First step of the salvage: remove any organic material.' She glanced outside then ran through the upturned craft, sliding on its angled floor.

'Where are you going?' Wynn called after her.

She looked back, gesturing for him to follow.

Wynn skidded towards her, losing his footing as he came to rest beside her.

A dark shape appeared at the twisted opening in the wrecked shuttle. The bulk of the spider filled the space, then it lowered its legs and its sensor head peered inside. Wynn tensed, not daring to move. The spider's head, twisted, searching the interior, letting out intermittent chirps and beeps, and its dark mass turned towards Wynn and Bara.

A red laser light shifted and found Wynn's boot. Another beam joined it and began to snake up his leg. The spider whirred as it forced itself in through the opening, stretching out one of its appendages towards Wynn.

SORTING

The spider's arm lunged at Wynn. Instinctively, he ducked, rolling across the sloping deck to avoid the machine's extending claw. The spider adjusted its aim and turned towards him, stretching another of its appendages in his direction.

'This way,' Bara cried from behind him. Wynn followed her voice, avoiding another strike from the spider's talon. The spike embedded itself into the shuttlecraft's bulkhead, slowing the spider's chase for just a second.

Wynn ran after Bara. She had already crawled through an exposed service hatch and disappeared inside the craft. Wynn squeezed through the hole, sensing the recovering spider scratching along the deck behind him. As he retreated into the narrow space he heard the recognizable hiss of the metal arms telescoping after him, hammering into the hull, pulling at the panels. Wynn crawled on his belly, hardly able to move his arms and legs, squeezing past wires and cables, deeper into the dark unknown depths of the ship.

The spider's assault stopped, and, for a moment, there was silence. Wynn rested, trying not to make a sound.

A razor-sharp spike penetrated the crawl space, tearing through the metal like it was paper, and pierced Wynn's shoulder. He cried out, the pain unbearable. He could hear the spider making noises, whirs and chirps, as if it was communicating with its counterparts, then it pulled the spike out, ripping Wynn's skin. Desperately, he scrambled along the tiny space, ignoring his shoulder.

Another spike stabbed into the space, passing between his legs. It pulled itself out and struck once more, impaling the wall close to his foot. Wynn dragged himself away, adrenaline suppressing the pain, knowing that hesitation meant certain death. In the blackness, he felt his hands drop away from him and he began to fall through a void in the crawl space. He tumbled through the ship, hitting the lower deck, sliding along its tilted floor towards a large tear in the ship. As he fell through the fissure he could see the grey misty light of the hanger once more. He landed uncomfortably on a pile of rubble, tumbled down its slope and rested in its shadow, catching his breath. Already he could hear the spiders clawing over the wreckage, converging on him. Wide eyed, he picked himself up, looking for a new hiding place. There was Bara, just ahead of him, waving for him to join her. She was at the hatch of what appeared to be another lifeboat, similar to his own but much larger.

'Help me,' she said as he fell against the open hatch. She led him inside, to a circle of seats. There were three people in the chairs, sitting upright, their heads held back against the cushioned seats, but Wynn could tell that they were dead. Bara began to release one of the bodies from its harness, lifting it towards the hatch.

'Put this outside,' she barked, already working on the next corpse.

'What happened to them?' Wynn asked as he dragged the body away.

'I don't know. They're dead, that's all,' Bara said as she deposited another body at Wynn's feet.

He hauled the carcass outside, dropping it close to the first. He returned to Bara, asking, 'Why are we doing this?'

'Computer logic,' she explained as the last body fell from its chair. 'The spiders are looking for organic matter, so we give them some. They'll deal with this lot first, then come for us. It buys us time.'

Together they lifted the third figure out of the lifeboat and dropped it with the others. Wynn looked down on them, feeling remorse at these three lives, discarded like rubbish.

The sinister shape of a spider appeared on the crest of a nearby hill, and Wynn felt his body tense.

'C'mon, we don't have much time.' Bara said.

They retreated into the lifeboat and pulled the

hatch shut.

Wynn stared at the confined circular space. 'We're just going to wait in here?'

Bara shook her head. 'It looks to be in decent condition . . .'

'You think it can fly?'

'Maybe.'

'But those people, they died in here.'

Angrily, Bara replied, 'I know that! You've got a better idea?'

Wynn laughed. 'No.'

Bara turned away from him to peer out of the tiny window built into the hatch. 'They're coming,' she noted.

Wynn saw it too. The spiders were converging on the lifeboat. Each one collected a body and dragged it across the field of debris.

'Okay,' Bara whispered, 'we don't have long till they come back.'

She turned to study the control panel set into a column at the center of the pod. 'Main power is still online . . .' A low hum vibrated through the space as subdued lighting illumined the seats. 'Fuel seems fine . . . Ah.' Bara's face furrowed.

'What is it?' Wynn asked, feeling helpless.

'No oxygen left. They had to purge due to a toxin leak. By the time the air was clean there was nothing left to breathe. That's why our friends died.' She looked up at Wynn, her eyes full of despair. 'We're not going anywhere.'

'There's air in here now,' Wynn replied. 'We can breathe this for a while.'

'A while?'

'Long enough to get out.'

'It beats staying here,' Bara mused as she scrolled through the control panel screen.

'Can you get us airborne?'

'That's the easy part. If we want to survive we'll have to get out of this hanger, and we can't ram our way out of that door.'

'We need to wait for another junk drop?' Wynn asked.

Bara nodded grimly. 'When the door opens we launch . . .'

'And fly through the junk.' Wynn added.

'Making sure we're outside before the hatch closes again.'

Wynn laughed darkly. 'You make it sound easy.'

'It might just be possible, if not for those spiders out there.'

Wynn checked the small window: he saw movement from over the rise of junk. 'They're coming back.'

Bara nodded silently, checking the screen. 'I'll shut everything off. These walls should hide our bio-signals, unless they look closely.'

The power ebbed out of the lifeboat. The lights

dimmed, and the subtle moan of activity faded away to nothing.

'Keep watch,' Bara whispered. 'Let me know when that door opens.'

Wynn nodded, then turned back to the window, almost jumping at the sight of the dark mass of a spider directly outside the hatch. He froze, not daring to move.

The spider scanned the lifeboat, its sensors checking over the exterior. One of its lights flicked over the glass, catching Wynn's eye. Every nerve in his body cried out for him to retreat, to drop down and hide behind the metal door. But he did not dare to move. The light played over the glass, illuminating Wynn's face in its red glow. One of the spider's tendril arms reached out and scratched at the door, tapping, tapping. More spiders surveyed the scene, moving closer. One of them climbed onto the top of the lifeboat, its arms clanging against the hull. Wynn and Bara stared upwards, listening to the slow, deliberate banging from outside. Then the spider at the hatch began to claw at the door's release mechanism. Wynn watched as it gripped the handle and began to turn it. Slowly, it rotated, letting off a menacing whine. Wynn gripped the door from the inside, hoping he might be able to hold it, but it was no good. Air hissed around the seal as the door began to open. It turned slightly, revealing a narrow gap at the edge, and a metallic pincer tested the opening, inching its way inside. Wynn watched in horror as the mechanical fingers gripped the door, ready to pull it open.

Somewhere, a feeble alarm began to tone. Vibration resonated throughout the hanger and the spider's claw stopped. It let off a series of chirps and the other spiders responded, withdrawing from the lifeboat.

Wynn peered through the thin gap in the hatch and realized why they had retreated. 'The door's opening,' he shouted.

Bara worked at the control panel, bringing the craft to life. 'Get that hatch shut!' she barked.

Wynn pulled at the mechanism, satisfied when a red light pinged to confirm it was sealed. In the same instant, the lifeboat tilted as it began to rise from the wreckage.

Wynn rushed to one of the seats and strapped himself in. Bara did likewise, pulling the control panel towards her chair. The screen lit up with a representation of the hanger bay and the opening door somewhere above them. A dark mass was already coming through the hatch.

'More junk,' Bara noted.

'Warning,' a synthetic voice intoned. 'Collision alarm. Stand by for avoidance routine.'

'No!' Bara shouted. 'It'll hide us away from the junk. We need to go through it.'

'I am unable to allow that,' the voice commanded.

'The lifeboat would sustain too much damage. Your chances of survival are higher if I move us to a safe–'

'Computer,' Wynn shouted, 'override computer safety measures and give me manual flight control at this station.'

'Authorization?'

Wynn spoke without thinking, the information coming from somewhere deep within him. 'Command Obsidian, red nine T-H-Y axis, four, one, three, K.'

'Authorization confirmed.'

A screen rotated towards him, control and navigation icons already forming. He felt a trembling excitement as he began to punch a series of commands into the computer. *He knew how to fly this thing!* It was as instinctive as breathing.

He settled into the chair, letting his fingers trace his impulses into the computer's system.

The lifeboat responded, lifting, turning towards the vast door.

'Viewer,' Wynn demanded.

The ceiling above the chairs rippled with light as an image began to form. There was the distant door, half-open now, debris already plummeting through the gap. His chair tilted back so that he could see it, and, as his fingers danced over the control screen, Wynn felt that he and the lifeboat were one.

Bara watched as he navigated his way closer and closer to the vast opening. Beyond was the inky blackness of space, just visible in between the tumbling debris coming towards them.

'Collision alarm,' the computer droned.

'Acknowledged,' Wynn replied, already shifting the lifeboat with ease. On the screen, a twisted bulkhead fell past them, making Bara jump in her seat.

Wynn weaved through the field, avoiding the largest pieces of metal. From time to time smaller fragments pinged off the hull, tiny musical notes that rattled and chimed through the interior.

Bara stared at the approaching mass of plastic and metal. 'There's too much. We can't–'

'We can!' Wynn insisted, his eyes never moving from the view. His fingers glided over the control panel, maneuvering, guiding, shifting their flight. Ahead, the dark mass seemed to break apart, revealing a star-encrusted portion of space. Wynn responded and pushed the little craft towards it. At the same moment, a giant fragment of burned hull smashed into another piece of debris, and the gap began to close.

'We'll never make it,' Bara warned.

Wynn didn't reply, his entire focus was on the screen. He saw the multitude of spinning fragments and calculated the best course to see them safely out of the hanger. The lifeboat ducked, rotated, shifting like it was alive under Wynn's command. He could see space clearly now, and he allowed himself a brief smile of satisfaction. They were going to make it.

'Collision alarm.'

It came from the edge of his vision, a giant slab of scorched alloy and girders, whirling towards them. The vision of stars disappeared, and only metal remained.

Wynn reacted, but it was too late. There was a sickening sound as the debris smashed into the lifeboat. For a moment the lights flickered out, plunging them into darkness. At least the hull hadn't ruptured, he thought as he fought to regain control of the vessel. Then he felt a breeze passing over his face. He twisted to see a tiny hole in the skin of the lifeboat, the air rushing out through it.

Bara saw it too and released her harness. She fell from the chair, plummeted towards the ceiling, then tumbled across the hull towards the hole as the lifeboat span. She pulled out a small canister from her overall pocket and squirted it at the finger-sized hole. A plume of grey foam filled the void, expanding and hardening rapidly, until the damage was sealed.

'That'll hold for now,' Bara gasped. 'Can you get us out of here?'

Wynn checked the flickering viewer above him. They had stopped spinning and were moving towards the door again. The debris fell about them, but there was less of it now.

'Yes,' he replied, 'I think I can.'

He adjusted his flightpath towards the exit and engaged the thrusters, watching as their velocity increased, satisfied that they had enough momentum to carry them out now.

That's when the door began to close.

THE INFINITE

'We can't make it!' Bara cried. 'Pull up!'

'It's too late,' Wynn said through gritted teeth. He ran through every on-board system, diverting all the energy he could spare into the thrusters.

'You'll get us killed!' Bara cried desperately.

The door inched closer. The gap became smaller and smaller, just a line of blackness blotted with the last fragments of debris.

It was hard to judge distances from the viewer, the door was so vast, so Wynn relied on the numbers counting down on the control panel. But something else guided him; the same intuitive knowledge he'd tapped into when he'd taken control of the lifeboat, an innate confidence in his own abilities. He could make this, he knew it.

The gap was almost gone now, a black edge between life and death. Wynn made his final adjustments and let go of the control panel. There was nothing more he could do. He let his head rest on the padded seat as they flew faster and faster towards the closing door.

Wynn squeezed his eyes shut, tensing as they came upon the exit.

The lifeboat rattled, vibrations rocking it as they thundered through the gap. Behind them the door rumbled shut, expelling the last of the hanger bay's atmosphere into space. The lifeboat tumbled on the currents, spinning away from the Bone-Grubbers' ship.

Wynn opened his eyes, realized he was holding his breath, and exhaled.

Beside him Bara laughed, trembling. 'How the hell did you do that?'

'I don't know,' Wynn confessed. 'I just did it.'

They both smiled with relief, taking a moment to compose themselves.

'Rear view,' Wynn ordered. The screen flickered, and he saw the vast ship they were retreating from. It was a huge elongated mass, an ugly jumble of connecting hulls and modules. It looked ancient, as if it had been added to and built upon for decades, possibly longer. In front of the giant door was a funnel of wire netting that extended out into space. About it was the vast debris field of the *Ark Royal Obsidian*, its remnants caught on the net and corralled towards the hanger bay.

Bara checked her screen. 'Fuel seems okay, we should be able to find somewhere safe to go to.'

'If we can get oxygen . . .' Wynn added.

'Computer, how long will the air supply last?' Bara

asked.

'Approximately twenty-three minutes of usable air supply remaining,' the computer replied flatly.

Wynn turned to face her. 'Any friendly ports in range?'

Bara smiled. 'Computer, scan for a ship with this transcode frequency.' She keyed in a long number sequence into the control panel.

'Scanning,' the computer diligently replied.

'What are you hoping to find?' Wynn asked.

'When they gave the order to evacuate I couldn't get to the main hanger, so I took a lifeboat instead. *Lexica* was in the hanger and–'

'*Lexica*?'

Bara looked up, pride in her eyes. 'He's my ship. When I couldn't get to him I signaled for him to launch and get to safety. If he's okay I should be able to get him to come and pick us up . . . if he's not still angry with me.'

Wynn stared at her, quizzically. 'Your ship . . . is angry with you?'

'Long story.'

'Transcode frequency found,' the computer said.

Bara whooped in delight, slapping her chair. 'Okay, patch me through on an encoded channel.'

'The vessel requires an authentication code to initiate communication.'

'Pickles,' Bara replied with a grin.

'Contact made.'

A faint com channel opened, filled with distortion. 'I'm not talking to you,' a smooth male voice said.

'Yes, you are,' Bara laughed.

There was a pause, then, 'What do you want?'

'I need a pickup, and quick. We're running out of air.'

'*We?*' There was a hint of accusation in the voice.

'Who is this?' Wynn whispered to Bara.

'Lexica. My ship. He's an acquired taste. A bit highly strung.'

'I can hear you,' Lexica moaned.

'Sorry, Lex,' Bara soothed. 'That's Wynn, he's okay, you'll like him. Can you pick us up? Please.'

'I'm damaged, remember?'

Bara winced. 'I busted his starboard flank in my last fuel scoop. That's why he's angry with me,' she explained to Wynn.

'And you managed to tear off my docking array,' Lexica said. 'I am unable to operate the docking clamps from here.'

'Then we'll have to open it from the outside,' Bara said optimistically. Her entire tone had lifted since she had contacted her ship. She turned to Wynn. 'We do have spacesuits in here, right?'

He undid his harness and let himself drift into the center of the lifeboat. He searched the space and pulled out a space suit from an emergency locker. He found a second suit and threw it to Bara. She climbed out of her seat and began to pull on the survival suit. 'Computer, plot a rendezvous course with *Lexica* and take us to him.'

'I have control,' the computer announced as the lifeboat began a new set of maneuvers.

Bara closed her suit around her neck. 'If we survive this, what will you do?'

'Do?' Wynn asked as he pulled his suit over his head and joined the seal at his waist.

'I'm going home, 'Bara explained. 'I wasn't from the *Obsidian*, I'm just a hired hand, I've worked there for just over a year. My home is . . . it's a long way from here. I think it's time I went back for a while.'

'I . . . I don't know where I'm from,' Wynn said. 'I need to find out who I am. And I want to find out who destroyed the *Obsidian*.'

'Revenge?'

Wynn tensed. 'They should pay for what they did.'

'That's a big fight you're stepping into.'

'Maybe . . . I don't know . . . I don't have any answers. I wish I did.'

'Well, you're a top-notch pilot,' Bara noted. 'You're a high-ranking Kenric who knows a few command override codes. If you're looking for answers, I'd start on a Kenric arkship; that's where you belong. And that's probably the best place to start if you really want to fight back.'

'Then maybe that's where I'll go,' Wynn said with a determined smile. He paused, thinking, then added, 'Tell me about the *Obsidian*.'

Bara sighed nostalgically. 'A beautiful ship. You know it was the family's capital ship, don't you?'

'The family?'

'The Kenric family. They're the last royal House. You must remember the Prince?'

Wynn tried to hide his frustration. 'I remember nothing, really.'

Bara studied him. 'Okay, right . . . well, the House of Kenric, it's the last royal household, and it's ruled by Prince Thyred . . .' She thought for a moment. 'If he's still alive, that is. He was on board the *Obsidian*.'

'Did you know him?'

'Me?' Bara half-laughed. 'No, I didn't know him. We moved in very different circles. I remember once, he came down to the engine deck for a tour. We spent days cleaning it all, making everything perfect, and the old guy only spent fifteen minutes there. Hardly looked around at all. I don't think he was interested.'

'Who do you think attacked the *Obsidian*?'

Bara looked down. 'I don't know. It all happened so quickly.'

'But what about the Gilgore grid? Shouldn't that have . . .' Wynn's voice tailed off. 'I don't know what that is, it just came to me.'

'You're remembering,' Bara said.

'But I don't know what I'm remembering!' Wynn seethed. 'It's just tiny fragments that are coming to me, and they make no sense!'

'A Gilgore grid is a lattice of torium plasma that hugs the skin of an arkship,' Bara explained. 'It protects it from an attack.'

'Yes,' Wynn replied, sensing a recollection. 'Yes, that's right. So why–'

'I don't know!' Bara cut in. 'But they got past it, and the *Obsidian* is gone.' Emotion took hold of her voice and she turned away from Wynn.

He watched her, wanting to reach out and comfort her, uncertain what to do.

'Approaching target,' the computer voice announced. 'Be aware, there is substantial debris outside. I may have to make appropriate course adjustments during rendezvous.'

Bara composed herself and lifted her helmet over her head. Wynn did the same, feeling the rush of air on his aching skin.

'Com check.' Bara's voice filled his ears.

'I hear you,' he replied.

'Okay, got you here too. Clip up,' she said, pulling out a cable line from her waist belt which she clipped into place on a metal ring by the hatch.

Wynn followed her lead, and braced himself against the hull.

Bara's voice radioed into his helmet. 'Computer,

decompress the lifeboat and open the hatch.'

'Decompression is a dangerous procedure and should not be undertaken without the appropriate training and precautions. Are you sure you wish to continue?'

'Yes,' Bara replied impatiently.

'Decompression can lead to death. Are you–'

'Yes! We know what we're doing.'

'I understand,' the computer replied. 'Decompression begins in ten seconds.'

Bara shook her head. 'Safety protocols will get us all killed.'

The computer finished its dispassionate countdown and Wynn heard the noise of pumps removing the air from the compartment. After several long minutes, the door light changed to green.

'Decompression complete,' the computer announced.

Wynn turned the hatch lock and pushed the door aside. The view caught his breath. In front of him, framed by the glittering starfield, was another spaceship, turning slowly so that its contours caught the light. Around it was the fragments of other ships, drifting in a collective orbit.

A surge of dread and vertigo poured through him, forcing him to grip the edge of the hatch. *Had he been on a spacewalk before?* His fear suggested that this was a new experience, but he had no way of knowing. The uncertainty frustrated him, only adding to his tension.

'Are you okay?' The voice was Bara's, coming from his helmet's speaker.

'I'm fine,' he replied, realizing he was breathing hard. He tried to calm his lungs, closing his eyes until the dizziness subsided. When he opened them again Bara was by his side, her helmet's visor close to his own.

'You don't look so good,' she said.

'I'll be okay, just need a moment.' He inhaled deeply, held it, then took in the rotating view again. The ship hung in a swarm of debris, all of it twisting and turning, bouncing off each other and finding new trajectories. And the light! The light was dazzling bright, casting hard shadows over the pitted hull in front of him. It was a modest sized craft with a flattened central body behind two elongated wing-like sections that pointed forwards in the direction of flight. The lights of the bridge windows sat between and above the two wings, giving off a warm yellow glow that illuminated the copper-colored hull. Along its length were the obvious signs of wear, tear and repair, and the entire starboard flank was scarred with long grooves that dug into the metal. An array of blackened engines bulked out the rear of the ship, making it look unbalanced, as if it was ready to blast away at any second.

'There he is,' Bara grinned. '*Lexica*. We'll have to jet over to the docking hatch and see if we can open it from the outside. Do you want to wait here till I'm done?' Bara offered.

'No, I'm better now. Just dizzy for a second.'

She hesitated, watching him. 'You sure?'

'Yes, really. I'll be fine.' He forced a smile, raising his hand in a 'thumbs up' gesture.

'Okay, great. Just follow my lead.' Bara stepped out of the hatch and her suit began to propel her towards her ship.

Wynn watched her go, then took a step forward, his boots poking out over the threshold. Beyond was nothing, just empty space and dead spaceships. He unclipped his safety line and pushed himself out of the hatch.

Immediately the systems of his suit took over, the tiny backpack steering him forwards. A glowing target appeared on the inside of his visor, locked onto *Lexica*'s docking hatch. There was nothing he needed to do, just relax and wait for the brief journey to be over.

'Still okay there?' Bara asked.

'All good,' Wynn replied. The nausea had subsided, and he felt better now, well enough to take in the scope of it all. He could see the island of metal, turning slowly, revealing its underside to the light. About it, small pieces of wreckage drifted, and here and there were the tiny shapes of bodies, frozen in their last desperate grab for life. He felt minute, insignificant next to this vast silent graveyard.

Wynn looked away, feeling like he was defiling something sacred. He turned to the light, feeling it's warmth on his skin. His eyes narrowed, momentarily blinded as his visor adjusted to filter the brightness, then he could see again.

'Ah!' he cried.

'Wynn? What's happened?' Bara asked, her voice broken by static.

'It's . . . it's . . .' Wynn struggled to put into words what lay before him. There, against the darkness of space was a snaking line of pulsing light. At first, he thought it was two glowing circles, one larger than the other, but then he saw that they were one continuous, twisted form, a sinuous line of kinetic light that seemed to bore into his eyes, even with the visor's adjustments. 'It's . . . beautiful.'

He heard Bara chuckle over the radio. 'Yes, I suppose it is. You really don't remember anything? Not even that?'

'What is it?'

'It's called *The Infinite*,' Bara said, her voice low. 'It used to be a star, just like any other, until about two hundred years ago. Then that happened.'

Wynn couldn't take his eyes off the hypnotic view. 'What could do that to a star?'

'There's lots of theories, but no one really knows. But whatever happened, it created a black hole at the center of The Sun and destroyed every single planet in the solar system. There's nothing left now but rocks and gas and dust.'

Wynn felt a wave of sadness overcome him. It was as if that strange sight was looking back at him, communing with him, filling him with sorrow, and he had to look away.

The ship came into view again, a vast wall of metal. His visor counted down the distance to the hatch until his hands touched the surface.

'Made it,' he said to Bara who was resting next to the docking hatch's entry panel.

'Okay, good. I think the mechanism is intact, but the com lines to *Lexica* are severed. I should be able to . . .'

The hatch turned slightly, then it began to slide into a recess in the hull. A soft bellow of released air pushed past them, rattling his suit, then silence once more.

The interior was hidden in darkness until Bara shone her helmet light through the opening. 'Funny . . . internal power is supposed to kick in when the hatch is triggered. Maybe that's broken too.'

She pulled herself through the opening and disappeared into the ship. Wynn drifted inside after her, glad to be out of the inquisitive stare of The Infinite. He switched on his helmet lights and followed Bara along a short corridor that led to a wide equipment store. Junk floated in front of them: tools, equipment, clothing, paper. He pushed them aside, watching as they floated away from him and ricocheted off the walls.

'No grav either,' Bara noted, as if she was making a mental repair list. 'Lexica? Can you read me?'

The ship did not reply.

'This is gonna a be a bigger job than I realized,' Bara moaned as she powered up a small console built into the wall. She scrolled through a series of options, then the docking hatch began to close. Light flickered overhead as a second interior door sealed off the connecting corridor and air started to fill the room. After a few seconds, the control panel beeped and went dark. The dim lights above their heads died as well, leaving just their helmet lights to guide them.

'Power overload,' Bara sighed.

Wynn waited in the darkness as she set to work. Power returned, and the lights overhead blazed into life. Artificial gravity dragged the floating junk to the floor, and Wynn stumbled as he found his balance. The air pumps hummed as they began to work again.

'There!' Bara explained. 'First job done. We should have coms now as well.' She pressed a button on the control panel. 'Lexica, it's me. Can you read me?'

'Yes, Bara,' the ship replied. 'I suggest you make your way to the bridge, immediately.'

'Lex, I've got a million jobs down here to look at. Can it wait?'

'No, it most certainly cannot. We have company.'

DRAIG

Orcades Draig gazed out of the arkship *Fenrir's* observation deck window at the wreckage of the *Obsidian*. As he watched the burning ruin he clenched and unclenched his hands, trying to contain the rage that grew within him. He knew that decisions made in the heat of the moment were always flawed, that cool thinking was needed to find the right solution, but the urge to strike out, to kill that fool Waffron for his error, was almost too strong to resist. That was why he had come here, away from the tension of the bridge, to his observation deck. The transparent barrier towered over him, the largest continuous wall of glass on any arkship by some considerable margin. The density of space filled his vision, making the demise of his prey even more appalling. Usually the giant vista calmed his mind, allowing him insight and strategy, but not today. This wasn't helping, he realized.

He turned his back on the destruction and walked down the steps to a semicircle of cushioned seating. There was his mother, exuding her typical calm majesty as she waited for him. Her cool blue eyes pierced him, her face concealing her thoughts.

Orcades dropped into the sofa, unable to hide his own rage. 'A waste,' he muttered bitterly. 'A pointless waste.'

'Unfortunate,' Sinnsro Draig noted without emotion, 'but not pointless.'

'An arkship destroyed! And not just any arkship. How can this be anything but a waste? There is nothing to be gained from this.' Orcades jabbed at the new constellation of metal. About it a dust cloud had formed, stretching out into space, obscuring the stars.

'Tell me what happened,' his mother said calmly.

'Waffron is a fool! He should—'

'The facts,' Sinnsro urged. 'Do not let emotion rule you.'

'You knew the plan; we were to take the *Obsidian* with minimal loss of life. Thyred was to be captured and he would have endorsed my claim.'

'And what went wrong?'

'Waffron had access to the Gilgore grid,' Orcades said slowly. 'With their defenses down, it should have been a simple matter to disable the *Obsidian's* engines.'

'A simple matter?'

Orcades reddened, conceding his mother's point. 'There is always the possibility of a miscalculation . . .'

'Arkship engines carry an enormous amount of fuel. With the grid down, it is hard to estimate the damage inflicted from a bombardment. A stray charge could easily ignite a fallorite rod . . .'

'Yes, I know the theories,' Orcades barked. 'A burning rod can cause a cascade that could rip an arkship down its spine. But it's just a theory!'

'Until now,' Sinnsro said, gesturing towards the window.

'So, you're saying Waffron should go unpunished?'

'No, that is not what I'm saying, Orcades. Commodore Waffron should have anticipated the potential risk and reduced his bombardment, focusing on the command section rather than the engines. He must pay for his mistake.'

'Exile?'

Sinnsro chuckled. 'Child, you are always so dramatic.'

Orcades reddened. 'I am not a child!'

Sinnsro waited for Orcades to compose himself. 'A demotion is suitably humiliating for a man of his age and experience. Commander, I think. And move him off the *Fenrir*, to a less prestigious ship. That should send the right message. Who is his second?'

Orcades smiled to himself; she knew already. 'Thorwald.'

'Yes, Captain Thorwald, a stern sort, trustworthy. Make him your Commodore.'

Orcades nodded, thinking.

'Do not lead by fear, Orcades, lead with love.' Sinnsro added with a maternal smile.

'But, the *Obsidian*, none of this changes the facts. It is destroyed, and our plans lay in ruins with it.'

His mother waited, her nostrils flaring as she exhaled. 'This is not what we planned, but if you are to be Valtais you must learn to adapt to unexpected situations.'

Orcades stood up. '*If? If?* I will be Valtais. This is just a setback. I will overcome . . .'

Sinnsro raised a hand, stalling Orcades' outburst. He blustered, then sat down once more.

'You *will* be Valtais,' Sinnsro confirmed, 'but this is a critical time, Orcades. What you do next could affect the timing of your accession.'

'I know that, I am sorry,' he replied quietly, trying to emulate his mother's control. He envied her discipline, and hated her for it as well. She sat before him, her spine upright, her sinewy hands clasped, laden with the rings of office, her robes stately and formal, her long neck heavy with jewelry, holding her head steadfastly towards him, impaling him with her unblinking eyes. He lacked her serenity, her conviction, her detachment.

'The destruction of the *Obsidian* was unplanned, not even Reader Durante foresaw such an event,' Sinnsro said, rising from her seat. 'It complicates our plans, but it is not an insurmountable problem. A setback, that is all. In time, you can still rule both houses and claim what is yours.'

'I cannot wait for tomorrow, I must act now!' Orcades

seethed. 'You see in eternity, mother, I do not.'

Sinnsro turned to face him, irritation furrowing her brow. 'Your impulsiveness will be your undoing. Do not rush into this without consideration.'

'Tell me then! Tell me what I should do?'

Her face softened. She smiled benevolently at him then returned to the carnage outside. 'We have taken the *Tephrite*. You will plant your flag there instead of the *Obsidian*. You will say that the *Obsidian* was the center of a cult plotting against the Church, that they worshipped only themselves, that they practiced abominable things. You had to act to cast off this darkness. You tried to reason with them, but they destroyed themselves rather than face justice.'

'But Thyred is—'

'Thyred is dead!' Sinnsro interrupted. 'His rule is over. This is your opportunity. This is what we have worked towards. Do not let sentiment for an old man cloud your decisions.'

'But to say he was a godless . . .' Orcades protested. 'It lacks honor.'

Sinnsro waved her hand dismissively. 'Once you have power you can rewrite history any way you see fit. Say he was coerced . . . say whatever you like. But for now, until you have authority, you must have the people behind you. They must believe you have saved them, not enslaved them. You have defeated Thyred the man, now you must destroy Thyred the symbol.

Do you understand?'

Orcades let his eyes settle on the view. Explosions and fire dotted the wreckage, just distant islands of color in the dissipating dust cloud. It all seemed so fragile, so insignificant.

'I understand, mother,' he replied.

'Good. Do this, declare your heritage and take the House of Kenric. Become their prince and you will have proved your worthiness. No one can lay claim to the throne once you sit upon it.'

Orcades stared at his mother. 'You think the rumors are true? Surely the prince-in-waiting is dead.'

'The *Demon Star* was destroyed in the attack. Thyred's son is most certainly dead. The House of Kenric has no prince . . .'

'And yet you hesitate.'

Sinnsro's eyes looked away. 'Something the Reader said to me, about the future.'

'You put too much faith in the Church, mother.'

'That is the point, Orcades, is it not? Do not underestimate the power of faith, on the individual, or as a tool for the ruling elite to wield.'

Orcades scowled. 'What did he say?'

'It was more what he did not say. He would not be drawn on the fate of Prince Halstead,' Sinnsro said, thinking. 'Perhaps your impulsiveness, in this instance, is a good thing.'

Orcades studied the battlefield, spotting lifeboats

retreating from the maelstrom. 'Perhaps, we might mop up any survivors, just in case.'

'A wise precaution.'

The Infinite broke at the edge of the window, startling the view with its radiant light.

'And perhaps you could have another chat with your Reader,' Orcades said, 'see if he can be more . . . specific.'

'I will speak to him, but the Church will only be pushed so far. And we will need their blessing before your coronation.'

'They have too much power.'

'Perhaps,' Sinnsro conceded, 'but you might try to cultivate their favor, and some of their power will come to you. We need them, if you are to be prince. When, Gods willing, that day comes I will concede the Valtais to you. I will become your Varjot Valtais, forever by your side, and you will rule over both houses, Kenric and Draig joined at last.'

'Yes, mother.' He ran his fingers through his dark hair, pushing it away from his forehead.

The light from The Infinite became overwhelming. Automatically the view tinted, shielding them from the glare. The room became aglow with ochre shades that reminded Orcades of the artificial turn towards night that all ships followed.

Sinnsro stood, straightening her robes. 'I will speak to Reader Durante and inform him of your plans. It is a good day, my son, the start of greatness.'

Orcades smiled politely, bowed, waiting for her to leave. He heard the familiar fizz of the holograph and the image of his mother was gone. It was easy to forget; the simulation was so accurate. Alone, with only the window for company, a wave of sadness took hold of him. The task ahead seemed gigantic, too large to complete alone. But he could not show doubt, he could not show weakness. He straightened his back, letting his chest rise as he took a breath, then he pressed the communicator on his wrist and summoned Commodore Waffron to inform him of his decision.

LEXICA

Wynn followed Bara onto the bridge. It was a wide space, dominated by a wall of large windows that overlooked the bulk of *Lexica*. He stood in the doorway as Bara threw herself into one of the three seats that faced a bank of consoles under the imposing view. Out of the windows Wynn saw the giant shape of a ship drifting towards them. It was another arkship, he guessed by its size, a hulk of curved stone and metal crafted into a domineering whole. Immediately it reminded Wynn of the *Obsidian*, although this vessel was perhaps half its size.

'It's a Kenric arkship,' Bara confirmed with a relieved smile. 'Looks like you got lucky.'

'Bara.' The voice was Lexica's. 'It is good to see you again.'

'You too. Tell me what I've missed.'

'My records suggest this is the arkship *Tephrite*, a Kenric vessel. I have tried to establish contact but, so far, they have not responded.'

'You don't have my charm, Lex.' Bara smiled

contentedly as her hands played over the console. She was at home here.

Wynn moved closer as she flicked a switch and spoke into a small com unit. 'This is Captain Sēbarā Delaterre of the merchant vessel *Lexica*, registration MC-89409-LX, out of the *Ark Royal Obsidian*, request permission to dock.'

The dull noise of background static filled the bridge. Bara reclined in her seat, watching the approaching mass.

'Odd . . .'

'What's wrong?' Wynn asked, sitting next to her.

'No response. Even if their com was down they would be sending out their transponder code automatically.'

'Could their transponder be damaged.'

Bara shook her head. 'No, multiple redundancies all over the ship. It's a failsafe. The only way you can disable the transponder is if you do it manually, shut down the entire system from the flight deck. But you wouldn't do that unless . . .'

'. . . unless you wanted to be hidden,' Wynn said.

Bara leaned forwards, checking her console. 'Lex, are we flight-ready?'

'Close enough. Engines standing by.'

'Okay.' She fastened her seat harness around her chest and turned to Wynn. 'You might want to strap in.'

'You think they're hostile?' Wynn asked, looking back at the silent arkship. It almost filled the windows now.

'I don't know, but they're not being very friendly so far, are they?' She pressed a button and a control column unfolded in front of her seat.

'Control yoke deployed,' Lexica said. 'You have navigation, Bara.'

'Got it, thanks,' Bara replied as she gripped the control yoke handles.

'Please, remember my limitations,' Lexica cautioned, his tones almost human.

Smiling, Bara turned to face Wynn. 'Let's give them one more try.' She pressed the com button and spoke into the mic again. 'Hi *Tephrite, t*his is Captain Sēbarā Delaterre of the merchant vessel *Lexica*, registration—'

A flash of light erupted from the front of the arkship, followed by another.

'Tracking hostiles,' Lexica warned, 'two inbound, locked on.'

Bara jerked the yoke and *Lexica* responded immediately. Wynn felt himself pressed into his seat as the ship began to turn and accelerate rapidly. The arkship disappeared from the windows but Wynn could see a representation of it on a three-dimensional holograph projecting from the console in front of him. At the center of the map was *Lexica*, with two bright flashing points of light approaching.

'Hostiles closing,' Lexica announced. 'Launching countermeasures.'

'Wait!' Bara barked, her full focus on the readouts in front of her.

'I really can't endorse this plan, Bara,' Lexica replied, his voice amplified to be heard over the increasing noise and vibration of the engines.

'Come on,' Bara said through gritted teeth. 'You love it!'

'Eight seconds to impact.'

The ship tilted under Bara's guidance, diving towards a cluster of debris, building speed.

'Four seconds.'

'Countermeasures!' Bara shouted.

Wynn felt a rumble from deep inside the ship. On the holographic display, he saw a new constellation of flashing lights appear between *Lexica* and the two chasing signals. Out of the window he saw the husk of a destroyed ship – remnants from the *Obsidian* – approaching rapidly. Too rapidly. Then, all at once, there was a flash of light, then another, and *Lexica* began to shake. The noise and vibration became unbearable.

Bara slammed the yoke forwards, and Wynn felt his chest thump into his harness. His head filled with blood as pressure grew behind his eyes. His vision began to tunnel and, for a second, he thought he might pass out. Then, as the pain decreased he saw that the wreckage had disappeared. Now, all he could see from the windows was darkness.

'Lexica,' Bara whispered. 'Full shutdown.'

'Done.'

The engines whined, rumbling as they powered down. The lights died, every single console screen went out. Everything stopped, even the air pumps fell silent. All Wynn could hear was the slow creaking and pinging of the ship as it began to lose heat to space. As his eyes adjusted he could make out details in the darkness outside; structure, fragments of hull, drifting debris.

'Where—'

'Sshh!' Bara interrupted.

Wynn obeyed, resting, waiting to see what might happen. Several long minutes past, neither of them making a sound. Outside, a light began to grow, illumining more details, and Wynn realized they were hiding inside the remnants of the destroyed ship. The searchlight passed over them, adjusting from time to time, then moved on. Beyond, through the torn hull and wreckage, he could make out the ominous shape of the arkship *Tephrite* as it cruised by. They watched in silence, waiting long after it had gone before either dared to speak.

'I think it's moved on,' Bara said eventually, her voice barely audible. 'We should wait here for a while longer until we're certain.'

Wynn nodded, feeling cool in the dropping temperature. 'Why did they attack us?'

Bara thought, looking uncertain. 'Maybe whoever

attacked the *Obsidian* has taken over the *Tephrite*.'

'How do you know?'

'I don't. But a Kenric ship wouldn't fire on unarmed merchants. It looks like whoever is in charge is trying to pick off any survivors from the *Obsidian*. Which means we need to get as far away from here as possible, and we can't trust any Kenric ships.'

Wynn's mind raced. 'But I need to make contact with someone from Kenric, I need to find out who I am.'

Bara rolled her eyes, hardly hiding her irritation. 'It's not safe anymore.' She took a breath, calming her voice. 'Look, I can drop you somewhere else, if you like . . . maybe a Merred arkship, or a Ciation outpost? You can find out what's going on from there. But I'm not risking contact with any more Kenric ships.'

Wynn didn't reply. His mind was clogged with frustration and uncertainty. Bara stood and opened a storage locker at the rear of the bridge. She pulled out two grey blankets and passed one to him.

'We'll have to wait a while longer before we risk going,' she said. 'They might still be in attack range. Air should be fine for a while, but it's gonna get cool in here.'

Wynn pulled the blanket round his shoulders, watching as Bara returned to the locker and found two square packets. She shook them by the edge and offered one to Wynn.

'Doesn't taste great,' she confessed, 'but it's food.' She read the back of the packet. 'At least I think it's food.'

Wynn smiled as he accepted the packet. He removed a small plastic spoon from the back of the pouch and tore at the seal. Aromatic steam rose from the opening.

'Smells okay,' Wynn said, feeling his mouth water. He poked at the contents with his spoon and lifted out a lumpy brown paste.

'Some sort of protein,' Bara said in between chewing. 'Says it's beef flavor. I don't know what beef is, but it won't kill you.'

Wynn tested the edge of the spoon against his lips. The paste was slightly metallic, with a powdery consistency, but it was warm and edible.

'This might be the best thing I've ever tasted, for all I know,' Wynn joked.

'Let's hope you're not allergic to beef.' Bara quipped in return.

They both smiled, watching the drifting view as they ate.

'Does the House of Kenric have enemies?' Wynn asked.

'I didn't think so, not before today. There hasn't been a major war between the families since . . . well, I don't know when, but it was ages ago. And it makes no sense to destroy an arkship! They're so valuable. If this was a hostile takeover by another family they'd do everything they could to take it without too much damage. And it's not like the Ven Cord or C-Waac to do anything like this, it's not their style, it's gravel-headed.' She looked at Wynn. 'Is any of this making sense to you?'

'Some,' he laughed.

'Sorry, it must be tough.'

Wynn put down his food. 'You could say that.' He gazed out of the windows, letting his mind drift, hoping something might come to him, some lost memory that might help him to make sense of everything.

Movement caught his eye, and he bolted up from his seat. 'Did you see that?'

Bara glanced from her meal. 'What?'

'Out there . . . I thought . . .' He suddenly felt foolish.

'What did you see?'

Wynn rubbed his eyes. 'Nothing . . .'

'Tell me.'

'It looked like . . . for a moment, I thought someone was out there. It was just a dark shape moving across that piece of hull – probably just some debris.'

Bara put down her food and stood up, leaning in towards the windows. 'Out there?'

'Yes,' Wynn confessed. 'But it's gone now. I think I'm seeing things.'

Bara didn't reply, her attention fixed on the view.

'What is it?' Wynn asked.

'You were right,' Bara replied, 'there is someone

out there.'

Wynn squinted, scanning the wreckage about them, spotting the tiny movements of debris. Yes! There it was: a strange human-like figure scaling a length of twisted bulkhead, keeping to the shadows, concealing its shape from their viewpoint.

'I didn't imagine that,' Wynn said.

'It's too thin to be someone in a suit. More likely a hunter bot left behind by the *Tephrite*.'

'A robot?' Wynn checked.

'A robot sent to look for us,' Bara said as she activated her console. 'Lex: power up, now!'

'Start-up initiated,' Lexica replied.

The ship began to hum as the lights stung Wynn's eyes. Warm fresh air filled the bridge as, one by one, the ship's systems came back online.

Bara hit a switch and the exterior was illuminated by the ship's spotlights. The strange shape froze in the glare, then scrambled towards them, leaping from one piece of junk to the next, propelling itself closer and closer.

'If that thing gets hold, we'll never get rid of it,' Bara said, 'it'll rip through the hull, get in here and . . .'

She pulled at the yoke, commanding the ship to retreat, and a crunching noise reverberated through the ship.

'Proximity alert,' Lexica said.

'A bit late, but thanks,' Bara replied dryly.

'Do you have any guns?' Wynn asked.

'Yes,' Bara said, focusing on her console, 'but it's damned tight in here. We'd never hit it at this range, not without blowing holes in *Lexica*.'

Under Bara's guiding hand, the ship rocked from side to side, trying to retreat from the hunter bot. As the vessel turned the bot disappeared from view.

'Where the hell is it?' Wynn cursed.

There was an ominous thud on the exterior.

'I believe it is on the hull, Bara,' Lexica said dispassionately. 'I can feel it.'

'Where?' she asked, sounding desperate.

A holograph display zoomed in on a patch of hull on the starboard side of the ship.

'I see it,' Bara said to Lexica. 'Sorry about this.'

She yanked the control yoke and the ship crashed into the scarred wall of their hiding place. Bara scraped the ship through the debris, grinding and tearing at *Lexica*. Behind them the door to the bridge slammed shut.

'As you're being liberal with my hull I've taken the liberty of closing the bridge, in case of accidental decompression,' Lexica said coolly. 'I trust this meets with your approval?'

Bara winced. 'Sorry, Lex, I'll fix it, I promise.'

As the ship cleared the debris Wynn focused on the holograph again. 'Has it gone?'

'Sadly, no,' Lexica replied.

'Where is it now?' Bara muttered.

A glowing icon appeared on the display.

'Over the cargo bay?' she checked.

'Yes.'

'Blow it, Lex!'

Wynn felt the ship rock, turning violently as a message flashed over the display: *Decompression Warning*. The vibration subsided and Bara regained control of the wayward ship. A multitude of warning lights flashed. One by one Bara checked them and shut them down, cursing. 'Gravel-headed idiot!'

'Did you get it?' Wynn asked.

'I can no longer feel anything attached to the hull,' Lexica said, adding, 'I can no longer feel large sections of the hull either. I have sustained considerable damage, Bara. Again.'

Bara sighed heavily. 'I'll fix it. Better than new.'

'I am also low on fuel.'

'Okay,' Bara replied.

'And oxygen.'

'Right. Hell of a day. Any ships we can get to?'

She adjusted the display, widening the scan. Nothing appeared on the screen.

'There is one,' Lexica noted. A new icon pinged onto the display.

Bara saw it and began to smile. 'Can you make it?'

'Barely. I'll need to shut down life support to all sections except the bridge.'

'Okay,' Bara said as she rubbed her face. 'Set a course. Do what you need to do.'

Wynn leaned closer. 'Where are you taking me?'

HUNTER

Gofal watched the stars rise and fall overhead, their dots of color stretching to slice the blackness. He felt the hull of the ship shake, turning under him, building speed. He glanced from the stars to the ejected cargo canisters drifting away, becoming a new micro-constellation. As they retreated he scanned them, cataloguing their contents. Clothing, books, toys, spices, medicines, toiletries, an odd assortment of items. He wondered if they were for trade or for personal use. He calculated how long the medicines might last, depending on the number of patients, their age and afflictions, then he researched the purpose, effectiveness and side-effects of each item. Next, he read some of the books, retrieving their texts from his database. Some of the poetry he skipped over. Finally, he looked at the spices and decided what sort of meals might be enhanced by their addition. He reviewed the cultural significance of the menus, noting any that he had not sampled for later indulgence. He wasn't sure why he did it, but it helped to pass the seconds.

The compression point was coming. This would be the most dangerous moment, when the vibrations from the engines grew to their maximum, surging through the hull, threatening to shake him off. He prepared himself, moving slightly to reduce his profile. There was a great deal of damage to the cargo bay, he noted, and he guessed his presence was no longer being tracked by the occupants of the ship. He looked down at what remained of his right arm, wondering if he should eject it rather than allow it to hang from his shoulder. It would only slow him down, it might even lead to his detection. Better to get rid of it now rather than risk it complicating his predicament later. But no. He would keep it, hoping he could repair it at a later stage. Sentimentality, perhaps? Maybe.

The vibrations grew about him, shaking him as the compression point came over the ship. For a second, his vision stalled, then the vibrations subsided, and his optical system came back online. The ship was at full speed now. Destination? He plotted the stars and calculated a selection of potential targets. He scanned for ships along their current trajectory but found none, just a few isolated asteroids. Were they going there? he wondered.

As the ship rumbled on Gofal worked through the list of repairs he'd have to endure when this was over. It was an extensive list, far too many items for his liking. His ability to carry out his orders had been severely compromised, but he would not give in. His mission was clear: he would track his targets to their destination then deal with them there.

SHIP OF SHADOWS

Wynn stirred from a troubled sleep. He had been dreaming of fire and screaming faces rushing towards him. He recalled the noise of twisted metal, the smell of burning, the sensation of falling, the taste of blood in his mouth. Already the details were evaporating, leaving behind just the shell of the dream, nothing more than a feeling, a blurred shape without detail. He opened his eyes and remembered where he was: in a chair on the bridge of *Lexica*. He watched his icy breath drift from his lips, and he pulled the blanket tight under his chin.

The bridge windows were obscured by a fine fracture of frost, and the air was sharp against his nose. He looked about him, hoping to see Bara, but he was alone on the bridge. He stood, wondering where she had gone, and walked towards the hatch that led to the rest of the ship. He pressed the control panel but the door remained shut.

'I wouldn't do that, if I were you.'

'Lexica?' Wynn called.

'Hello, sleepyhead,' the ship replied. 'What's up?'

'Where's Bara?'

'Making repairs. She's suited up on level three.'

Wynn pressed the door button again.

'I can't let you out, sorry,' Lexica replied. 'The bridge and the adjoining corridor are the only parts of the ship with an air pocket and life support now. Bara shut down life support to the rest of the ship after she left. You wouldn't like it on the other side of that door.'

'But it's freezing in here,' Wynn moaned.

'But there's air, so that's good. Every cloud . . .'

Wynn returned to his chair. Already the padding was cool against his body. 'Where are we headed?'

'See that dark black nothing up ahead?'

Wynn leaned over to the windows and rubbed a circle out of the frost. 'No,' he replied. All he could see was the gloom of space and the bright dots of stars and nebula.

'Well, that's where we're going.'

He sunk back into the chair, wondering how long he'd have to suffer that computer. The cold was making his skin ache. He touched the scars and wondered how long his face had looked this way.

There was a rush of air and his ears popped as the hatch slid open. Bara appeared wearing a lightweight environ-suit. She stepped through the door, closed it again and removed her helmet. About her, the atmospheric pumps forced air back onto the bridge, equalizing the pressure.

'Sol!' she exclaimed. 'It's cold in here. Lex, turn the heating up, will you?'

'If I must.'

Bara smiled. 'Thank you, Lex.'

Almost immediately Wynn felt a warm current of air drifting from beneath the console, rising past his legs and warming his icy fingers.

'I don't think your ship likes me,' Wynn said in a cautionary whisper.

'He doesn't like anyone, not really,' Bara teased. She squinted at the windows, watching as the frost began to thin.

'Still on course?' she checked.

'Straight and true,' Lexica replied.

Wynn checked the window again, wondering if he was missing something. 'Does someone want to explain where it is you're taking me?'

Bara's face lit up with a broad smile. 'Melchior, my home.'

He checked the view once more. 'But there's nothing out there.'

'Look closely.'

He rubbed the closest window panel with his sleeve, clearing it of frost and moisture, and stared into the darkness once more. He saw the familiar background of stars breaking the blackness apart. The longer he looked the more stars he saw until he realized the black wasn't absolute. Everywhere he looked he saw stars.

Almost everywhere.

His eyes rested upon a patch of space where he couldn't find any starlight. He let his eye describe the shape, checking to make sure it wasn't a trick of the light. There was a cylindrical area devoid of stars.

'What . . . what is that?' Wynn asked, pressing a finger to the window.

'An arkship,' Bara grinned. 'Melchior. It has no exterior lights, no emissions, no radio noise, nothing. To all but the most inquisitive eyes it's just a piece of rock floating through space. And not very interesting rock either; nothing worth mining. Its orbit it finely adjusted so it always sits in the shadow of an asteroid orbiting closer to The Infinite, that way its surface receives no light, and there's no thermal difference between the night and day sides. It's invisible, hidden in shadows.'

'Bara . . .' Lexica's voice cautioned.

'Yeah, I really shouldn't be telling you this,' she said to Wynn with a frown. 'Probably have to kill you now.'

Wynn tensed.

'Sol! I'm kidding! And I don't have much of a choice but to tell you about it, do I? We've got nowhere else to go. Which reminds me . . .' She jumped into her seat and began to check the scrolling information on her console. 'Normally we plot an indirect route to avoid being tracked, but we don't have enough fuel for a walk round the park, so coming straight at them is going to spook a few folk.'

Wynn watched as she tapped out a rhythm on the console. Out of the window he saw the glare of their spotlights flashing.

'It's a really old form of communication,' Bara explained. 'Dates back to before the Fracture, when the Cluster was actual planets and moons with solid earth beneath your feet. Can you imagine? It's called Morse code. I'm sending out a message by flashing my lights at them. Hopefully they know I'm friendly.'

'Will they respond?' Wynn asked.

Bara shook her head. 'No. But hopefully they'll let us in now.'

She changed the display's view and a holograph of Melchior appeared above the console. Bara was right: there was nothing that marked it out as anything but a natural clump of rock. No technology, no obvious form of propulsion, nothing to see except a pitted grey surface marked by craters and dust.

Outside the dark shape grew, blotting out the stars, but still no details of the surface became obvious. The holographic display was the only way to discern surface contours and scale.

'It's huge!' Wynn gasped.

Bara smiled proudly. 'Over twenty thousand people in there, all living outside of the hierarchy of the families, outside of the scrutiny of the Church.'

'You're self-sustaining?'

'Almost. What we don't make or recycle we trade from the outside. There are a few of us, like me, who choose to live outside. We find work, we trade for things we need and return home when we've got enough supplies.' She sighed wistfully. 'They're not gonna be happy that I jettisoned most of my cargo into space.'

'I've logged its location,' Lexica noted. 'When we have finished my repairs, we can attempt a retrieval.'

'If it's not been picked up by scavengers first.'

Ahead the view was split in two; below was darkness, above was the grey-black of space filled with stars. Wynn could see a clear dividing line, a ragged horizon of mountains and valleys. All of Bara's attention was on the holographic display now, watching as the terrain rolled beneath them.

'Marker one approaching,' Lexica said.

'Got it,' Bara replied. She tilted the ship, slowing their approach.

'Marker two . . . '

Bara nodded. 'I see it. Shut down everything but thrusters. I have control.'

'You have control. All auxiliary systems shut down.'

The lights on the bridge dimmed. Only Bara's console remained illuminated, casting a cool green glow over her face. Wynn felt the ship dropping towards the rocky exterior. Outside the stars had disappeared. They were close to the surface now, gliding into a depression.

'Marker three,' Lexica said, his voice softer now.

'Locked on,' Bara whispered.

The ship turned slowly, descending.

'Landing gear down. Docking clamps ready . . .'

A cloud of dust pushed past the windows, coating them in a grey ash that obscured their view.

'Contact light,' Lexica noted.

'Clamps engaged . . . cutting thrust . . . touchdown.' Bara let go of the control yoke, shut down the engines and leaned back as the ship became still.

Outside the dust settled, drifting back towards the surface.

'Two meters off center,' Lexica noted.

Bara frowned. 'Think you could do better?'

'Yes.'

'Well . . . maybe you could . . .'

'I could.'

'Lex, don't you have something to do?'

'No, not particularly.'

'Well, find something!' She turned to face Wynn. 'Welcome to Melchior.'

Wynn stared out at the blackness. 'What happens now?' he asked.

Bara smiled, her eyes twinkling. 'You'll see.'

Wynn heard a series of distant bangs followed by a low vibration. He felt a sickly sensation in his stomach, as if he was moving, and grabbed the back of the chair.

'It's okay,' Bara smiled. 'We're going inside.'

He looked to the holograph display. The icon

representing *Lexica* was descending through a circular chamber dug into the rock.

'We're going down to the main hanger bay,' Bara explained, pointing to the holograph. Wynn heard a grinding noise coming from above them – the landing pad hatch closing, he suspected. They were completely hidden now.

'How will your people take to a stranger coming here?' Wynn asked.

Bara took a moment to reply, her face tense. 'I'll be honest, they won't like it, but I'll deal with it. When we stop I'll go out and talk to them. You stay in here until I come for you, okay?'

Wynn nodded, feeling hemmed in.

Outside was a faint glow of light, getting stronger as they descended. He could see detail in the rocky wall of the chamber as it passed by the window – long shadows defining the jagged surface. As the light grew their decent slowed until, with a jolt, they came to a halt. Outside of the windows was a vast hanger bay, its far wall hidden in the distance. He saw other ships, resting on individual pads connected by raised walkways. A central tower dominated the hanger, a circular structure with a ring of illuminated windows at its peak.

Tiny dots of people approached their berth along one of the walkways. Wynn saw the weapons in their hands and couldn't help feeling a tremble of anticipation.

'Right,' Bara said as she stood, 'I won't be long.'

She opened the hatch and disappeared from the bridge. The door hissed shut behind her, and Wynn noted the ping of a lock being activated. He wasn't going anywhere.

He rested in the chair and closed his eyes, trying to remember something from before the attack. He lost track of time, feeling his mind drift towards sleep, when he heard voices inside the ship. They spoke quickly, in a language he didn't understand.

The hatch door opened and two men entered, both holding long weapons pressed into their shoulders. Their faces were covered by black scarfs wrapped over their mouth and nose, but their keen eyes were exposed and locked onto Wynn.

'Out of chair . . . slow!' the first man said, his voice deep and imposing.

As Wynn stood he caught sight of Bara on the other side of the hatch. She shrugged apologetically at him.

The first man lowered his gun and pulled Wynn's hands behind his back and snapped something onto his wrist. 'Not try anything, okay?'

'What would be the point?'

The strap around his wrist tightened, then he felt it pull at his other hand, drawing them together.

'Good,' the man replied. 'Keep it good.'

He took Wynn by the arm and led him off the bridge, through the ship to the lowest deck. Ahead of him he saw an open entrance ramp bathed in light. He walked down it, squinting his eyes, adjusting to the glare, towards a group of waiting people. At the center of the gathering was a stout woman in her late fifties with long silvery blonde hair. Wynn's captor delivered him to the waiting congregation, pulling on his arm to stop him a short distance in front of them.

'Forgive the shackles,' the woman said to Wynn. 'We get so few visitors here, and we do cherish our isolation. We must be cautious.'

'I'm not here to hurt you,' Wynn said.

The woman nodded, taking a step towards him. 'You say that with conviction, and I'm sure you believe it. But belief is a powerful thing, and it can hide many truths.'

Wynn glanced over his shoulder: Bara stood behind him, listening.

'My name is Selena Varjo,' the woman said to him. 'I am Chancellor of Melchior.'

'I'm Wynn.'

'Just Wynn? No other name?'

Wynn tensed, trying to dig up something about his identity.

Chancellor Varjo sighed, avoiding his gaze. 'Bara has explained who you are, and about your lack of identity. This worries me.'

Wynn stared at her, puzzled. 'Worries you? Why?'

'You are a man who does not know himself. If you

cannot trust your own memory then how can I trust you?'

Wynn hesitated. 'I don't know.'

'Neither do I,' Chancellor Varjo replied sadly. 'So, we must take certain measures to protect ourselves.'

'Measures?'

Chancellor Varjo turned away from him. 'The chief will explain. I am sorry, Wynn. We have worked far too long here in Melchior to risk you damaging what we have achieved.'

Behind him he could hear sobbing. Was it Bara? He was about to turn around when he felt heavy hands pushing on his shoulders, forcing him to his knees.

'I don't mean you any—'

There was a sharp pain at the base of his neck, a jolt of electricity that rattled through his spine, and his world dissolved away to nothing.

CIRCADIA

The cell was perfectly spherical, a white space of soft padded walls. Wynn floated at the center, drifting gently in the zero-gravity bubble. He'd given up trying to move: each time he tried to reach for the walls he felt the inevitable tug of artificial gravity keeping him in the middle of the space. Every movement was checked and counteracted. He could do nothing but float and wait.

Distant music haunted him, a melancholic voice singing in a language he didn't understand, drifting through the walls from somewhere else. He heard muffled voices as well, getting closer. A break in the smooth cladding appeared, a fine line that became a circle. The newly-defined shape sunk away, revealing an opening, and Wynn felt his body being gently pushed towards it. He gripped the edge of his prison and fell through the opening, landing on a cold metal floor beyond.

'Sol! You look rough.' He saw Bara staring down at him. Beside her was a broad-shouldered man in his forties who lifted Wynn to his feet, supporting him as he recovered.

'Thanks. That was one hell of a night,' Wynn quipped. 'Have I missed breakfast?'

'It is middle of afternoon,' the man replied as he guided him to a pod-like vehicle. Wynn dropped into one of the seats inside the pod, feeling the novelty of gravity dragging at his muscles once more.

Bara joined him, as did the burly man.

'You might remember the chief,' Bara said, gesturing to her companion. 'He had a scarf over his face the last time you saw him.'

'And a gun,' Wynn added.

'Oh, I still have gun,' the chief chuckled.

The pod door closed as it began to accelerate into a tunnel.

'Where are we going?' he asked.

'We've got you set up with a room,' Bara smiled, 'but you're free to go anywhere you want now.'

Wynn stared at her. 'No interrogation? No questions first?'

'It is done,' the chief said. 'We go over everything. You seem okay.'

'I . . . I can't remember that.'

'Deep . . . deep . . .' The Chief hesitated and turned to Bara, speaking to her in a different language.

'Brain scans,' Bara replied.

'Yes!' the chief laughed. 'Deep brain scans. All done

with deep brain scans. Not conscious . . . unconscious while we work. Lab men happy with results, but they can't get past memory block. Professional job.'

'A memory block? It's not from the battle?' Wynn checked, his mouth dry. 'It's not just concussion?'

The chief laughed. 'No: on purpose . . . deliberate. Someone does not want you to remember. You have enemies? An ex-wife, yes?'

Wynn's mind raced. Instead of answers he just had more and more questions. He rubbed his aching neck, and his fingers sensed a fine cut to his skin.

The chief smiled at him. 'Insurance, in case you're not as safe as we think.'

'What is it?'

'Kill switch. Step out of line, be naughty, we switch you off for good.'

'It's more than that,' Bara added. 'It's an implant plugged into your brain. Once you leave here, if you try to come back uninvited, or disclose information about Melchior, it will activate the kill switch.'

'Clever thing,' the chief noted proudly.

'You people are insane!' Wynn muttered.

'Not insane, just cautious,' Bara replied. 'I've got the same implant as you, had it for years. It won't do you any harm. We've got a lot to look after here. Come on, I'll show you.'

Beyond the windows, he saw lights whizzing by against the blackness of the tunnel. They began to slow, giving way to a brightly lit concourse, full of people and other pods. The door opened and they stepped outside. The air smelled sweet here, a thick perfumed scent catching his nose.

'Where are you taking me?' he asked.

'I want to show you what we have here,' Bara replied. 'I want you to understand why we have to protect ourselves.' She turned to the chief and smiled, speaking again in her own language. The chief replied, sounding doubtful. He eyed Wynn, bowed politely to Bara, then returned to the pod, leaving the pair alone.

Bara led Wynn through the square, past the inquisitive stares of the other people there.

'Ignore them,' she said,' they don't get to see many new faces.'

At the end of the promenade was a large bulkhead hatch with thick protective doors. The aroma was stronger here, carried on the warm breeze that came through the hatch. It was a sweet smell, distinctive and pleasant. Bara stopped by the doorway and smiled. 'I think you'll like this.'

She held out her hand to him. Wynn hesitated, festering in his temper, but her smile was infectious and he didn't have the will to resist. Together, they stepped over the raised door seal and walked into another world.

Wynn stood there, just staring, trying to make sense of what he saw. Then he began to laugh. It was an involuntary reaction of joy, a way for him to process the complex emotions he felt on seeing this strange sight.

The space was vast and must have accounted for most of the volume of Melchior. It was a cavernous void that seemed to go on forever, and all around the interior he could see life: houses, roads, buildings, open spaces, all following the contours of the space.

'They must have . . . did you . . .' Wynn struggled to find the right words.

Bara smiled, squeezing his hand. 'This was hollowed out long ago, before the Fracture. Melchior was one of the first-generation ships, full of people who wanted to leave Earth for somewhere better.' Her features changed, a mournful expression on her face. 'If only they'd known how good they had it.' Bara's eyes drifted. She shook herself, forcing a smile. 'They dug this chamber out of an asteroid, mining everything they could use. The gravity is created by Melchior's rotation, so we can live on the interior skin.'

Wynn looked up: instead of a rocky cavern ceiling he saw the tops of buildings, pathways and roads laid out like a map, all of them in darkness, just tiny lights bleeding from their windows.

Through the center of the vast space ran a giant rod-like structure that emitted a yellowy light onto one half of the cavern.

'That's the Circadia, our day/night system,' Bara

said, watching Wynn. 'It rotates over a twenty-four-hour period, so we can honor and observe the ancient rhythms of the first planet. Up there,' she pointed to the ceiling, 'is night-time. Down here, it's mid-afternoon. As Melchior rotates it gets darker. We even have seasons.'

'Seasons?'

'The planets had seasons, when the temperature changed. There used to be four seasons on Earth. We simulate the changes from the old records, adjusting the heat and light from the Circadia so our plants grow as they once did. Autumn is my favorite time.'

Ahead of them was a wide boulevard with steps that led down to a broad expanse of water, a fountain at its center. The surface glinted in the warm light, as gentle ripples lapped at the edge. Wynn could feel the moisture in the air, kissing his skin. There was the scent again, haunting him.

'What is it? What is that smell?' he asked.

'Smell?' Bara thought for a moment then laughed. She led him down the steps, past the fountain, towards an avenue of formal rectangles that exploded with color.

'Flowers. Our gardens are the best in the entire Cluster.'

Wynn knelt in front these alien objects. He studied a clump of yellow stalks with white protrusions facing the light. He leaned closer to smell the odd structures, marveling at their delicate shapes. His hand rested on the ground and he touched a fine green growth that covered the space between the flowers. It was soft to the touch, calming to his mind.

'Grass,' Bara explained.

Wynn laughed again. He stood up, spying a larger growth ahead. He ran to it and touched the pitted surface of the cylindrical object. Above him the shaft divided into a number of smaller offshoots. These too narrowed and divided, filling the air, and from each one grew thin green shapes that danced in the breeze.

'What is this?' he asked, stretching his arms out to embrace the dark mass.

Bara smiled, joining him to touch the brittle skin. 'A tree.'

Wynn felt a calmness inside him, certain he had never experienced anything like this before. This place was alien to him, and yet it felt like home.

'I knew you'd like it,' Bara laughed.

They walked further, through an avenue of trees, feeling the coolness of their shadows, listening to the whisper of their branches as they swayed, and Bara explained every new thing to him.

The gardens ended at a low wall. Beyond was a series of large open spaces planted with more growths in ordered lines.

'These are our crops,' Bara said. 'We still use hydroponics and growth tanks to feed ourselves, but our best food comes from here. And the crops help to regulate and recycle our air supply.'

'And all of this has been working for hundreds of years?' Wynn asked.

'We've improved it, and we're still learning. There's nothing like this on any other arkship. You see now why we must protect it?'

'Yes, I see. I understand,' Wynn replied. He felt insignificant walking through this majestic space. He looked up again at the Circadia overhead, marveling at its design. The light had changed since they had started their walk. It was softer now, more orange than yellow, and the shadows about his feet were longer. The buildings overhead caught the first blue rays of dawn, as night became day.

Bara checked the time. 'We should go.'

'Go? Go where?' Wynn asked, feeling remorse at having to leave this place.

Bara pointed up to a portion of the cave falling into the shadow of night. 'Chancellor Varjo is throwing a dinner in our honor. I'll show you to your room first, you can wash and change there.'

'I don't want to go to a dinner,' Wynn replied. 'I need to find out who destroyed the *Obsidian*, maybe then I can get some answers . . . maybe then I can find out who I really am.'

'We will, I promise, and this is a good place to start. Chancellor Varjo may know what has happened. And there will be some other couriers there as well.'

'Couriers?'

'People like me,' Bara explained. 'We travel out there, we trade, we bring back supplies and information. I hear that Derward Tarkkail came home only yesterday. He seems to know everything that's going on across the Cluster.'

'Then I must speak to him,' Wynn said quickly.

Bara smiled, her voice calming. 'You're still recovering, Wynn. Take it slowly. A few hours won't matter. And you stink, do know that?'

Wynn laughed, his impatience easing. 'Then I'd better get washed.'

VAMPIRE

Gofal waited, gathering data from his hiding place. He had managed to tap into some of the ship's low priority systems without making his presence known, but he dared not penetrate any further. This was an advanced ship that could easily detect his presence. It hadn't noticed the discreet power syphon which was restoring Gofal's systems, but that was only because of the severe damage the ship had endured. Once it had repaired itself the ship would sense the power drain, would feel Gofal feeding off its veins, and do everything it could to stop him.

His arm still bothered him. He did not have the resources to fix it, and without it his performance was impaired. He would need to be in prime condition if he was to complete his mission. He wondered if he might find the parts he needed in this hanger. There was no way of knowing without leaving the relative safety of the ship's hull. He wasn't ready to do that, not yet. He needed more time to feed. Then, when he was sated, he might explore. This place was unknown to him, and therefore unknown to anyone in the Cluster. His database was extensive . . . Why was this arkship not listed? The inconsistency bothered him, and he tried to compose some poetry to take his mind off it.

No, it was no good. He just didn't like poetry.

Instead he tried to access an internal system for this place. If he could find some information it might prove useful in the future.

There, an unprotected network drifting in the air. He tapped into it, cataloguing the data he found. It was a music channel, broadcasting across . . . this place was called *Melchior*. He listened to the songs as he searched his database. The language was new to him, but he sensed its origins in three distinct Earth tongues.

Melchior . . . there it was, an archaic bit of information buried in a barely accessed database. This was a generation ship that set out from Earth – one of three constructed by an ancient religion to take their holy teachings to the stars. It was interesting, but of little importance to his mission. His prey was somewhere on-board Melchior, that was all that mattered.

Gofal turned off the music. It was a distraction. He must prepare, he must focus for the important task ahead.

THE COURIER

Wynn was relieved to see the gathering was smaller than he had expected, just a dozen or so people in a secluded courtyard. As he and Bara entered the square the overlapping conversations dipped as people discreetly observed the arriving guests. Bara smiled politely to the onlookers as she guided Wynn to a chair at the long table set in the middle of the square. He lowered himself into the seat, feeling old and tired. Bruises covered Wynn's body and, despite the soothing bath he had just taken, he ached all over. His escape from the *Obsidian* was catching up with him.

Bara sat next to him, comforting him with her smile as strangers took their seats around them. She had changed out of her blood-stained overalls into a loose-fitting dress with a thick leather belt that pulled the material in around her slim waist. Her dark hair was clean and, for the first time, Wynn saw how beautiful she was. She was tall, like most he had encountered on Melchior, and she carried herself with a poise and dignity that seemed at odds with her youthfulness.

'This is Derward Tarkkail,' Bara said, indicating an older man who had sat next to him. 'He's the courier I told you about.'

'Always a pleasure to meet a new face in Melchior,' Derward said warmly, grasping Wynn's hand. He was thin-faced with pronounced cheekbones and a piercing stare. His tawny face was framed by a stubbly silvered beard and short tousled hair, but his posture and manner hinted at order and discipline.

'Bara tells me you were on the *Obsidian*,' he continued in a hushed voice. 'Terrible business.'

'I think I was,' Wynn replied hesitantly. 'I can't remember much.'

Derward nodded. 'Bara explained about your memory loss, and your wish to contact a Kenric arkship. That may be harder than you expect.'

'Why? What have you heard?'

'I travel far around the Cluster, and I hear—'

A waiter came to pour drinks, and Derward paused until he had passed over them.

'I hear many stories,' he continued. 'Most are untrue, but some have truth hidden within them. This last three months I have been trading with the Merreds and the Sinclairs. They talked about a lot of activity on the Draig arkships; higher than usual trades, unusual shipments, unscheduled orbit deviations of their fleet . . .'

'You think the Draig family are behind the attack?'

Bara asked.

'Speculation, that is all,' Derward said, adding, 'but informed speculation. And since the attack on the *Obsidian* there has been a communication blackout with the other Kenric arkships. I fear some may have changed allegiance.'

'We were attacked by the *Tephrite*,' Bara said darkly.

Derward pondered this, scratching at his stubble.

'Who are the Draig family?' Wynn asked, feeling frustrated.

'Let us talk after the meal, I think I can help to fill in the gaps,' Derward said, his mood lightening.

As he spoke there was a rustle of chairs as the other guests stood. Derward and Bara did likewise, and Wynn followed their example as he saw Chancellor Varjo coming to take her seat at the head of the table.

'Please, be seated,' Chancellor Varjo said with a wave of her hand. 'Tonight, we have honored guests, so we will speak in the trader's tongue.'

Wynn sensed an air of disdain from the other guests, as if this was a language beneath them.

Chancellor Varjo raised her glass in a toast. 'To old friends, and new.'

'And to the poor souls lost on the *Obsidian*,' Derward added.

Chancellor Varjo bristled before smiling diplomatically. 'A dreadful loss,' she said. 'You have met Wynn.'

'Yes,' Derward replied. 'I am not surprised his mind has blanked out such horrors, but in time I hope his identity will return to him.'

'Our best neurologists have already scanned this young man's brain. His memories are not lost, Mr Tarkkail, they are suppressed. Deliberately blocked. And not by Wynn; someone did this to him.'

The waiting bots attended the table, bringing out plates of sizzling hot food that tempted Wynn with their smells. As the guests began to eat, Derward leaned back in his chair, thinking. 'Deliberately blocked, you say? That does raise some interesting questions.'

'Indeed, it does,' the Chancellor replied. 'Motive seems the most pressing question to my mind.'

'Yes. Why would someone want to block this young man's memories? Who would gain from suppressing his former life? Or course, we are working on the presumption that this was a deliberate act,' Derward said, raising his eyebrows.

'It's obvious that it is deliberate,' the Chancellor replied, irritated.

'Really? Is it obvious?'

Wynn leaned closer. 'What do you mean?'

Derward sipped from his drink, composing himself. 'We know from the Chancellor's study that your memories have been blocked by some medical procedure. That suggests two possible scenarios. The first is that it was a deliberate action intended to block you – or anyone else for that matter – from accessing your mind. This suggests that there is something to hide there, either from yourself or from others. There could be valuable secrets hidden in that head of yours, Wynn! This is the theory that the Chancellor believes to be true.'

'But what's the alternative?' Bara asked. 'You said there were two scenarios,'

'Yes, I did, didn't I.' Derward smiled, pausing for a moment. 'The other scenario is that this was an unintentional outcome.'

Chancellor Vargo tutted, unconvinced. 'How so?'

'Let me paint a picture: young Wynn here has some minor neurological disorder that needs treatment. The arkship *Obsidian* is an impressive vessel, I'm told. I'd imagine they have the expertise and equipment to treat his condition. He is prepared for surgery and taken to the operating theatre. The procedure begins, just as the attack on the *Obsidian* starts.' Derward turned to Wynn, adding, 'Forgive me, but the scars on your face are new, correct?'

'Yes, I think so,' Wynn replied, his hand touching his damaged skin.

'Then perhaps they provide an answer to your problem. During surgery, the attack began. The operating theatre sustained damage, and you were badly injured. The operation was curtailed, leaving you with the memory block, and the scars to your face.

Someone must have placed you in a lifeboat and managed to get you to safety.'

Chancellor Vargo shook her head. 'The brain is a delicate organ, Mr Tarkkail, I can't imagine a botched operation would have such a specific outcome.'

Derward held up his hands. 'I am not an expert, Chancellor, I am merely putting forward an alternative theory, one that does not require a sinister conspiracy of secrets.'

'No one suggested a conspiracy.'

'Not directly, but that is the ultimate outcome of your theory, is it not? If this was a deliberate act on Wynn's mind then someone has secrets to hide. Someone doesn't want Wynn to remember. Someone conspired to hide information from him. And yet, if someone wanted certain information to be kept secret then they could have easily killed him. This mind block is far more elaborate and difficult than simply extinguishing a life. Therefore, if this was not an accident then you are implying a conspiracy of several people: a neurosurgeon and the medical support staff – one does not cut up a brain alone. And a single neurosurgeon would not choose to hide secrets in a patient's mind, would they? That implies a network of people, a hierarchy where the medical team are the end solution to the problem, not its source. A lot of people would have worked very hard to protect Wynn and the secrets in his head. Is that not the definition of a conspiracy? Do you see how far-fetched this starts to become if we simply extrapolate your supposition? Now, what do you think is the more feasible origin of Wynn's problem: an accident or a conspiracy?'

Chancellor Varjo listened, swilling the wine around her glass as she pondered the courier's words. 'As always, you speak well, Mr Tarkkail, but you are yet to convince me of your theory.'

'Then we must come back to motive, Chancellor. Who would do this? Who would gain from it and how?'

'The Church?' Bara suggested.

Derward sighed, shaking his head.

'Why not?' Chancellor Varjo added. 'It is the sort of thing we know they do.'

'Forgive me, Chancellor, I don't want to sound rude,' Derward said, half-smiling. 'What we have created here is one of the greatest wonders in the entire Cluster. We have protected it with isolation, but sometimes our views suffer for it. We can be . . . provincial in our thinking. We look for monsters and point to the Church, it is an easy presumption that requires little thinking.'

Wynn sensed the tension around the table as the Chancellor eyed Derward.

'You spend a great deal of time away from Melchior,' the Chancellor said in a whisper. 'You travel across the Cluster. You provide a vital service to our society, and for that we are grateful . . .' She inhaled, her voice becoming stronger. 'But I think you often forget the sacrifices we have made to preserve this haven of peace. Our society grew out of faith and belief, and that doctrine almost lead to our destruction. We fought to remove its vile teachings from our home and since then we have prospered, in peace and love and understanding. We do not need a god, or infinite gods to make us better people. We do not need the corruption of religion to keep us living in fear. We have grown beyond such things. Does our history make me distrust the Church? Does it make me question their motives? Yes, it does. But does that make me provincial? No, I do not think so.'

Derward smiled passively. 'You are right, Chancellor. I spend too long away from our home, and I am grateful to be back.'

'Perhaps you should consider extending your time here.'

'I would love nothing more, but I'm scheduled to leave again in a few days. The arkship Meyer will reach its aphelion soon, and I can get a good price for our fruit. Its orbit is close by.'

'That is a shame.' Chancellor Varjo noted, her eyes narrowing. 'At least we will have Bara for a little longer, I hope?'

Bara nodded. '*Lexica's* repairs will take some time. Besides, I'm looking forward to seeing my family.'

'Please pass on my regards to them. It has been too long since I saw your parents.'

'I will,' Bara smiled.

About them the diners finished their meal, breaking into smaller groups to talk further. The Chancellor drifted away, taking time to speak with others at the dinner.

Wynn, Bara and Derward took their drinks to the edge of the courtyard where a long chair rested under a thin tree. Wynn admired the dazzling view overhead. The Circadia obscured the daylight shining on the opposite quadrant, letting just a handful of star-like islands of light through its vast cowl.

'What are you thinking about?' Bara asked.

Wynn laughed, feeling embarrassed. 'I was wondering what it was like to stand on a planet. Imagine being there, no helmet or visor, air to breathe, and that view.' He pointed upwards at the artificial lights. 'Imagine seeing stars from a planet.'

'I've seen pictures,' Bara replied, 'but I don't think it's the same.'

'I met a man who says there's a planet out on the edge of the Cluster, he said he'd been there,' Derward said with a mischievous smile.

'Oh, we've all met guys like that,' Bara laughed. 'There's been stories like that since the Fracture!'

Derward nodded. 'I'd like to think there's some truth in those old stories, Bara. Maybe there are still parts of the Cluster left to discover. Doesn't that make life more interesting?'

'After the last few days I don't think I want it any more interesting.'

Wynn laughed, feeling the effects of the wine on his head. 'Earlier, you said you'd tell me about the Draig family.'

Derward's eyes widened. 'Yes, I did. Now, let's see . . .' He waved to get the attention of a bot, waiting until it had filled his glass. 'Thank you,' he said, then continued. 'Draig . . . yes, Draig. I've never been on a Draig arkship, they tend to trade with other arkships rather than independent merchants like me, but I hear plenty. They're a small family, just four or five arkships to their name. They're mineral miners around the Jupiter ring, always in territory disputes with the Li-Zhang family. But it's a big ring, room for plenty there, right? What was the name of the old girl in charge? Sinnsro . . . something like that. She was Valtais until she died last year. Since then they've been in transition. Her holograph is still in power, but her son is soon to take charge. Orcades Draig: He's the one to watch. Young guy with big ideas about expansion. Bit of a hot head, from what I hear.'

Wynn listened, hoping some of this might revive a lost memory. 'So, you think he's the one who attacked the *Obsidian*?'

'Maybe,' Derward shrugged.

'And you think this has nothing to do with Wynn's memory loss?' Bara asked.

Derward laughed. 'Sol! It's connected! I'm sure of that.'

Wynn stared at him. 'But . . . what you told the Chancellor . . .'

'Was a complete lie,' Derward grinned. He lowered his voice, aware of the other guests nearby. 'I just like to wind the old girl up. An accident during surgery? Oh, come on! How likely is that?'

'So, you think it was deliberate?' Bara checked.

'Of course it was deliberate! There's secrets inside that brain, and I'd bet good fruit on it being connected to the destruction of the *Obsidian*.' He tapped Wynn's head playfully as he spoke.

'I have to find out,' Wynn muttered in frustration. 'I need to remember.'

'Maybe I can help you with that,' Derward replied quietly.

'How?'

Derward glanced at the other guests, noting the position of the Chancellor, then swung his arm round Wynn's shoulder as he spoke in a loud voice. 'My ship? It's the best little ship in the Cluster. But I don't have time for tours, I'm a busy man.'

The chancellor watched as Derward emptied his glass, swaying slightly as he drank.

'No, no, far too busy,' he continued. 'But!' Derward handed his glass to Wynn and walked towards the exit. 'But . . . come to the dockyard tomorrow around eleven, maybe twelve, and I might be able to show you round, as long as you don't get in the way.'

Bara laughed. 'If you're awake.'

'Awake? I'm always awake.' Derward grinned, turned to find the chancellor and bowed theatrically towards her.

Chancellor Varjo nodded politely, her face fixed.

Satisfied, Derward turned to leave, bumping into the wall as he made his way out of the courtyard.

LEUGHADAIR

Derward Tarkkail's ship was an oddly-proportioned vessel, larger than Bara's *Lexica* but its mass was in its height rather than its length. Most of its bulk came from the stocky cargo containers that hung beneath the body of the ship, dwarfing the slender legs that held the ship above the dockside platform. The hull was a mess of reds and browns, discolored by years of travel. High above, Wynn saw the soft lights of the upper decks and the bridge of the ungainly ship.

A steep entry ramp extended from the rear of the craft, squeezed beneath two dirty-looking engines that dripped oil into puddles on the platform.

'It's an ugly ship,' Wynn noted.

Bara turned to him, her eyes wide. 'Don't say that to Derward, he won't be happy. Besides, it's bad luck.'

She gazed up at the stained hull as she waited by the ramp. 'Don't listen to him, he didn't mean it.' She kissed her palm than slapped it against the engine, removing a layer of dust in the shape of her hand from its pitted surface.

Wynn smirked, joining her by the ramp.

'What are you laughing at?' she asked as she patted his shoulder with her dirty hand. 'Say hi to Derward from me.'

'You're not coming?'

'No, *Lexica* needs me. If I don't give him some attention soon he'll never speak to me. Besides, I get the feeling Derward wants to talk to you alone.'

'Oh,' Wynn said, feeling nervous. 'Will I see you later?'

'Sure. Call by when you're done. I'm on platform 39A, just over there.' She gestured into the distance, to the characteristic shape of *Lexica*.

Wynn smiled his thanks before turning to climb the ramp. Inside was a narrow corridor with a low ceiling that forced him to stoop as he entered. Ahead, steam vented from a pipe, hissing as it spread through the passageway.

'Welcome aboard the *Leughadair*,' a voice bellowed. 'She's a little beauty, isn't she?'

Wynn peered under a large pipe and saw Derward grinning at him from beyond the billowing steam.

'Come, this way.' Derward disappeared up a narrow ladder. Wynn squeezed past the grey-white gas and followed him up through deck after deck until he emerged into a wider space at the top of the ship. The noise of the dockyard was all but gone now, and Wynn could hear faint background music drifting from the bridge, just ahead. Old rugs hung from the walls, softening the edges of the room, and a thick carpet cushioned the floor. Derward pulled at the hatch, cutting them off from the rest of the ship as he waved Wynn into the space.

'Please, sit, make yourselves comfortable,' he said, gesturing towards a collection of assorted cushions that littered the floor.

'You don't believe in chairs?' Wynn asked.

'Oh, I believe,' Derward laughed as he climbed the short ladder that led up to the bridge, 'but this is much nicer, don't you think?'

Wynn watched Derward as he searched through a crate, his host just a dark shape against the large windows. After a moment, Derward returned to the top of the ladder, grinning.

'Relax, make yourself at home, Wynn,' he encouraged as he leaped down the steps and joined him on the carpet. In his hand was a cylindrical container which he placed between them on the floor.

'You like my ship?' Derward inquired, his eyebrows raised.

'She's beautiful,' Wynn lied.

'Beautiful? You think?'

'Y–yes.'

'Hrmm,' Derward thought. 'Really? I always thought she was a bit dumpy, but – Sol! – she's a gem of a ship! Now, I don't have a lot of time, but I can give you the tour, show you the bridge.'

'I came to talk,' Wynn said urgently.

Derward leaned forward and picked up the canister in front of him. 'Oh, yes, we can talk. I'll tell you about the engines, how I keep them running so quietly . . .'

As he spoke he pressed the base of the canister and twisted it. The device clicked and Wynn heard a high-pitched vibration. Derward put his finger to his lips. '. . . This is an excellent ship and I'm sure you'll like it.'

The device pipped twice, and Derward smiled with relief. 'It's okay, we can talk openly now.'

'What is that?' Wynn asked, pointing to the device.

'A jammer,' Derward explained. 'Old habit, I don't like eavesdroppers.'

'But we're in Melchior's dock. Isn't it safe here?'

'Indulge me,' Derward replied. 'I feel more comfortable with it on.' He looked up from the device, his eyes scrutinizing Wynn. 'So . . . you want your memories back?'

'Of course! You know how to do it?'

Derward laughed, rolling up the sleeves on his loose shirt. 'Well now, I'm not going to make any boastful claims, in case this doesn't work, but I have some meditation techniques that might help.'

'Meditation?' Wynn asked skeptically.

'A method I've picked up on my travels. Calms the mind, helps you unlock things that are hidden.'

Wynn said nothing.

Derward noted his doubtful expression and added, 'You don't have to try it if you don't want to.'

Wynn sighed. 'I don't have anything to lose, do I?'

'No, you don't' Derward grinned. He pulled out a small disc from his pocket and offered it to Wynn. 'Here, do as I do.'

Derward produced a second object and placed it in the center of his forehead. The device took hold and throbbed softly with a bluish light.

Wynn looked at the little device in his own hands. 'What is this?'

'Theta state inducer. It adjusts and amplifies your brain wave frequency, helps to generate a meditative state. These two devices are linked. I act as a sort of pacemaker, to help to get you to the right state of mind. It doesn't hurt.'

Wynn placed the device onto his forehead. It was cool to the touch and vibrated gently on his skin. 'Okay, what happens now?'

'Just relax,' Derward said quietly, 'Close your eyes and follow my instructions. I'm going to start bringing you down from a gamma state to beta. You should start to feel calmer.'

Wynn sensed the device sending a cooling wave through his brain, slowing his thoughts. It was as if the rest of the world faded away; Melchior, the dockside, the ship, one by one they became insignificant, until only Wynn and Derward remained.

'That's good,' Derward said, sounding distant. 'We're coming down through alpha state . . .'

Images began to form in his mind, appearing as if from nowhere, hazy at first but soon they were clear and vivid. He saw the *Obsidian*, frozen in time, moments before its destruction. Then he saw himself inside the lifeboat, adrift in space. His fear was gone, he felt in control. It was almost as if he could step out of the lifeboat . . .

'Theta state,' a voice said from somewhere far away. 'I can see your thoughts now.'

Wynn was in space, adrift amongst the wreckage of the *Obsidian*. He turned to see his lifeboat: he was still inside, his face frozen in a scream.

'. . . that's good. Focus on the moment . . .'

He turned back to look at the *Obsidian*, at the pockets of red and orange that erupted from her skin.

'. . . good. Hold that moment. Now, take us back, slowly . . .'

The explosions tumbled back towards the ship, pushing their way inside. The holes in the hull closed up around them. Something moved past him, towards the ship: it was his lifeboat.

'. . . go with it. Follow it . . .'

Wynn moved with the lifeboat, past the maelstrom of debris, towards the *Obsidian*. As he got closer it became harder to move, as if he was pushing against some resisting force.

Ahead was the tiny dot of the launch bay. The lifeboat dropped towards it, getting smaller and smaller. He couldn't follow it; the force was too great.

'. . . keep going. This is the start of the wall in your mind. You have the power to go through it. I am with you . . .'

Wynn felt a surge of energy pulse through him and the resisting force gave, just a little. He began to chase the lifeboat, watching as it grew in size. He fell into the launch tube, through the lifeboat, and into the *Obsidian* itself. The force grew again, trying to repel him, and he felt as if he might tumble out of the vision at any moment.

'You can do this. You are inside the wall now. Hold this moment . . .'

Wynn tried to focus. The lifeboat sat in its launch silo, the main hatch open. He saw himself sat in the chair, his chin resting on his chest, his eyes half-closed. He turned to see another figure, close by. Their shape was blurred and dark, devoid of detail.

'. . . concentrate on them!'

Wynn gazed at the dark shape. Its arm was outstretched towards the lifeboat. What were they doing? He moved closer to the figure and he saw the fingers appear out of the murk. There a hand, strapping his unconscious body into the lifeboat. His eyes followed the hand, up the arm, towards the shoulder. As he did more and more detail revealed itself.

The arm wore a uniform, grey and red with a rank of office on its shoulder. Then the chest and neck formed out of the darkness. It was a man! He let his eyes trace the head, revealing the face. He was dark skinned with a bald head and broad nose. He hoped he might know the face, but there was no instant of recognition, no flood of memories unlocked.

Wynn moved back to see the man properly. His uniform was formal, with dark boots and a thick leather belt pulling the buttoned jacket in. Along his chest was a line of badges . . . medals, perhaps? The details were blurring again, it took so much effort to focus. He felt the edges of the world begin to crumble.

'Let time go forwards . . .'

The figure began to move, fastening the harness around the unconscious Wynn in the lifeboat. He was aware of another figure moving nearby, of splinters of conversations between them. The military man stood over the lifeboat and said something to Wynn. The words were far away, just distorted noise coming from the man's mouth. Wynn forced the image back. He let the words play again, trying to decipher them. Nothing. Again, he forced the vision to replay itself, and he moved closer to the man's mouth, listening intently, watching as the lips formed syllables. Still, it was little more than a discordant noise, but one fragment of a word came to him: *Hal.* Confusion broke his attention and the edges of the vision frayed.

'. . . hold your focus!'

The image began to collapse. The deck of the *Obsidian* buckled and fractured. The man dissolved into dust until just his hand remained, grasping the harness to Wynn's seat. The colors shifted, blurring into one until all that remained was Wynn in a storm of noise. A shape came to him, drawing him out of the mayhem, a golden line of light: The Infinite. He followed it, feeling its warmth as it grew. Wynn reached out, sensing it change from a twisted star into a piece of golden jewelry hanging from a chain. His fingers touched it and the last of the vision collapsed.

Derward knelt over him, his face full of concern.

'Finally!' he said, relived. 'you've been out for ages.'

Wynn sat up, feeling groggy.

'You passed out,' Derward said as he handed a bottle of water to Wynn. 'Can you remember anything?'

'I . . . I saw the moment before the lifeboat launched, and a man in military uniform.'

'Did you recognize him?'

Wynn pictured his face again. 'No.'

'A pity,' Derward said. 'It seems the memory wall is substantial. We could try again but I don't think you'll be able to get through it.'

Frustration overwhelmed Wynn. 'Then how am I going to find out what happened to me?'

Derward thought for a moment. 'Whoever did this will no doubt have some way of removing it. A keyword, an image, perhaps. Something that will trigger your subconscious to eradicate the wall to your memories. But until you know what that trigger is I don't see how you're going to get past the memory wall.'

Wynn nodded, feeling exhausted.

'You should go,' Derward said briskly. 'You've been here far too long for a simple guided tour. We don't want to raise any suspicion.'

'Are you always this nervous?'

'Cautious, not nervous. It's kept me alive this long.' Derward straightened, staring at Wynn. 'Look, I'm leaving the day after tomorrow. Perhaps you might like to join me? I can always use an extra pair of hands. In return, maybe we can test that memory of yours some more . . . and I can see what I can find out about the Kenric arkships.'

Wynn thought about Derward's offer. It felt like Melchior was a dead end for him now. He needed to be out there, to find other Kenric survivors, to learn about the Draig family. Then he pictured Bara and doubts clouded his mind. He didn't want to leave her, but he couldn't live without knowing who he was.

'Yes,' he said eventually, 'I'd like that.'

'Good. Now go, get out!' Derward laughed. 'I'll be in touch when I'm ready to launch.'

Derward's smile fell away as he watched the boy leave, replaced with a sense of foreboding. He had shared his vision, he had seen Wynn's last moments on board the *Obsidian*. The boy had not known the other figure in his vision, but Derward had. Long ago, he had been on board the *Obsidian* and had met many of the royal household. The uniformed man Wynn had seen in his vision was Cam Tanis, the Lord Chamberlain to the House of Kenric, second-in-command to Prince Thyred. Derward had recognized him immediately, his surprise almost breaking the vision. He had suppressed his knowledge, wondering as to why such a high-ranking individual would be tending to Wynn in his lifeboat.

Then, as the vision moved forward, he had seen Tanis speak. His voice was inaudible but Derward had read his lips as easily as if they had been words on a page.

'. . . Hal, my Prince.'

My Prince.

Wynn didn't know who he was. But Derward did. He had no doubt anymore: this strange boy was Prince Halstead, rightful heir to the House of Kenric.

MEMORIES

It was always strange to come home. Bara Delaterre had not been in this house for over a year, but after just one night she was already feeling the confines of its small walls. This was the room she had grown up in, sharing it with her sister until . . .

She still missed her, even after all these years. Bara had been so young when Guin had died, it was hard to recall a genuine memory that she hadn't stolen from photos and home movies. The pictures still hung on the wall, her face haunting her even now.

She loved coming home. She hated coming home.

Bara walked through the house to the little patio with its view over the park. She rested in her mother's old wicker chair, smiling at its familiar shabbiness. They'd been threatening to throw it out for years.

'Don't let her catch you sitting there.'

Bara looked up, glad to see her father walking through the house. His overalls were covered in dirt from his shift in the processing plant.

'Don't let her catch you walking through the house

125

in those clothes,' Bara teased. She kissed his cheek, tasting oil and chemicals.

'Good day?' he asked.

Bara shrugged. 'I put *Lexica* on a diagnostic sequence. I've switched off his core intelligence to do a full sweep of his main drive.'

'I bet he wasn't happy,' Leo said.

'Furious! He'll be down for a few more hours. There's nothing much I can do until he's back online again, then I can see what's left to fix.'

Leo perched on the low wall that marked the edge of the patio. 'Hatch all done?'

'Like new.'

'And the micro stabilizer?'

Bara nodded.

Satisfied, Leo smiled. 'He'll be as good as new.'

'Better.'

'Better? I doubt that.'

'Dad,' Bara laughed, 'you might have built him, but I've ripped out almost every system in there and upgraded it. He's twice the ship you gave me.'

Leo sighed wearily. 'I suppose he is. How long you hangin' around for?'

Bara hesitated. 'Not long.'

He tried to hide it, but she saw the disappointment on her father's face.

'Not straight away,' she added quickly, 'but we're short of medicines. I can get some work on a Ciation ship; they're always hiring, and they pay well.'

'Ciation.' Leo said it as if it was a curse.

'They're not so bad . . .'

'They're rich! Know how they got so rich? Slavery, that's how.'

'Dad, that was ages ago.'

Leo squeezed his fingers together. 'Not so long ago, I can still remember. They do a good job of making themselves sound proper and decent now, but it ain't that long since they had plenty of blood on their hands. Them and C-Waac, and don't try convincing me otherwise.'

Bara knew better than to argue with him when he was like this. The Cluster might have changed but her father never would.

'You eaten yet?' he asked, straightening his back.

'Not yet. I think Wynn is coming over.'

'Wynn?'

Bara shook her head. 'Dad, I told you. He's the one from the *Obsidian*.'

Leo's eyes widened. 'Ah, the stupid one.'

'He's not stupid, he just can't remember.'

'There's a difference?' Leo teased.

'Look, if you're gonna be like this then I won't introduce you to him,' Bara laughed.

'Best behavior, I promise.' Leo stood, checking his clothes. 'I should change.'

'Before Mum gets home, yeah, good idea!'

The food was delicious. Bara had become so used to processed nutrients that she'd almost forgotten how different freshly grown vegetables tasted, especially when her mother was cooking them. Tonight, it was steamed broccoli with callaloo, seasoned potatoes, grated carrots and daikon. The aroma of spices and seasoning wafted through the house, setting her taste buds on fire long before the meal arrived at the table.

Bara sat back, contented and sleepy. Her parents hadn't embarrassed her, in fact her father had been quite the host. He'd asked questions, but not too many, and when Wynn had taken an interest in her father's engineering background he had known to curtail his stories before he'd lost his audience.

'Did you enjoy it?' Bara asked Wynn as the house bot cleared the table.

'Of course!' he grinned. 'This was the best meal I can remember eating.'

Bara's mother beamed with satisfaction, the irony of Wynn's statement missing the mark. 'There's plenty left. I'll vac some for you to take with you.'

'Thank you,' Wynn replied.

'How did it go with Derward?' Bara asked as her parents left the table.

Wynn frowned. She had gotten used to the scars, and bruises were going down. It was easier to see the face beneath it all now. He had kind eyes, she thought, the sort that could look sad sometimes. He had a strong chin, and a mouth that looked like it might break into a smile at any moment. He had probably been handsome, before his injuries. The broken nose, the scars, the burns: most of it looked treatable. In time, he would be handsome again.

Bara realized she was staring and blushed as she looked away. Wynn was talking and she hadn't been listening.

'. . . managed to remember a bit more about the attack, of sitting in my lifeboat before I got out, but that's all. There was a man helping me, but I didn't know him.' Wynn sighed. 'I'm sorry, it's just so frustrating, not knowing who I am.'

'I know,' she said, putting her hand on his. She had done it without thinking, but now she felt uncomfortable, and pulled it away.

'What sort of person am I?' Wynn continued. 'Am I good? Am I likeable? What do I do? What's my last name?'

He stood and went to the open door that led to the patio, taking in the air and the view.

Bara joined him there. 'Well, you're good, I know that. You saved me, didn't you? And, yes, you're likeable,' she laughed. Wynn managed a tiny smile in return. 'And last names are overrated, aren't they?'

'But it's not just that. A name means family, doesn't it? I don't know anything about where I come from. Being here, with you and your parents, it's obvious how much they mean to you, how important Melchior is to you. It defines you, it makes you who you are.'

'True, but I think you already know who you are, Wynn.'

He turned to look at her. 'What do you mean?'

'You're a proud Kenric man, aren't you? I can see the anger driving you. You want to find out who destroyed the *Obsidian*. You want them to pay for what they did. You might not know your last name but you know where you came from. You came from a Kenric arkship. You're one of them, so you know who your family is. That's what defines you, that's what drives you.' Bara moved closer, her voice softer. 'You're a good man, Wynn, that's all you really need to know.'

'Thanks,' Wynn replied. 'I wish I was as sure as you are.'

The house bot came to the door and made a small apologetic cough.

'Yes, Mr Boo,' Bara said.

'Can I get you a drink?'

Bara shook her head. The bot turned to Wynn. 'Something for you, sir?'

'No, thank you,' Wynn replied.

The machine bowed slightly and returned to the house.

Wynn, stifling a smile turned to look at Bara. 'Mr Boo?'

She laughed, blushing. 'My sister named him, when

she was little. She couldn't say *bot* properly. It came out as *boo*, so he got called Mr Boo. Doesn't seem right to change it now.'

Wynn laughed. It was a warm, deep laugh that seemed to dispel his worries.

'Is your sister still on Melchior?' he asked.

Bara felt the familiar knot in her stomach. She hadn't had to explain this to anyone for years. News spread quickly on Melchior.

'She . . .' Bara faltered, took a breath. 'Guin died, when I was very young.'

'I'm sorry,' Wynn said. It was his turn to touch her hand, but he didn't remove it. His skin was warm, comforting.

'A stupid accident, that's all,' Bara continued, trying to keep the emotion out of her voice. 'She loved to explore, going on adventures to see the world. She'd drag me along with her. We'd find hatches, airlocks, service ducts, all the places little kids weren't supposed to go. Really dangerous, but she just loved to discover new places. One day, she fell . . . she fell down a ventilation shaft. I tried, but I couldn't reach her, I was so small. I raised the alarm but it was too late. They found her in the vent system close to the dockside. Her legs were broken but she'd dragged herself there, trying to get out. The ships pump their waste gasses into that system . . . she didn't stand a chance.'

The emotion of the memory overwhelmed her, and

Wynn took her in his arms. She didn't resist, letting her head rest on his shoulder as she cried.

Eventually, she pulled away, wiping her face. 'Sorry, I don't talk about it too much.'

'Don't be sorry.'

She shook her head, feeling exposed. 'Coming home, it brings it all back.'

'It's okay,' he soothed.

Bara tried to shake off the feelings of regret. 'I could use some help tomorrow. *Lexica* needs some love and attention. I could use another pair of hands.'

'Sure,' Wynn replied. 'You'll have to teach me what to do.'

'I get the feeling you're a quick learner. A few more days, maybe a week, and I think I'll be ready to go. I'm going to try a Ciation ship, there's one not too far away. You could come with me, maybe see what we can find out about the attack from them.'

Wynn grimaced, glancing away. 'I'm leaving . . .'

'What?'

'With Derward. Day after tomorrow, I think. I'm not sure where he's going – I don't think he's too sure yet either – but he can help me with my memory, I think. And I can't just stay here, Bara, I need to get back out there. I need to find some answers.'

She hesitated, uncertain of her emotions.

'But I can help you with the ship,' Wynn added, 'until I go.'

'Sure, fine,' Bara replied, trying to sound casual. 'Whatever you think.'

Wynn smiled, those sad eyes of his pitying her. It was as if he could see though her, know what she was feeling even before she did. 'Shall we have coffee?' she asked, turning into the room, desperate to break his gaze.

Wynn shook his head. 'It's late, and I'm feeling tired. I think I should go.'

Bara nodded solemnly.

'But I'll see you tomorrow, okay?'

'Yes,' she replied, watching as he found her parents, exchanging pleasantries, thanking them for the meal. He was at the door, saying goodbye, smiling, and then he was gone, and Bara felt more alone than she had in years.

BETTER TIMES

Reader Pace Durante sat on his bed and stared at the oil painting hanging on the far wall. He had acquired it many years ago when he was stationed on the edge of the Neptune Wastes. Perhaps it was the bleak hostility of that place, or maybe he was getting sentimental, but the painting had struck a chord deep within him and he had to own it. Since then it had moved with him to every new posting, finding a home at the foot of his bed where he could stare at it and let his mind wander. It was one of the few material possessions he had, and no-doubt it was frowned upon by his superiors, but he was compelled to keep it with him anyway. A tiny act of rebellion.

The image depicted a long-forgotten fairy-tale popular before the Fracture, of a prince finding a sleeping maiden in the heart of a castle frozen in time. A shaft of light intersected the painting, bringing with it a host of angelic spirits who banished the dark forces that had made the citadel their home. The colors were golden, the figure-work exquisite, and the picture had occupied his eye for many hours, its romance and innocence warming his pessimistic soul.

But not tonight. He could find no peace in those pre-historic brushstrokes. He looked away from the painting, back to the report in his hand and read it once more, letting the details sink in, trying to control his anger. The arkship *Obsidian* had been destroyed, hundreds – maybe thousands – of people dead, and it was his fault. He had foreseen this outcome, he had noted it in several reports, all of which were now safely stored and indexed forever in the Church's archive. And yet he had done nothing to avoid this eventuality.

Pace Durante had observed Orcades Draig for many years, recording his personality index in great detail, forecasting his development, and adjusting it when necessary. He was ignorant and arrogant; that made him pliable, and Durante was sure he had contained his more excessive potential. He had kept him to the plan, that was all that mattered.

Until yesterday.

Yesterday, Orcades Draig had deviated from the plan, and the Scribe wanted to know why. Durante had no answers. He had underestimated Orcades Draig, or perhaps he had overestimated his influence on him and his mother. He stared at the painting, trying to decide where he had gone wrong.

The pad on his bedside table pinged urgently; the Scribe again, he guessed, or perhaps Librarian Okuda with another report. He picked it up; the call bore an authorized Church ident mark and was coming through on their secure network, but the caller's name was missing. He thought about ignoring it, but he decided there was little point hiding from his folly. He let the call connect and waited until a face appeared on the screen.

'Reader Durante? Are you there?' a voice asked.

Durante kept himself away from the screen until he could place the caller. The face was familiar, like a distant memory from a long-forgotten place. The hair was flecked with grey, and the short beard was new to him, but he recognized the pronounced cheekbones and those piercing eyes.

'Reader Vurig?' Durante spoke in a whisper as he picked up the pad. 'Or do I call you Tarkkail now?'

The caller looked down regretfully. 'Not Reader, not anymore, but yes it's me. Is this a secured com?'

Durante checked his device and nodded. 'It's good to see you. How long has it been? Since the *Conquistador*?'

'It has been a while. I am sorry I'm not calling you in better times. I presume you know about the *Obsidian*?'

Durante's stomach fluttered. How quickly had word spread? 'Yes, I have heard.'

'Do you know who is behind the attack?'

Durante hesitated. Derward Tarkkail may no longer be a Reader but he was obviously still part of the

Church. A Watcher, perhaps? Even so, he should be cautious. 'The investigation is ongoing,' he replied.

Derward Tarkkail shook his head, obviously frustrated. 'I don't have long, Durante. I think this is a Draig plot against the House of Kenric. You're stationed on a Draig arkship, correct?'

Durante didn't reply.

'Look, Pace, I'm not asking you to compromise your position,' Derward continued, 'but I need to tell you what I know, and I need your advice.'

'My advice?' The last time Durante had met him Derward Tarkkail had been the more senior Reader; he had not asked for advice then. He wondered what had happened to his old friend in the intervening years.

'Yes,' Derward replied, moving closer to the screen. 'I can't contact *Icarus* directly, and you're the only one I can trust with this information.'

The image fractured into a matrix of color, then reformed again.

'. . . must be quick, before they spot my com.'

'What is it you need to tell me?' Durante asked.

'The House of Kenric, I believe the heir survived the attack on the *Obsidian*.'

'Prince Halstead is alive?' Durante gasped.

'I believe so, yes.'

'And you know where he is?'

'He's on Melchior.'

Durante's mind raced with new possibilities.

'I am watching over him,' Derward continued. 'He does not know who he is, there's a memory wall keeping his identity from him. Pace, I need your help. What should I do with him?'

'You were right to bring this to me, Derward, thank you. I will consult the plan and–'

'Forget the plan!' Derward interrupted. 'I need your advice, now! Should I keep him hidden here or take him to *Icarus*?'

'Neither,' Durante replied. 'I will come for him. He shall have the Church's protection.'

Derward's face broke with relief. 'How long till you get here?'

A series of co-ordinates scrolled across the bottom of the pad. Durante checked it against his current position and said, 'There are some things I need to do first.'

'Any delay could be–'

'I will be swift, you have my word. Can you keep him safe till I can get there?'

'Yes . . . yes, I can,' Derward replied. 'Thank you.'

'I presume Melchior is as secretive and as hostile as ever?'

Derward nodded. 'Contact me when you are close. I'll come in my ship to meet you.'

The picture fizzed with interference.

'It was good to see you once more,' Durante said, smiling. The com ended and the room fell into silence.

Durante stood in front of the painting, letting his eyes absorb the smallest details. Sometimes, he thought, by studying a fraction of the picture he could better appreciate the image as a whole. 'Details,' he muttered, turning to find his pad. He waited as it confirmed his identity and then he accessed the Church's core database. There was the plan in all its fine detail. Orcades' move against the House of Kenric had caused some deviation, a section of equations flagged in red. Durante wondered what the return of a Kenric heir might do to the predictions. He inputted the new information and waited as the plan realigned itself. More red. More deviation. More war. More death. Orcades had set in motion a chain of events that could not be easily corrected by the return of a Kenric to his throne. What then? What was the best option? Killing the heir would not improve things. The columns of red remained.

Durante stepped back from the painting and stared at it for several minutes.

Melchior. What was Melchior's role in the plan? That arrogant little cluster! They thought themselves hidden, but the Church had been aware of them for many years, tolerating their isolationist heresy. But . . . *what if they – and the Kenric heir – were removed from the plan?* Durante wondered. He entered the data and waited. The wall of red turned green, just a small cluster of numbers remained an annoying crimson now.

A more agreeable outcome. Their deaths would help to avoid many more. It was a price worth paying . . . He was saving people. The Gods willed it.

He should consult with the Scribe, he told himself. But then the glory would be diluted. This was his solution. Durante alone was purging the plan of deviation. He alone should take the glory for his good work.

He said a prayer to the Infinite Gods asking for their guidance and, when no reply came, he decided it was a sign that he should work alone.

So be it. If that was the Gods' will.

Reader Durante contemplated his actions, mourning the deaths that would come, then he called Valtais Sinnsro Draig to arrange a meeting. Through the mother he would control the son.

ENLIGHTENMENT

The banquet hall was vast, like all the state rooms on the arkship *Fenrir*. Orcades Draig took in the excessive splendor as he walked towards the table at the center of the room. The hall sat at the top of the arkship with a view out to space along three sides. Orcades gave it only a cursory glance; he felt the slow turn of the stars unbalance him and he looked up to the giant chandeliers that decorated the high ceiling instead. He had no interest in the finery of the room, no interest in the family history that underpinned it, but it was either the ceiling or having to look at the two people waiting for him at the table. He was only expecting one.

His mother stood to greet him. Her guest remained seated until the last possible moment. Orcades saw the insult and ignored the old fool, leaving him to wait with his hand outstretched. 'I did not know we had a guest tonight, mother.'

'Reader Durante is always welcome at our table,' Sinnsro Draig said to her son as she gestured to the purple-robed man by her side.

143

Orcades took the other man's hand but refused to look at him.

'That is my fault,' Reader Durante said, offering a seat to Orcades as if he was the host. 'Valtais Sinnsro and I had a meeting earlier today and, after our discussion, I begged your mother to permit me to join you this evening. I hope that is acceptable?'

Orcades sat, eyeing his mother with suspicion. 'More prophecy, mother?'

Sinnsro tutted, indicating to the waiting bots to serve them. 'Not prophecy, Orcades: strategy.'

The machines attended the table, pouring wine into ornately decorated glasses and placing one in front of each person.

Orcades sighed impatiently, knowing what was to come.

Sinnsro's eyes narrowed, scolding him as she raised her glass. 'To the Infinite Gods.'

'May their reflections shine upon us all,' Reader Durante added solemnly.

They both waited for Orcades. He picked up his glass and gestured towards theirs. 'May their blessings shine upon us,' he muttered.

'Infinite blessings,' Sinnsro and Durante said in unison. They both paused then sipped at the wine.

Orcades drank all of his and put the empty glass on the table. Almost at once one of the bots appeared and refilled it.

Reader Durante smiled, his thin lips tightening. 'Your faith is not as vital to you as it is to your mother, is it?'

'I have no issue with your Church, Reader,' Orcades replied. 'I do not object to its existence—'

'That is wise,' Reader Durante injected.

'—or to those who wish to believe in its teachings, but I do object to its habit of interference in the affairs of others. No, Reader, I do not share my mother's unswerving faith in your Church.'

'Belief is an individual's luxury,' Reader Durante said, eyeing Orcades with intent, 'but you are not an individual, and your lack of faith troubles me.'

'Not an individual? How so?'

'You are Orcades Draig, Heir Valtais, leader of your people—'

'When the time is right,' Sinnsro added.

Reader Durante bowed respectfully. 'Of course. But one day you will lead the House of Draig and your people will look to you for direction. You are a figurehead, a beacon, a guiding light. You are not an individual and you cannot afford the luxury of an individual's indifference. You must be clear in your beliefs, you must lead by your opinion. The Church would not look favorably on anything but complete devotion.'

'Are you threatening me?' Orcades asked.

'Orcades!' his mother scolded.

'Threatening you? No,' Reader Durante said, his

smile fading as he stood to take in the view. 'But the Church is concerned by your recent actions, your attack on the House of Kenric, the destruction of the *Obsidian*. These are matters that affect the Church, and your refusal to accept our counsel is . . . troubling. But no, the Church does not threaten. This is merely a word of caution from one friend to another.'

'Friend? You are a guest here, nothing more,' Orcades scoffed, emptying his glass again, 'I do not require your counsel. You remain here at my pleasure, but I think perhaps you forget your place. Do not presume–'

Orcades' chair fell backwards as a hand found his throat. Reader Durante knelt over him, a knee pushing into Orcades' chest as he slowly choked him.

'It is you who presumes, Orcades,' Reader Durante whispered. 'You forget yourself, and you forget who it is you talk to. I am a Reader of the Church of The Infinite. The Gods speak through me. My will is their will.'

Wide eyed, Orcades searched for help, but his mother and the bots did nothing.

'You may be the heir to a great and noble family, young Orcades,' Reader Durante continued, his mouth close to Orcades' ear, 'but you exist at our pleasure. The Church bestows its love on you so that you might live. Do you understand?'

Orcades, unable to find his breath, nodded quickly.

'Good, I am glad.' Reader Durante released his hand and straightened, adjusting his robes.

Orcades gasped for air, his face red. He pulled himself to his knees, his mind racing, full of impulsive thoughts of retaliation. He glanced up; there was Durante's hand in front of him, waiting for his submission. Orcades glanced to his mother and realized he was on the wrong side in this battle. He buried his feelings and kissed Reader Durante's hand.

Satisfied, Durante turned his hand over and offered it to Orcades.

'The wine is good,' Durante said as he pulled Orcades to his feet. The Reader returned to his chair, acting as if nothing had happened. 'You have had a good harvest this year?'

'I . . . I believe so,' Orcades replied, still uncertain what just happened.

A bot stepped forward and righted his chair, waiting until Orcades was seated to place a napkin on his knee. He stared at the Reader, trying to hide the vengeful thoughts pushing blood to his cheeks.

'You did not come here to discuss crops. What is it you want to talk about?' Orcades asked.

Reader Durante smiled to himself.

'Rumors,' Sinnsro said. 'About Prince Halstead of the House of Kenric.'

'The dead prince?'

Sinnsro frowned. 'There are rumors he is still alive.'

Orcades sneered as he took a drink from his glass.

'More than rumors,' Reader Durante corrected. 'Intelligence.'

'What sort of intelligence?'

'The Church stands outside of quarrels between houses,' Durante said as he pondered his glass of wine. 'We do not interfere–'

Orcades scoffed, then saw Durante's steely glare and he looked away.

'We advise, we guide and steer. We do not get involved, unless it is the will of the Gods, of course.'

'Of course,' Orcades smiled icily. He was looking forward to planning this man's downfall, when the time was right.

'But,' Durante continued, 'if we can help our friends then we will. This . . . dispute between you and the House of Kenric–'

'It is not a dispute!' Orcades barked. 'It is my right to rule.' He turned to stare at his mother. 'Tell him! Tell him of the prophecies.'

Reader Durante held up his hand, silencing Sinnsro. 'Child,' he said to Orcades, 'the Church is the origin of all prophecy. We are the keepers of history and doctrine and projection. The Church will write your legends. But remember, there is a difference between divine prophecy and wishful thinking.'

Orcades clenched his fists, trying to keep his temper in check. He wanted to beat this man's skull to pieces, watch as his brains stained the expensive carpet. He took a breath and smiled. 'There are things even the Church does not know.'

'Really? You think we do not know of your claim to the Kenric throne, that your father was the recently departed Prince Thyred – killed by your actions, I might add – that you seek to take what you believe is rightfully yours by birth?'

Orcades stared at the man, unable to respond. He turned to his mother. She sat with her hand to her mouth, tears streaming down her face.

'Forgive me, Valtais Sinnsro,' Durante said softly, 'I did not wish to upset you. Perhaps we should continue without you.'

Sinnsro's holograph flickered then broke apart, evaporating into the air.

'What did you do?' Orcades demanded.

'Turned her off. Oh, don't worry, her matrix is safe. I have deleted the last few moments so as not to upset her.' Durante chuckled to himself. 'It's funny how much respect we give such simulations, isn't it? We treat them as flesh and blood, worrying about their feelings, when in fact your mother has been dead for over a year, has she not?'

Orcades stood, his rage boiling.

'Oh, do sit down, boy,' Durante said. 'We both know you'll end up on the floor again.'

Orcades glared at the Reader, locking eyes with his,

and his anger seemed to leave him. An overwhelming compulsion to obey flooded his mind, soothing his thoughts. He would sit, he decided, and listen to what this man had to say. 'Please, continue.'

'As you wish,' Durante replied. 'The Church knows many things; the Church sees all. The Church sees a boy with ambition to rule, but he is stupid and impulsive. His ambition, left unchecked, will start a war, a war that will spread throughout the entire Cluster. We see death and destruction . . . possibly the end to our fragile race. The Church does not wish that. The Church needs believers, otherwise . . . the Church will have no purpose, and without purpose the Church will cease to exist as well, Gods or no Gods. You are the pinnacle, a vertex of uncertainty. The calculations are too erratic. Without guidance, without our support, you may be the death of us all. But I bring good news, child. The Gods have spoken, and they have bestowed their love upon you, Orcades Draig, Heir Valtais to the House of Draig, son of Thyred Halstead Kenric.'

'They . . . have?' Orcades asked. He sensed an embrace of love washing over him, and he felt whole for the first time in his life.

Durante walked round the table and stood over him. 'Yes, child, they have. They see your mission to claim your birth right and the Infinite Gods' reflections shine brightly upon you. Through me they will help and guide you, but you must know that there remains an obstacle in your path to enlightenment.'

'An obstacle?' Orcades repeated softly.

'The son of Thyred still lives.'

Orcades shook his head. 'His ship was destroyed along with the *Obsidian*. He is dead.'

'No, the heir to the House of Kenric is alive. Prince Halstead, the second son of Thyred lives. He is the legitimate child of Thyred and Evanine Kenric, ordained to rule. He is the rightful heir. Your claim is invalid as long as Halstead lives. You cannot sit on the Kenric throne until he is dead.'

'Then . . . I must seek him out,' Orcades replied, thinking quickly. 'I will hunt him down and kill him.'

Durante beamed malevolently. 'The Gods smile upon you, Orcades. The Church knows where he is.'

MOVEMENT

The dockside was alive with activity, even at this early hour. Wynn walked past a giant ore mining vessel that was unloading its cargo onto a conveyor belt. The clumps of rock trundled out of the craft, throwing up dust that danced in the ship's spotlights, and disappeared below the dock to be crushed and processed. He heard the miners shouting from inside the ship, talking and laughing as they went about their work, just tiny dots high above him inside the vessel.

He weaved past a wall of containers waiting to be loaded onto a smaller craft, and followed the steps down to the next level. Sparks fell through the grating, their little lights dying as they dropped close to Wynn. A dock worker hosed down a patch of spilled oil while a bot brushed it clean. The man nodded to Wynn as he maneuvered past the slick. Ahead, he saw the distinctive shape of Bara's ship, *Lexica*. Its repaired hull seemed to glisten in the harsh spotlights of the dock, making the ship stand out from its grey-black mooring.

A grinding noise drifted on the slow breeze, bringing

with it the metallic smell of burning. He followed the sound and saw a helmeted figure perched on top of *Lexica*, half hidden in a cloud of billowing smoke.

Wynn called up, waving his arm.

The figure switched off the grinder and revealed her face from under the protective helmet. Bara acknowledged him and shouted, 'Hatch's open. C'mon in.'

Wynn smiled to himself as he found the entry ramp and ambled inside.

'Morning, Wynn,' a voice said as he entered.

'Hello, Lexica,' Wynn replied. 'How are you?'

'Better, for the most part,' the ship replied in its disinterested voice. 'Bara has completed most of the repairs to my satisfaction, although there are still a number of minor fixes that need her attention before I am ready to leave.'

Wynn laughed. 'Good to hear. Where's Bara?'

'Keep going up, you'll find her.'

His memory of the ship was vague, and Wynn got the impression that *Lexica* wasn't in the mood to help, so he followed the faint trail of noises coming from the top of the ship. Eventually he found himself back on the bridge, looking out over the dock. He saw Bara on the hull and decided to join her. He left the bridge, found an open hatch and climbed out of the ship. The view was specular, he could see the entire vista of the dock from up here: ships being repaired, others unloading their cargo, people going about their work, service vehicles driving along the walkways, bots making sure everything ran smoothly. He took a moment to take it all in, then he walked towards Bara, making sure his footing was sound.

'Hiding from me?' he teased.

'Jobs to do, Wynn,' she replied without looking at him.

'It's great up here, isn't it?'

Bara stopped for a moment, looked down at the dock then returned to her work. She knelt at an open panel, replacing a box-like component with a dozen wires trailing from it.'

'What are you doing?' Wynn asked, trying to make conversation.

'Replacing the skin sensor,' she replied quietly.

Wynn hesitated, then tried again. 'What's that do.'

Bara sighed. 'Checks for impacts or things stuck to the hull . . .' She put down her tools. 'What do you want, Wynn?'

'Want?' The question took him by surprise. 'I don't know, I just came to see you, and to help, if I can.'

Bara returned to the sensor. 'That's great, but I'm kinda busy right now.'

'Oh, right,' Wynn replied. 'Well, okay. Derward's planning on leaving this evening. Will I see you before then?'

Bara attached the final wire and hit an intercom

switch on her wrist. 'Lex, how's that?'

'Skin sensor online again,' Lexica's voice came from the wrist communicator. 'Calibrating now.'

'Bara . . .' Wynn said.

She held up her hand to him.

'Sensor fully functional,' Lexica said.

'Okay, good,' Bara replied. 'Give it a test. You should pick up us two on the starboard wing.'

Wynn shook his head. 'Bara, please, can we talk?'

Lexica's voice broke over the com. 'Scanning . . . scanning. Scan complete.'

'Well?' Bara asked.

'I have detected two objects on the starboard wing,' Lexica said flatly.

Bara nodded. 'Good, that's us.'

'. . . and another object under the port wing.'

'What sort of object?''

'Unknown. Metallic with a low-level power source. It appears to be trying to mask itself from my scan . . . it is powering up now . . . Bara?'

'Yes, Lex?'

'Bara, the object is moving. It is moving towards you.'

MANEUVERS

Orcades Draig stood on the flight deck of the arkship *Fenrir* as it accelerated to full speed. The lights were dimmed, as was standard procedure during flight, giving the entire space an air of dread about it. The sea of consoles threw a sickly green light onto the faces of their operators, little floating heads in the darkness. At the center was the vast operations map which currently showed their flight progress to their target, a tiny flashing dot of red.

He looked out of the windows; there was no obvious sense of acceleration – no indication of movement of any kind – but he could feel the deep vibration of the engines cascading through his stomach. He put his hand to the bulkhead around the window: the vibration was more obvious now, a surge of power pushing the giant vessel faster and faster.

Satisfied, he walked back to the center of the flight deck and rested his hands on the ops map. Next to him stood Commodore Thorwald, doing his best to hide his nerves. He had only just been promoted yesterday, and this would be his first mission in command of the *Fenrir,* not to mention the rest of the Draig fleet. Orcades still had his doubts about Thorwald. He had risen through the ranks quickly, had proven himself to be a competent leader, but he had never been fully tested in battle. Today would be the making of the man.

Opposite him stood Reader Durante, his hands resting at his back. After their last encounter Orcades had found himself troubled. He had left the meeting with a sense of love and devotion towards Durante, and towards the Church as a whole. This was entirely new to him and, even though the sensation filled him with gratitude, he knew something just wasn't right.

Orcades made a habit of recording his meetings. It came in handy for future reference, as a learning tool, and sometimes, as a way of keeping his enemies in check. So, when he couldn't shake his feelings of unease, he had retrieved the data log of his last encounter with Durante.

What he saw had startled him. Reader Durante had tackled him to the floor, threatened him and deactivated his mother's holograph. That's not how he had remembered the meeting going. His recollection was of a robust discussion followed by a deep understanding by both men. They had agreed on strategy, and he had left the meeting with a newfound optimism and loyalty to Reader Durante.

Everyone knew about a Reader's mental ability, they were trained in the art of manipulation. Charm and suggestion were their weapons. But there were rumors of other abilities; mind-reading, telepathy, extra-sensory-perception. Orcades had never believed them, but after watching the recording of his meeting with Reader Durante he wasn't so sure.

As a precaution, he had started to take a course of maxidopamil, an antipsychotic drug that was said to have the side-effect of blocking a user's latent telepathic function. If he was under some sort of mental attack the drug should help to counteract it. The headaches had been terrible, but at least he felt like his thoughts were his own again. He knew the risks – this was the same medication found in Gravel – the drug of choice for the idle classes – and could be highly addictive and cause paranoia, but he was no feeble-minded waster. He was a Draig. He could cope.

Orcades eyed the three personal guards that he had assigned to the flight deck. They were dressed in standard crew uniforms, but they each wore a discreet sidearm. They had orders to disable Durante if he came too close to Orcades; an additional precaution in case the Reader tried to influence him again. Always have a back-up plan, he reminded himself.

He sensed Commodore Thorwald waiting at his side, and Orcades turned to face him.

'We are locked on to the co-ordinates you provided,

Heir Valtais. We are tracking for orbital drift but there's still no signal from the target,' Thorwald said in a hushed voice. He had already expressed concern about the validity of the location, and the doubt remained in his voice. Was he trying to avoid embarrassing Orcades?

Reader Durante approached the Commodore, his hand touching his arm. 'I do not expect there will be a signal. You must have faith, Thorwald.'

Commodore Thorwald turned to the Reader. 'Yes, of course . . . but–'

'Continue towards the target,' Orcades barked.

'Yes, sir,' Thorwald replied.

'The Gods will guide us.' Orcades smiled to Reader Durante and wondered if he knew what he was really thinking.

The Reader simply nodded his approval and turned back towards the windows.

Orcades grinned to himself, aware of three unassuming crew members whose hands hovered over their weapons. They went unnoticed, just three more people on a busy flight deck.

Preparations were underway for cube flight. This was the part Orcades always enjoyed; the rising tension as the moment approached, the increase in chatter as information was relayed quickly, the sense of anticipation that seemed to fill the flight deck.

'Cube drive is powering up, sir,' Commodore Thorwald said. 'You should strap in.'

Orcades nodded as he took one of the cable clips from the edge of the ops map and fastened it to his belt. He did the same on the other side, testing their grip by leaning back from the table.

'All hands, secure for cube flight,' Thorwald announced over the flight deck com system as he clipped himself to the table. An alarm sounded, heralding the imminent shift.

Thorwald picked up a pad and referred to its glowing screen as he spoke into the communication system again. 'All stations, this is the COM. Cube drive status check: give me a go, no go for flight.'

The responses came quickly over the flight deck speakers:

'FIDO is go, COM.'

'Guidance is go.'

'VIRO is go.'

'Go from EECOM.'

'GNC, we are go, COM.'

'Control, all systems green. Go, COM.'

'Network is go.'

Thorwald smiled. 'We are go for cube drive initiation.' He turned to face the station directly behind him. 'CUCOM, you have control.'

The young woman nodded, speaking into the communication system. 'COM, I have control. Initiating cube drive. Power levels are good. ST bubble is stable and growing.'

Orcades felt the uneasy shift in gravity, then the odd sensation of falling. Automatically, he held the edge of the table.

Voices overlapped as they relayed status updates.

'Stand by for cube drive flight in ten . . . nine . . . eight . . . '

'ADM looking good.'

'. . . seven . . . six . . . five . . .'

'Free fall.'

'Tachyon flow is green.'

'. . . four . . . three . . . two . . .'

'Hull stress is nominal.'

'. . . one.'

A moment of silence, of nothing, and then the ship was moving. The stars outside shifted, appearing to untangle into threads of color, and Orcades became weightless. His feet lifted from the deck, drifting upwards. In front of him a stray pad glided off the ops map. Thorwald pointed to it and an officer grabbed it and placed it under the table.

'Cube drive is running. ST bubble remains stable. All systems are green.'

'Flight time is thirteen minutes, ship time.'

There was sense of relief across the flight deck as people monitored the maneuver.

'Thank you, CUCOM,' Thorwald said to the young woman at her station. 'I have control again.'

'COM, you have control,' she acknowledged with a

small nod.

The Commodore checked a console screen and smiled with satisfaction. 'An excellent ship, don't you think, Heir Valtais?'

Orcades nodded benevolently. 'A ship is only as good as her crew.'

'Of course.'

A voice broke from the speakers overhead. 'COM, FIDO.'

Thorwald turned to look at a control station on the right hand side of the vast space. 'COM, go ahead.'

'COM, I'm picking up an object along our flight path.'

'Collision potential?'

'No, COM. It's at our destination. From my readings, it could be an asteroid.'

'Thank you, FIDO. Keep monitoring.'

Thorwald turned back to Orcades, his eyebrows raised. 'So, not empty space after all.'

'No, Commodore.' Orcades replied, aware of Reader Durante pulling himself along the table to join their discussion. 'That is our target.'

Behind him, the doors to the flight deck opened and a dark figure entered.

'Valtais on the flight deck,' someone called.

Valtais Sinnsro Draig, unaffected by the lack of gravity, walked towards the ops map.

Orcades acknowledged his mother, making room for

her by his side. Her face was stern, her eyes narrowed.

'Would someone care to inform me of our destination?' she asked, her voice like ice.

'Valtais,' Commodore Thorwald began, 'we are approaching an uncharted asteroid at a set of co-ordinates provided by your son. It is–'

'Reader Durante has been kind enough to supply us with information,' Orcades added.

His mother glared at each of them in turn. 'I am still Valtais, and yet I was not informed of this. I was not consulted. My heir, my Reader and my Commodore – newly appointed, I might remind you – did not see fit to seek their Valtais' advice. Why is that?'

Reader Durante stepped forward. 'Forgive me, Valtais, this was my error. I spoke to your son and told him of the urgency of this matter. I promised him that I would speak to you, but in my rush to confirm the details I have neglected my duty.' His voice was measured and hypnotic, and Orcades found himself wondering if Reader Durante was capable of manipulating a holograph as well as a human.

'Reader, what is so urgent that you could not find time to inform me?' Sinnsro asked.

'Unfinished business,' Orcades said.

'The Church has learned that the heir of the House of Kenric survived the destruction of the arkship *Obsidian*.' Durante explained.

'Yes, yes, I am aware of the rumors,' Sinnsro replied

sharply. 'You yourself told me of them, Reader.'

'Yes, I did. But new information has come to light, about the prince's whereabouts. We believe he is hiding inside the asteroid ahead.'

'Inside?'

'It is an unregistered arkship, ancient, from before the Fracture.'

'Populated?'

Reader Durante hesitated. 'Yes, we think so.'

'I see,' Sinnsro said, pondering the information. 'And you intend to apprehend the prince.'

A collective silence fell between the four people grouped together at the head of the operations map. Eventually, Reader Durante replied. 'No Valtais, it is the Gods' will that the target be destroyed.'

'Destroyed? Is the destruction of arkships becoming some sort of addiction?'

'No, of course not, Valtais. But the Gods have spoken. The people hiding there are non-believers . . . deviants. It is the will of the Infinite Gods that this asteroid be destroyed so that their souls can be saved.'

'Reader,' Sinnsro began, her face troubled. 'Does that not seem excessive to you?'

'It is not my place to question the will of the Gods, Valtais,' he replied, adding, 'nor is it yours.'

The Valtais Sinnsro Draig bristled. It was easy to forget she wasn't real, Orcades noted.

'Very well,' she said eventually, her words clipped. 'If the

Gods wish it.'

'They do,' Durante confirmed.

Sinnsro glared at him. 'Then who am I to stand in their way?'

'Approaching target, COM.'

Commodore Thorwald bowed politely to the Valtais. 'Please excuse me.'

She dismissed him with a flick of her gnarled hand. The Commodore turned to the ops map and spoke to his flight deck crew. 'All stations, this is the COM, stand by for cube inversion. Go, no go for inversion?'

The responses were rapid, and the ship began to vibrate as power built.

'. . . cube drive power curve-down beginning in five . . . four . . .'

'Prepare for superluminal threshold.'

'. . . three . . . two . . . '

'Shockwave displacement deployed.'

'. . .one.'

There was an instant of violent vibration which quickly subsided to a low background noise.

'Inversion is go!'

Gravity began to reassert itself, and the ship creaked and groaned in response. Orcades watched the stars become dots once more, glad to feel his feet pushing against the deck.

'Particle displacement complete.'

'Cube drive shutdown.'

'Locking Tachyon funnels.'

'Zero shockwave.'

'. . . normal drive redeployed . . .'

'Location is confirmed. Target coordinates achieved.'

Ahead, out of the window, Orcades saw a grey rock, hidden in shadow. They were at the edge of the Cluster, far from the prying eyes of the other families. Whatever happened here today would go unnoticed.

Commodore Thorwald turned to face the others, pride on his features. 'Valtais, Heir Valtais, Reader. We are at the target location. It is possible they have detected us. We should take countermeasures, disable their systems.'

'Very well,' Orcades said.

Thorwald activated his com. 'Weapons, target the asteroid. Two Black Stars.'

A voice responded. 'Confirmed, two Black Stars ready for launch. EMP shield is activated. Gilgore grid powering up. Black Stars away . . . locked on target . . . running true.'

HUNTED

'It's moving towards me?' Bara shouted into her wrist com.

'Yes,' Lexica said. 'I suggest you defend yourself and return inside.'

Wynn scanned the ship's surface, looking for movement, but could see nothing unusual.

'Damned hunter,' Bara seethed, picking up her tools and running for the hatch.

Wynn hesitated, still looking over the hull.

'C'mon,' Bara shouted after him.

He began to make his way towards the hatch, his fingers twitching to find a gun at his empty belt. *Did he know how to shoot?* he wondered.

A metallic clatter caught his ear and he turned to see an object rising over the wing. At first, he couldn't tell what he was looking at. Strange tube-like shapes telescoped over the edge and dug into the hull, followed by a longer segment. An arm! A thin robotic arm with pistons driving it forwards. It seemed to struggle for a moment, trying to force itself higher, then it gained purchase and pulled itself up so that Wynn could see its face.

Two dark blue eyes locked onto him, and the hunter stopped. A fragile laser light scanned over Wynn's body, then it pulled itself up to full height. It was over two meters tall, its frame a thin mass of wires and parts sitting atop two powerful-looking legs. Its right arm was damaged, just a splinter of it remained, a mess of exposed wires and tubes hanging from the socket. It had other damage as well; scorch marks along its right side, cracks and dents to its outer casing, but its movements were sudden and agile. It jolted towards Wynn, its feet hammering along the wing top.

A rush of adrenalin pushed Wynn into a sprint, sliding towards the hatch. He fell into it and his fingers hammered on the control panel. The hatch door began to close, its progress desperately slow. The gap narrowed, just a thin line when four metal fingers shot through the slit, halting the hatch. The door mechanism whined, complaining loudly, then it gave in and the hatch was forced open.

Bara pulled at Wynn, dragging him away as the hunter pushed its narrow frame through the hatch and fell to the floor in a clumsy heap.

Wynn looked around and saw a long wrench in Bara's toolkit. He picked it up and swung it at the bot, catching its head. The hunter's eyes rocked to the side, then it corrected itself and its arm lunged at Wynn, dragging the tool from his hand.

He felt Bara pulling at him again, and he didn't resist. They stumbled through a bulkhead door as Bara hit the emergency close pad. The door slammed shut, cutting the hunter off from its prey. Through a narrow window in the door Wynn could see the machine. It scanned the bulkhead before working at the door's control pad.

'What's it doing?' Wynn said.

'Trying to override the control,' Bara replied. She raised her com to her mouth. 'Lex, it's on board.'

'I know that,' the ship's voice replied. 'I can feel it trying to access my functions.'

'Can you stop it?'

Lexica didn't reply.

The hunter stared through the glass, its blue eyes watching them as it worked on the door.

'Sol!' Bara exclaimed. 'Those things are programmed with military combat tactics. It'll break into Lex's command code and open the doors. We need to go, now!'

The pair retreated, moving through the ship.

'Aren't we going to the bridge?' Wynn asked as they ran down to the lower decks.

'It's already got access to some of the ship's systems. We need to get out before it uses them against us.'

Ahead was the entry ramp that led to the dockside. As they approached it the ramp began to close.

Bara rushed towards it, down its length and jumped out of her ship. Wynn followed, trying to make it to the end. He fell to his knees as the opening narrowed, pushed himself through the gap, and tumbled to the deck, landing uncomfortably on his shoulder. Wynn lay there, watching the sealed entry ramp.

'It's got the ship,' he said desperately.

'It doesn't want the ship,' Bara replied, helping him to his feet. 'It's just being methodical. Once it figures out we're no longer aboard it'll come out here to find us.'

'Why does it want us?'

'Just doing its job, I think. Mopping up survivors from the *Obsidian*.'

There was a hiss of expelled gas, then the entry ramp began to open again.

'Sol, it's fast!' Bara exclaimed.

They ran through the dock, past the other ships, retreating into the shadows.

'We need weapons,' Bara noted as they crouched behind a stack of cargo boxes.

A distant alarm sounded, echoing through the dock. People ran past their hiding place, shouting as they came.

Wynn whispered. 'I think it's been spotted.' He peered over the edge of the crates and saw the metallic skeleton walking towards them. Its shape was dark against the lights of the dock, but it's blue eyes burned out of its silhouette.

Wynn took Bara's hand and ran. He didn't know where he was going, he didn't have a plan, he just hoped they could stop this thing from killing them. Behind him he heard the deep thud of footsteps getting faster and faster, closer and closer.

Wynn turned right, then left, weaving through the lines of cargo. He heard crates falling behind him, but he didn't dare to stop and look. He threw himself down a flight of stairs, checking that Bara was still with him.

'This way,' she shouted, turning in a new direction.

Wynn followed, keeping at her heels as she rushed towards a large elevator. The doors were already open. They slipped inside and pressed the button to close it.

The hunter appeared at the end of the deck. It turned, saw them cowering inside the elevator, and marched in their direction, just as the doors juddered and began to close.

'We're not gonna make it,' Bara said desperately.

The machine rushed towards them, two malevolent eyes blurring to meet them.

The elevator door pinged shut. The hunter slammed into it, shaking the carriage. Then, with a creaking of metal, the elevator began to descend.

'Do you have a plan?' Wynn asked Bara.

She didn't reply.

As the elevator slowed to its destination a deafening thud shook the carriage.

Bara looked up. 'It's on the roof!'

An arrow of blue flame pierced the ceiling, cutting a perfect circle into the elevator.

The doors pinged open and Bara and Wynn scrambled out. They were on the lowest deck now, a dark space filled with machinery, pipes and junk. Behind them, Wynn heard the clatter of the elevator as it gave way to the hunter's assault. As they searched for a hiding place there was a growing sense of inevitability to the chase. They couldn't hide from this thing. They couldn't stop it. But Wynn wasn't ready to give in.

They weaved through the machinery, looking for anything they could use to slow the hunter down, finding nothing.

'There's *Lexica*,' Bara said, pointing up through the grated ceiling. Seen from down here the ship was a dynamic sight. 'Maybe if we can get back up there—'

'We need weapons,' Wynn interrupted. 'That's the only way we'll stop that thing. Don't you have police or army here?'

'We have custodians,' Bara replied. 'They'll be on their way, but they don't carry the sort of weapons to knock that thing out. We'll be dead before they can stop it. We need to buy us more time.'

'Any ideas?'

'Keep moving, keep running.'

Ahead was a wall of vents, giant fans that sucked out the dirty air and pushed it into the filtration system.

At the side of the colossal turbines something caught Bara's eye.

'This was the place,' she said quietly. 'This was where Guin died. I've never been back down here since . . .'

Wynn took her hand. 'We're not going to die here,' he said adamantly. 'Okay?'

She nodded, her eyes distant.

'We'll get out of this, we'll figure something . . .' Wynn's voice trailed off as he turned to look along the walkway: the hunter was rushing towards the vents.

They began to run, but already they could hear it behind them. Wynn turned, stumbling to the floor as the hunter approached. The machine stood over him, it's one remaining arm outstretched. Something sharp fired from it and impaled Wynn's chest. He cried out, more in surprise than pain, and tried to remove it, but the hunter pushed down on his chest with its arm, holding him there while the needle-like device extracted his blood. Bara tried to pull it off but the bot dismissed her with a rapid swipe of its arm, returning to hold Wynn in place before he could react.

Bara fell on the floor, not moving. Wynn struggled to be free, but there was nothing he could do but stare as the red liquid was extracted from his body.

ANALYSIS

Gofal waited as the blood was extracted, trying not to harm his struggling captive. He had already injured his companion, something he regretted immediately. They were surprisingly fragile.

The shard began its analysis, testing the blood. It would take just a moment, then he could confirm the identity of the boy. He hoped he was right. He hoped this would be the one. If not, if he was wrong, there would be no chance of finding his quarry now. His mission would be a failure.

While he waited, Gofal conducted a scan of the female. Her pulse and breathing appeared to be normal. He must have knocked her unconscious, but she should recover, he hoped.

Once the test was complete – if it was a positive match – he had to plan an escape. He plotted a route back to the female's ship. He had already checked its systems: the ship was space-worthy and could be launched quickly. He extended his scan, testing the edges of his abilities to see beyond the rocky walls of this world. Something was not right there, something was approaching, something he did not like.

The shard pinged as it completed its scan. It relayed the results to Gofal, just as his entire system shut down.

BOMBARDMENT

Wynn stared at the inert machine. The light in its eyes had flickered and died, its body just an immobile statue of metal.

He stretched to reach the little needle and pulled it out of his skin. Then, he tried to move from under the bot. The weight on his chest was increasing, becoming more and more painful. He grabbed the bot's arm and forced it to one side. The entire machine began to sway, tipping towards his head. Wynn pushed again, and the hunter bot came crashing down to the ground on top of him, its giant head just inches from his own. Wynn pushed at the body of the machine and managed to crawl out from under it. Panting, he lay beside it, catching his breath. Then he remembered Bara and he scrambled to his feet.

But everything was dark, the last glow of the overhead lights had ebbed away, leaving the entire dockside in darkness. The alarm had stopped as well. Nothing worked.

'Bara?' he cried. 'Can you hear me?'

He felt with his hands, trying to remember where she was. 'Bara?'

Wynn kicked something and fell to his knees. Searching with his hands he felt a body on the floor. 'Is that you?'

The body groaned and turned on its side. 'Who else would it be?' Bara asked. 'You're still alive?'

'For now. The power's off. The lights are all out.'

'Everything's out?'

'Yeah, I think so. Unless I'm just blind,' Wynn quipped.

'No, it's me too,' Bara confirmed. 'Must be an EMP weapon. Knocks out power generation.'

'A weapon?'

'Or some sort of stellar radiation burst, but we're a long way out, and we'd have a warning before anything like that came our way.'

'Gravity is still okay.'

'That's because of Melchior's rotation. That's not going to change any time soon.'

Above, a tiny light appeared, flickered, then went out. It flashed again and grew this time.

'Someone's lighting a fire,' Bara noted.

In the feeble glow Wynn could see the frozen body of the hunter. 'Do you think it'll come back after us?'

'Its central matrix is fried. It'll have some protected core systems, but it'll take a while for it to re-route all its other functions through them. I think we're okay for now. I'm more worried about what might happen next.'

'Next?'

'An EMP's often used as the first wave of an attack. With all the systems knocked out it'll be almost impossible to defend Melchior.'

Voices shouted out overhead as tiny pockets of fire began to illuminate the space.

'I have to find my parents, make sure they're okay, then we can go to *Lexica*,' Bara said. 'Most of his systems are shielded, I should be able to get him up and running, but it's not going to be easy.'

Wynn helped Bara to stand and they found a ladder up to the next level. Confusion seemed to be spreading as people tried to make sense of what was happening.

'Bulkhead doors are stuck open,' Bara said. 'Sol, I hope this is just an accident. We're in bad shape.'

She stopped one of the mechanics who was rushing past them. 'Do you know what's happened?' she asked.

The man caught his breath. 'Circadia has gone dark. The whole place is a mess.'

'We need to get people to the dock–'

A distant rumble interrupted Bara. The space shook, casting equipment and cargo free. People ran, screaming as dust fell from the ceiling. Wynn and Bara held onto each other, tensing as the tremor passed over them, waiting until the vibration subsided.

Wynn looked at Bara, his eyes wide with fear.

'We're being bombed now?'

Bara nodded grimly. 'That was just the start.'

HOMECOMING

'Are you sure we're going in the right direction?' Wynn checked. Everything looked so different now it was hidden in near darkness.

'It's just ahead, Bara confirmed, leading the way. In her hand was a glowing lamp, an ancient device that had no circuits to fry. A few were kept in the dock in case of power disruption, but Bara could not remember them ever being used before.

Another impact struck the outer surface of Melchior, sending shockwaves cascading through the rock to the interior. Wynn and Bara dodged falling rubble as they pushed through terrified families, their possessions dragged along with them in hastily-packed bags.

'Go to the dock,' Bara shouted at them as they passed by. 'Get everyone to the dock!'

Ahead the path widened and the vast expanse of the Circadia cavern came into view. A faint greenish glow emanated from its length, casting a sickly light on the parks and fields under it.

They rested at the threshold, catching their breath

until another impact shook Melchior. The floor tilted, throwing Wynn and Bara off their feet. They slid to the side, sheltering from the falling debris. As the vibrations subsided they crawled out of their hiding place. All about them people ran in panic as smoke billowed from a cracked ventilation pipe, adding to the disarray and confusion.

'Do you think your parents will still be at home?' Wynn asked, wiping dirt from his eyes.

'I don't know!' Bara shouted as another impact shook the space. 'I have to do this, you don't!'

'I'm staying,' Wynn replied. 'We stick together, okay?'

Tears pooled in her eyes, and Bara pulled him towards her in a clumsy embrace. As they broke apart, she planted a small kiss on his cheek. 'Thanks. I don't want to do this alone.'

Wynn smiled and took her hand. The ground shook again, and a wall of fire erupted close to him. A wave of heat singed his face, and he retreated from it, losing touch with Bara as a crowd of desperate people pushed between them. Wynn forced his way through, catching sight of Bara at a flight of stairs.

'We need to go up,' Bara explained, coughing as the smoke caught her throat.

They began to climb, just as another shockwave hit. Wynn held on, waiting for it to pass, listening to the horrible noise of metal twisting. He looked out to the Circadia, still giving off a green afterglow. As he watched in disbelief, part of it broke away, smashing free in a cascade of explosions that lit up the entire cavern. The section hovered there in the shifting gravity, then it began to fall. Slowly at first, then accelerating, it tumbled towards the fields below, spearing into the land, throwing a cloud of dirt into the air as it came to rest at a dangerous angle.

Wynn turned away and sprinted up the steps with Bara by his side, not stopping again until they had reached her parents' level. On the last flight, the stairs had twisted from their housing, and they shook under their weight.

They ran into an open park with a commanding view along the Circadia. Fragments of it were falling away from the core, drifting down, across, up, and impacting the houses and streets around the cavern walls. It was almost as if the Circadia was throwing itself apart.

Another impact, and Wynn saw a crack in the rock overhead. He saw air rushing through the gap, and he felt his ears pop.

'We don't have long!' Wynn shouted over the noise.

They ran through an avenue of upright stones, past a line of uniformed trees that shook in the growing wind, to a promenade scattered with burning debris.

'This way,' Bara cried, leading him towards a cluster of small houses. She weaved through the narrow, rubble-strewn streets, past burning houses, over corpses, dodging demolished walls, until they came upon a familiar building and its small courtyard.

At first Wynn thought the structure had survived the attack, but as they rushed through the courtyard he saw the jagged crater where most of the house used to be, only part of the outer wall remained standing. A crumpled shard of the Circadia rested at the center of the hole, its length dotted with fire.

Bara screamed as she scaled the edge of the wall and fell into the crater, pulling at the rubble with her fingers. Wynn followed behind, scanning the space for signs of life. There, at the far side he saw the outline of a body. He skirted the edge of the depression towards the ash-covered shape, stumbling as the debris shifted under his weight.

As he approached, the smoke seemed to part for him, revealing the faces of two bodies in the ruin of a kitchen. He knew them at once, two grey sculptures of Bara's parents resting in the ruins of their home.

He turned to find Bara, but she was already at his side. Wynn held her, feeling her legs buckle at the sight of the bodies in front of her. She collapsed, sobbing as she cleaned the dirt from their faces, screaming her hopes at them, willing them to move with every fiber of her being.

But the bodies lay still.

Wynn shared in Bara's grief, feeling overwhelmed by her loss. He cried for himself as well, for the family he couldn't remember – the family he was sure had perished on the *Obsidian*. All he had left now was Bara.

CHURCH AND STATE

Orcades stood at the window, observing the unidentified rock that filled the view. There were no obvious signs of life, no technology, nothing that would set this asteroid apart from any other. Even their broad scans didn't find anything of interest. Any passing mining ship would take one look at this asteroid and deem it unprofitable and move on. Only a deeper scan revealed the truth: there was life inside, and lots of it. At least twenty thousand people, an entire society, no doubt self-sufficient, for the most part. That meant food production, life support, an entire eco-system hidden from view. This place could be useful, Orcades mused.

'Black Stars have disabled eighty six percent of the electrical grid,' Commodore Thorwald said as he approached him. 'The first wave of the bombardment is underway, Heir Valtais. Three waves of Slaan-hammers should be enough to crack it apart.'

'Good,' Orcades replied, watching the tiny flashes of light erupting on the dark surface. He observed them grow – beautiful little explosions of yellow and red and black – then fade to nothing, wondering what it might be like inside there. 'This could be quite an asset to our fleet, couldn't it?'

'The asteroid? Well . . . yes,' Thorwald faltered.

'A place to grow our numbers. A new Draig arkship.'

'But my orders are for complete destruction. Those are *your* orders.'

'Yes . . .' Orcades glanced at his mother. 'I am changing those orders.'

'Sir?'

Orcades turned his back on the view. 'You will capture this asteroid for the House of Draig, but kill all the men.'

Reader Durante marched towards them, his face reddening. 'My dear Orcades, may I speak to you alone?'

'No, you may not.'

Durante faltered, then composed himself. His voice was lower, rhythmic, compelling. 'Heir Valtais, the Gods have spoken. This asteroid is to be destroyed. You must fulfil their plan.'

Orcades smiled. 'Do I?'

'Yes, they move through you. They speak to you now. Your only desire is to please the Gods. You will do as they wish.'

'No, I will not.' Orcades replied, enjoying this moment. 'We have already seen the wasteful destruction of the *Obsidian*. That was a mistake, and I see no sense in the destruction of this place as well. The women and children will be taken into our care. They will become Draig. The men will be killed. The problem we discussed will be solved without the senseless waste of a strategic asset.'

'No, you cannot–'

Orcades felt his temper rise, and he had no desire to hold it in. 'This is the will of the House of Draig! These are my orders. *My orders!* Do you oppose them?'

Reader Durante stepped closer, his voice a spiteful whisper. 'Do *you* oppose the Infinite Gods?'

'I oppose you!' Orcades laughed. He nodded to his covert guards and they seized Durante, strapping his hands behind his back.

'You defy the will of the Church!' Durante shouted as he was dragged from the flight deck. 'The House of Draig will be burned by the Infinite Gods! All who oppose them will suffer an eternity of pain.'

The elevator doors closed and all eyes turned to Orcades Draig.

'This is a glorious day! We will capture this asteroid in the name of the House of Draig.'

Commodore Thorwald hesitated.

'Those are my orders,' Orcades added in a calmer voice.

Thorwald nodded and turned towards the operations map, almost bumping into Sinnsro Draig as she approached her son.

'What do you think you're doing?' she scolded him in a whisper. 'You cannot defy the Gods.'

'He is manipulating us,' Orcades replied. 'He does not speak for the Gods, he speaks for himself. You will stand with me on this, mother. Your time as Valtais is coming to an end. My moment approaches. Do not make that moment come more quickly than it should. Do not make that moment today.'

Sinnsro did not reply, but her eyes were wild. 'You risk everything that I have built, son. And for what? A rock?'

'If I am to be Valtais I must make my own way, mother. I must choose my own path. I must decide what is best for our family. Already our arkships suffer from overcrowding, and now we aim to take over the House of Kenric. More people to feed! What we need most of all is space. Space to expand, space to grow. This rock supports over twenty thousand souls! Don't you see the potential?'

His mother tutted. 'This is a dangerous plan! It will not go well. There will be war with the Church.'

Orcades straightened his back, glaring at her. 'You will support me in this, mother.'

She shook her head sadly. 'You leave me little choice.'

Sinnsro stared out of the widows at the asteroid, her face full of remorse. She glanced at The Infinite setting behind it, and tears fell from her eyes. She wiped her face as she turned to leave.

Orcades ignored her. She was old and scared. He would not reside over a family living in fear of the Church. He would be his own man or nothing at all. This rock would be his first great step.

'Commodore Thorwald,' Orcades barked. 'Prepare for a ground assault.'

REFUGEES

'The bombardment, it's stopped,' Wynn said, looking up at the ruined cavern. A constellation of fire dotted the view, their flames fanned by the winds being sucked out of the rupture in the rock.

Bara wasn't listening, she didn't look up from her father's empty face. She stroked his forehead and kissed him tenderly, then turned to her mother and did the same.

'Bara, I'm sorry, but it's not safe. We have to go.' Wynn waited by her side, knowing how hard this must be for her. About them, the earth shifted, the remaining buildings groaning and creaking as fire painted the cavern in unstable orange tones.

'Please,' Wynn said, taking Bara's hand. She let him lift her, to guide her away from her parents' resting place. Bara clung to him as they climbed out of the rubble, glancing over her shoulder until the bodies were out of sight. As they retreated from her home she broke down, falling to her knees and sobbing uncontrollably. Wynn scooped her into his arms and carried her away. Her head rested against his neck, her cries becoming quieter.

'I can walk,' she said eventually, her voice gentle.

Wynn put her down. For a moment, her arm lingered round his neck. She glanced at him, finding a fragile smile, then she let go and straightened. 'Thanks,' she managed with a determined nod.

They continued in silence, mute witnesses to the destruction around them. In less than an hour Melchior had been almost torn apart, its beauty ruined, its people killed or left homeless, and Wynn felt his rage grow with every step. It was only a matter of time before the breech in the outer wall grew bigger. Melchior's atmosphere was leaking into space, the pressure and temperature was dropping. If left unchecked the interior would be a frozen wasteland in a matter of hours, and there was nothing he could do to stop it. Wynn felt powerless.

The crowds were quieter now, numbed by the shock of it all. They moved along the corridors as a silent mass, towards the dock and the hope of escape. Every junction brought more refugees, slowing the throng to a mournful shuffle. From time to time the groan of a collapsing wall, or the aggressive pop of a fire, pushed the crowd on with renewed urgency, bodies crushed against one another.

Ahead, the expanse of the dock came into view, and the noise of the crowd increased. Chaos reigned as people began to push and jostle for access to one of the ships. Some power had been restored here, and circles of light illuminated the pathways. People elbowed for space as two men fought each other.

'We have enough ships,' Bara noted. 'They don't need to panic.'

A line of vessels waited, the broad entry ramps already filled with people as their engines cycled for launch. Dock workers shouted at the crowd, doing their best to herd them into the ships, but their voices were all but lost in the noise.

Bara took Wynn's hand again and they parted from the crowd, pushing their way towards *Lexica*.

'Can you get him flying?' Wynn asked as the familiar shape of Bara's ship grew larger.

'Let's find out,' she replied, pushing her wrist communicator. 'Lex? You still alive?'

'Good to hear your voice, Bara,' the ship replied. 'Core systems are fine, everything else is offline. Unfortunately, I'll have to leave the flying to you.'

'That'll have to do. Get powered up for evac, we're two minutes away.'

'Confirmed,' Lexica replied.

Wynn felt a glimmer of hope, they might just make it out of here, he thought.

Then the ground shook again. Sparks flew as a gantry above them crashed to the floor. The screams of the crowd grew as the entire dock vibrated. At the same moment, the first of the evacuation ships raised its ramp and began to glide away from the dockside, heading for the airlock gates. The gantry crashed into the ship, spearing its bridge and upper decks. It tilted to one side, its engines whining to recover as it slammed into the dockside.

Wynn and Bara ran towards *Lexica* as the listing evacuation ship tore into the gantry, throwing debris into the air.

'Wynn!' Bara cried.

Behind him a giant loading crane was smashed from its base by the evacuation ship. The metal structure tilted towards them, twisting as it fell onto the dockside. There was no time to run, there was no way to avoid it. He grabbed Bara and pulled her to the ground, throwing himself over her. Wynn squeezed his eyes shut, tensing as he waited for death.

The sickly echo of metal filled his ears. Dust engulfed him, robbing Wynn of his vision. He coughed, wondering why they had not been crushed, and turned to look behind him.

There, stooped over Wynn and Bara, holding back the mass of broken metal with its body, was a bot with one arm, it's blue eyes glowing.

BROTHERS

There was no window in Reader Durante's room, no view to ponder. That was the way it was meant to be; a Reader was supposed to contemplate The Infinite through the teachings of the Church, through the writings of the Scribe, through meditation and prayer. Reader Durante had always found the requirements of devotion to be somewhat excessive, and he interpreted them as he saw fit. Usually, the painting on the wall was a good substitute for a view, but today he would have preferred a window so he could see what was happening outside.

He was alone, for now. Two guards waited beyond the door, but he had already spoken to them, and found them pliable to his persuasion. Fear of the Church was useful in situations like this. Orcades had gone against the Gods; that would not sit well with many on board the *Fenrir*. They may be loyal Draig men and women but their fear of the Infinite Gods outweighed their alliance to Orcades. He had underestimated the strength of their belief, and Reader Durante would make sure he paid for that mistake.

The door was not locked, he could leave at any time, the guards would not stop him. Instead he waited and planned. His message would have been conveyed to the flight deck by now. It would not be long before he had a visitor. He closed his eyes and relaxed. He did not need to check the plan to know he was doing the right thing. By the end of today Orcades Draig would be a loyal pet of the Church of The Infinite, or he would be dead. Either way their control on the House of Draig would be tighter, and that could only benefit the plan.

The door opened, and Durante sensed someone waiting there.

'Come in, Commodore, please,' Reader Durante said, standing to greet his visitor.

Commodore Thorwald entered, looking sheepish. He was a large man and his frame seemed to fill the doorway, blocking the harsh light of the corridor, but he appeared timid and uncomfortable in the Reader's presence.

'Infinite blessings,' Thorwald muttered, his head bowed. Good, Durante thought, he was a Church man. That would make this easier.

'May the Gods' reflections shine upon you, brother,' Durante soothed. He gestured towards two chairs and a small table close to his painting.

Thorwald sat, looking like he didn't know what to do with his hands. 'I don't have long, I'm needed on the flight deck.'

'Yes, I know.' Durante joined him at the table. 'I'm sorry to drag you away from your duties, Commodore, and I will keep this brief. You saw how Orcades spoke to me on the flight deck?'

Thorwald nodded, his cheeks flushing. 'I must apologize for your treatment, Reader . . .'

Durante held up his hand. 'It is not for you to apologize, brother. The fault was not yours.'

'I stood by . . .'

'Yes, you did.' Durante sensed the man's guilt, his torn loyalties, and he knew the Commodore was his. 'But you are a man of position, a man of rank and duty, and that boy is your superior.'

Thorwald hesitated. 'True, but . . .'

Durante put his hand onto Thorwald's, squeezing it rhythmically as he spoke. 'You are not to blame, brother, you are but a man after all. But the Gods shine in you, they reflect in your eyes, I can see it.'

Good, Durante thought, he had him locked to his gaze now. He searched his memory and retrieved the Commodore's first name. 'Ricktor, you are a good man, loyal to the Infinite Gods. They look upon you and are glad.'

'Thank you, Reader.'

'They call upon you to fulfil your duty.'

'My duty?'

'You wish to please the Gods, do you not?'

'Yes, of course,' Thorwald said quickly.

'To walk in the Gods' path is not an easy choice, Ricktor, but it is the right choice. The right choice.' Durante's voice was low, resonant.

'The right choice,' Thorwald repeated.

'Yes, the right choice. Orcades is misguided. He may be ill. We must help him to find the Gods' path once more. You and I, we can do this together, as brothers of the Infinite Gods.'

'Yes . . . yes, of course.'

Durante smiled. 'You will do their bidding? You will carry out the will of the Infinite Gods and forevermore dwell in their reflection?'

Thorwald's eyes glistened, filled with dedication. 'Yes, I will. Tell me, what must I do?'

RETREAT

Wynn blinked dirt from his eyes and stared up at the hunter bot, its metal frame shaking under the weight of the crane on its back.

He slid out from under it, dragging Bara with him, hardly daring to speak. They both got to their feet and stepped away, expecting the machine to strike them down at any moment.

'What's it doing?' Bara whispered.

Wynn held his fingers to his mouth, putting more distance between him and the bot.

Overhead the damaged evacuation ship hovered, its body listing as smoke billowed from its wound.

Bara turned towards *Lexica* and began to run. Wynn took one last look at the hunter and sprinted to follow her. *Lexica's* entrance ramp lowered as they approached and they scrambled inside.

Bara glanced back at the wrecked dockside and the blocked pathway. 'We can't get anyone else out on *Lexica*,' she noted regretfully.

'They'll have to get out on one of the other ships,'

Wynn replied, joining her on the ramp.

Bara looked away and slammed the ramp control. As the hatch closed they bounded up through the ship towards the bridge.

'Are we set?' Bara shouted into her wrist com as they advanced.

'Engines hot,' Lexica replied. 'You're good to go.'

Bara leapt into her seat on the bridge and yanked her harness into place. Wynn sat beside her, watching her take control of the ship.

Outside, the damaged evacuation ship sank down towards the bottom of the dock. Further away, another ship was leaving its moorings and heading for the lock gate.

'No response from the Harbor Master,' Bara noted. 'We're just gonna have to do this on the fly.'

'That sounds like it might get messy.'

Bara grimaced. 'Yeah, probably.'

Power surged through the ship and Wynn felt it tilt forwards. *Lexica* drifted behind the larger ship as it entered the lock. They watched as the giant doors closed.

'We should be next,' Bara said, 'as long as the power to the doors holds out.'

Wynn viewed the dockside. The other evacuation ships were powering up and preparing to leave. A few people remained on the dockside, but most had found refuge on board the waiting ships. He scanned the platforms, searching for movement.

'You're looking for it, aren't you?' Bara asked.

'The bot?' Wynn nodded. 'Did it save us? Or was it just in the way?'

Bara sighed. 'I think if it had wanted to kill us we wouldn't be having this conversation now.'

'It . . . it felt like it was protecting us,' Wynn agreed, 'but it doesn't make–'

'Proximity alert!' Lexica barked.

There was a vicious crunch and the ship was rammed upwards.

'Sol! Something's hit us!' Bara shouted as she tried to control the ship.

The damaged evacuation ship limped into view, rising past the bridge windows, its hull dangerously close to *Lexica's*.

Bara yanked the controls and the ship responded, moving back from the other craft.

Bara shouted, 'She's moving for the lock gates!'

The ship rammed into the gates, tearing through them. Beyond was the second vessel making its way through the open exterior lock doors, heading towards space.

Bara cursed. 'Hang on!'

The dockside atmosphere rushed through the broken doors. The sudden wind, and the drop in pressure, pulled at *Lexica*, turning it away from the opening. Bara tilted the ship back, ramming it towards the exit. As the craft turned, Wynn caught a glimpse of the dockside; he saw tiny specks being pulled over the dockside wall, and he realized they were people.

The other ships were leaving their ports, each moving towards the shattered doors as *Lexica's* engines pushed them forwards. The lock gate doors were strewn with the wreckage of the downed ship, leaving just a fraction of it clear. Fire licked the opening, it's angry red tendrils being sucked out towards space.

'This is gonna be tight,' Bara said through gritted teeth as she rotated *Lexica* to squeeze through. They were almost at the lock gates when Melchior shook again.

TRUST

Derward Tarkkail checked the *Leughadair's* systems, relieved to see they had survived the EMP attack. His ship was well protected, more so than a simple courier would usually need.

He powered up the main drive and lifted away from the dockside as debris rained down on the ship. The lock gates were wide open, the atmosphere was dissipating and he knew he only had seconds to spare. Ahead was another small merchant craft; he recognized it as Bara's ship, *Lexica*. He knew his prey was aboard: the tracker he had implanted under Wynn's skin was relaying his location clearly.

He slammed the ship forwards, towards the burning lock gates. About him Melchior was in ruins, and he had a terrible feeling this was all his fault. He had trusted Reader Durante, given him information on Wynn's location. This attack couldn't be coincidence. Derward had been a fool to trust him, he realized now. But it was too late for regrets. He had to survive, he had to protect Wynn at all costs.

He put the boy out of his thoughts and focused on the approaching lock gates, trying to ignore the new bombardment that was threatening to destroy Melchior.

CHAIN OF COMMAND

The broad windows of the *Fenrir* lit up with flashes of white light.

Orcades Draig looked up from the operations map and stared at the view outside. The giant asteroid was being pounded by Slaan-hammers. He watched in disbelief as a chain of new explosions sliced across the rocky surface, tearing off chunks of rock that tumbled into space.

'What is this?' he demanded, his eyes fixed on the bombardment.

No one answered.

More explosions cut into the asteroid, dust and debris orbiting it in a thickening cloud.

Orcades whipped round, searching the flight deck for answers. 'Thorwald?'

The commander was at the far side of the space at the weapons station. Orcades marched over, his face filled with rage.

'What is happening?'

Commodore Thorwald straightened, turning slowly

to look him in the eye. 'The bombardment is going well, Heir Valtais.'

'I didn't order a bombardment!'

The commodore did not reply.

'Cease fire, immediately,' Orcades shouted.

'I am sorry, sir, but it is the will of the Church that the asteroid be destroyed.' Commodore Thorwald's voice was even, calm and controlled. No hint of fear.

'You will stop this immediately! You answer to me, not the Church!'

'Sir, in this instance I cannot carry out your orders.' He stood with his arms behind his back and looked out of the windows, as if that was the last word on the matter.

Orcades snapped. He pulled out the palm-sized gun he always carried, concealed in the small of his back, and raised it to Thorwald's face. 'You will comply, or you will meet the Gods you say you serve.'

The Commodore smiled, still gazing out of the windows. 'I dwell in the reflection of the Infinite Gods.'

'Dwell on this!' Orcades screamed as he pulled the trigger. There was a brief burst of red light, then Commodore Thorwald's head disappeared. His lifeless body fell to the floor. It shook for a moment, then was still.

Orcades turned to stare at the flight deck, taking a second to find each face, absorbing the shock and revulsion he found there.

'On this ship, I am God,' he said in a low voice.

He turned to the weapons console operator and aimed his gun at her head. 'Tell me you've stopped the bombardment?'

The woman nodded quickly, her hands shaking over the controls.

'Thank you,' Orcades added with a dry smile before walking back to the windows. Through the fog of destruction, he could make out explosion after explosion. The cascade of light ended and the dust cloud began to dissipate, revealing the asteroid fractured into pieces.

ADRIFT

The merchant ship *Lexica* accelerated through the inner lock gates, cutting through fire and smoke. All around it was the debris of the fallen ship, each piece spinning and colliding. Even the rocky walls of Melchior were crumbling now as the orbital bombardment intensified.

'Almost at the outer doors,' Bara noted, fully focused on keeping the ship on course.

Wynn could hear the debris dancing off the hull, a cacophony of bangs and scrapes and rumbles that shook his stomach. The vessel lurched, throwing him into his seat, then gravity seemed to shift and he felt himself dragged towards the view. His harness kept him in place, digging into his skin as the ship swayed under the shifting gravitational eddies. They passed the exterior gate, debris hammering into the ship, alarms sounding. A large fragment of rock drifted towards them. Bara hit a button and a protective shield dropped over the windows. The console simulated the exterior view, helping Bara to navigate, but there was no avoiding the impact. The noise was deafening, a stomach-churning crunch that seemed to go on forever.

'We're spinning,' Bara said quickly.

For a second the power failed, and the bridge became dark. One by one the systems came back online, and Bara had control again. The noise of the debris lessened and she opened the shield again. Light flooded through the windows, but it wasn't the light of The Infinite, this was the blazing glow of dozens of explosions.

Out of the dock came the other ships, each one filled with the refugees of Bara's former home. The first ship limped clear of the explosions, but the next was crushed by rock. One by one the ships were consumed by fire until the entire view was filled with burning vessels.

'Melchior,' Bara whispered, watching as the asteroid broke into pieces. Wynn gasped as he caught sight of the beautiful gardens exposed to space, the giant Circadia burning up.

He looked past the conflagration and saw a massive ship watching over the destruction. He recognized it at once: it was the same arkship he'd seen during his escape from the *Obsidian*.

The lone surviving evacuation ship powered up its engines, moving away from the expanding cloud of debris. Two points of light erupted from the enemy arkship and made contact with the fleeing vessel. The ship's engines spewed smoke, and the craft stalled in its escape.

'They're rounding up survivors,' Bara said as she worked at her console. 'Lex, we need to look like debris.'

'Understood. Shutting everything down,' the ship replied. 'Good luck.'

The lights died once more, and with it so did the engines. Wynn felt the slow change in gravity as it ebbed away. The air pumps stopped and the ship became silent except for the intermittent rattle of objects hitting the hull. They were adrift in amongst the debris field, slowly rotating as their momentum took them away from the arkship. They watched in silence as the giant vessel docked with the disabled evacuation ship, obscuring it in its massive shadow.

Bara stared out of the windows. 'What are they doing?'

'Taking prisoners,' Wynn suggested.

'They'll kill them all.'

'No, I don't think so. They could have easily destroyed them without docking.'

Bara pulled her feet up onto her chair, lost in her thoughts. 'Twenty thousand people, Wynn. Twenty thousand, all living in peace on Melchior. That ship might have seven . . . eight hundred, if we're lucky. The rest are . . .' her voice faltered. 'The rest are dead.'

'I know. I'm sorry.'

'I just don't get it. We've managed to keep ourselves

out of sight, kept our home secret for more than two hundred years! Until today. Today it all goes to shit. And why? What for? We haven't hurt anyone. We don't have any enemies. Why would anyone want to destroy Melchior?'

Wynn festered in his thoughts. He had an uneasy feeling about all of this. 'Bara . . . that arkship out there, do you recognize it?'

She checked the view. 'No. If Lexica was online we could I.D. it.'

'I know it,' Wynn replied. 'Or at least I recognize it.'

Slowly, Bara turned to face him, her bloodshot eyes wide.

'It's the same ship that destroyed the *Obsidian*. I saw it from my lifeboat.'

'You . . . you're sure?'

'Positive. Bara, I think they're connected, the destruction of the *Obsidian* and Melchior . . .'

Bara's face contorted into confusion, then anger as she thought about Wynn's statement. The only thing that connected them, the only thing that linked the *Obsidian* and Melchior was–

'You!' Bara screamed. She unbuckled her harness and threw herself at him. 'This is your fault! They were after you!' She screamed as her fists bore down on him. 'My parents are dead, my home is gone, because of you!'

Wynn raised his hands to protect his face, but he

didn't fight back. He let her take out her anger on him, knowing that she was right.

'I'm sorry,' he managed. 'I'm so sorry.'

'Your fault!' Bara cried, her voice hoarse. Her grief overwhelmed her and her barrage slowed. She fell onto him, sobbing.

Wynn took her in his arms and held her to his chest, listening to her cries get quieter and quieter.

The spinning view turned away from the arkship, and the windows filled with the rising light of The Infinite.

'Did you realize?' Bara's voice was barely audible. 'Did you know they were hunting you?'

'No. If I had I wouldn't have come here.'

She looked up at him. 'Who are you, Wynn? What's so special about you?'

'I wish I knew.' He held back tears. The thought of so many dead people weighed heavily on him. He was drenched in the blood of others.

The Infinite drifted across the windows, rising out of sight. The stars turned slowly, marking time, and the air became crisp, cooling his skin. Eventually, Bara lifted herself up from Wynn's chair and floated over to her own.

'It's not your fault,' she said quietly. 'You didn't kill them, I know that. But I need time, Wynn. Right now, I'm . . . angry, and I can't look at you. I need to think.'

Wynn felt smothered in guilt. He understood her

feelings, but he couldn't help but feel wounded by her words. He let his eyes rest on the view. Clumps of debris moved with the ship, slowly rotating, catching the light, a hypnotic dance that pulled at his vision, luring him into a restless sleep.

He awoke to Bara cursing.

'What's wrong?' he asked, noticing her console was illuminated.

'I thought it was time to check the systems,' Bara said, angrily. 'I did a minimal power-up, so as not to get anyone's attention. I only wanted to check our air and power.'

'And?'

'We've got neither. We took a lot of damage on the way out of Melchior, more than I realized. The air tanks are almost empty, they've been venting out for the last few hours. I've stopped that now, but there's not much left in reserve. The power's down to minimal, ramscoop is fried, I can just about get the drive system working, if I'm lucky.'

'Sounds like our run of luck is holding,' Wynn said dryly.

'That's not our most pressing problem.'

Wynn's heart began to beat faster. 'It isn't?'

'No. My power-up, they spotted us.'

'Who? The arkship?'

Bara jabbed her finger at the console in front of him. A navigation holograph showed their position in the middle of a blizzard of debris, and a huge ship bearing down on them.'

'How long have we got?' he asked quickly.

Bara inhaled sharply. 'Not long enough.'

LOST

The flight deck of the arkship *Fenrir* was deathly silent. The body of Commodore Thorwald had been removed, but his blood still marked the floor where he had fallen.

Orcades walked amongst his crew, sensing their fear as he approached. He liked that. He had been too lenient with them, he saw that now. He had treated them as equals. That had been his mistake. He had allowed dissent to grow, for people like Durante and Thorwald to get close to him. He would have to be more cautious from now on. He made a note to have all his senior crew re-assessed. He would oversee their psych tests personally, and remove anyone who did not match up to his expectations.

Orcades turned aside, put his hand in his pocket and found the bottle of tablets. He would have to increase his mental defenses, in case someone else like Durante tried to manipulate him. He took three tablets from the bottle and swallowed them.

'All prisoners are aboard,' a crew member announced as Orcades approached his station.

'Good. The men?'

'Executions are ongoing.'

Orcades nodded, satisfied. 'Put the bodies back on the ship and set it loose. Let me know when we are ready to get underway.' He turned to speak to the guards at the doors. 'Where is Durante? I ordered him to be brought here.'

The two soldiers glanced at each other, hesitating.

'Sir . . .' the closest guard spoke. 'I don't recall your order.'

Orcades reddened. The Reader had manipulated them, it seemed.

'Give me your side arms,' Orcades barked.

The two guards faltered.

Orcades inched closer, his voice full of menace. 'Give me your guns. Now!'

The men obeyed. Orcades checked the weapons and held one in each hand. 'Come with me,' he shouted as he marched off the flight deck, the guards in tow.

He took a pod to the accommodation levels. After their confrontation on the flight deck, Orcades had ordered Reader Durante confined to his room, his door guarded. He turned the corridor and was satisfied to see the soldiers still in place.

'Where is he? Orcades asked.

'The Reader? In his room,' the guard said confidently.

'Open it.'

The guard obeyed and Orcades stepped inside.

The room was empty, the Reader had gone. He'd even taken the ancient painting that used to hang on his wall.

Orcades pressed his wrist com.

'Flight deck? Is Reader Durante's shuttle still in the hanger bay?'

'Checking,' a voice replied. There was a short pause, then, 'His shuttle's not in its berth.'

Orcades felt his anger growing, pushing on his skull. The headache was getting worse. 'When did it leave?'

'Sir, I'm sorry . . . I know this doesn't make any sense but his ship's not on our system. It says he never docked.'

Orcades took a moment, massaging the side of his head, trying to think. 'Scan for any ships in the vicinity. He can't be far.'

He returned to the corridor and gave the guns back to his guards. His vision blurred at the edges, but he couldn't show weakness. He inhaled, then marched back to the pod.

The flight deck's lights hurt his eyes, piercing his brain with needles of pain. He shielded his face as he approached the Traffic and Obstacle Control desk.

'Well?' Orcades asked the crew member on the scanning console.

'No ships in range,' the crewman replied quickly.

'Extend the range. Run the scan again. Increase the . . . increase the . . .' He couldn't remember the words.

'I'll run a high-resolution pass, sir.'

'Yes! Do that.'

'It will take longer.'

'I know that!' Orcades replied. He retreated from the console, finding solace in the dark view out of the windows. The Infinite was below the ship, its light out of sight. He saw the broken shell of the asteroid, surprised to see patches of rich color on the interior spaces. Were they fields? Parks, perhaps? When this was all over, he must ask some of the prisoners. He would like to hear more about this place. He focused beyond the debris and saw the great span of the Ouranos Cloud, a sliver of frosted blue that stretched to form a horizon. Its name sounded peaceful, but he'd been there once. He'd witnessed its arcane temper with his own eyes. It was a place of folklore and lies, but no sane captain would take their ship into it.

'Heir Valtais,' the TOC controller said politely as he approached. 'I have found something.'

RED LINE

'Drive system is online and ready,' Lexica stated. 'Destination?'

'Inside the Ouranos Cloud,' Bara replied, pointing to the thin seam of blue matter that stretched out before them.

'May I remind you that is an extremely unstable region. You've put a lot of time and effort into my repairs.'

'Sol! Just do it, Lex! If we stay out here there'll be nothing left of you to repair.'

'If I must,' Lexica complained.

'You must,' Bara muttered as she stared at the holograph of the approaching arkship.

Wynn felt the familiar pull of the drive as it accelerated, pressing him into his seat. This time the gentle pressure did not go away, it just kept on building and building until he couldn't move his head. Every part of his body ached.

'Maximum velocity,' Lexica said after a moment.

The view shifted from blackness to a cool grey-blue

as the cloud grew bigger. Wynn could make out denser regions within the expanse, dark patches of swirling gas that dragged at the material around them. Here and there were clusters of rock which seemed to shoot through the cloud with ferocious velocity.

Lexica said, 'We are outrunning the arkship. It's the *Fenrir*, by the way. Draig registered.'

'*Draig*?' Wynn said quietly. 'Derward thought the House of Draig might be behind the attack on the *Obsidian*.'

'Drive cut-off,' Lexica announced. 'That's all I have for you. We are low on fuel, Bara. Maneuvering thrusters only now, I'm afraid.'

'Thanks, Lex,' she replied. 'I'll try to get us out of this one.'

'Promises, promises,' Lexica said, sounding resigned to his fate.

Bara turned to Wynn. 'This place is rough. Gravitational eddies, plasma vortices, micro meteorites travelling at supersonic speeds. If we're lucky that arkship won't be stupid enough to follow us in here. A ship that size would get pulverized.'

'And we won't?' Wynn asked.

Bara wavered. 'Look, I wouldn't take us in here if we had any other options. Besides, we're smaller, we can react quicker.'

'The arkship is slowing,' Lexica noted.

Bara's face lit up with relief. 'See? Told you.'

'And now they're firing.'

A dozen new dots appeared on the holograph, bright green lines aimed at *Lexica*.

Bara hit the console. 'Launching countermeasures.'

A new group of signals blinked onto the holograph, spreading out behind the ship. Three of the approaching missiles made contact with the new icons and disappeared in a burst of light.

Ahead, the edge of the Ouranos Cloud stretched out to greet them. The wispy tendrils snaked up, jostling the ship. Bara aimed straight for the gas, ramming the ship into it. The shaking became violent, throwing Wynn from side to side.

'Three missiles still locked on.' Lexica warned.

Bara pushed the nose of the ship down, straight towards a twisting hurricane of gas. The noise grew louder and louder as the driving vapor buffeted the ship.

'Used to be a planet,' Bara shouted conversationally over the racket. 'Gas giant. Quite pretty. Big blue ball, thin ring around it. Not any more. Now it's this mess.'

A small rock smashed into the hull, just in front of the window. The impact tilted the ship to one side, throwing them into a spin. Bara fought against it, jostling for control of the ship. She turned them towards a larger asteroid, banking directly at it.

'You need to pull up, Bara,' Wynn warned.

'I concur,' Lexica said.

Bara did not reply. She navigated to the edge of the asteroid, skimmed over its surface then launched upwards. The rumble of an explosion chased them.

Wynn checked the holograph screen: one of the missiles had hit the asteroid. The screen blinked, and a mass of new signals appeared.

'Great,' Lexica observed, 'instead of one big asteroid we've now got hundreds of small ones to avoid.'

'And one less missile,' Bara reminded him.

'We still have two missiles locked on,' Lexica said. 'Impact in nine seconds.'

'Lexica, you always were a pessimist.' Bara pulled on the control yoke, spinning the ship in a violent turn.

'I'm not designed for that level of G,' the ship reminded her.

The missiles whizzed past them, corrected their course and turned to find their target once more.

Bara seized on her advantage and headed straight for the dark eye of a turbulent storm just off their starboard wing. She slammed the ship into it, holding on as they were tossed and thrown about.

Wynn watched the two missiles on the console display as they chased them into the storm. They were gaining, only seconds from impact. He held his breath, his fingers digging into the arm of his chair. There was a massive vibration and the entire ship began to spin. The holograph screen flickered then died, then the power blipped across the entire bridge. The ship fell through the storm, dropping past its outer edge. Gradually, Bara regained control of the ship and stabilized their path.

Wynn blinked rapidly. 'The missiles?'

'Destroyed,' Bara said, relieved. 'Lex, can they track us in here?'

'I've shut down everything but flight control and life support. We should be almost invisible to them now.'

'Good, they'll presume they got us,' Bara replied. 'I'll plot a course for the outer edge, away from them. It'll be rough, but we should be able to make it.'

Relived, Bara turned to Wynn and her face broke into a grin.

'Bara . . .' the ship said quietly.

She sighed, her eyes closed. 'Don't say it.'

'I've checked the level of fuel . . .'

'Don't say it.'

'We are past the red line, Bara. We do not have enough propulsion to get us out of this cloud any time soon.'

'How soon?'

'Sixty-eight days. The air will be gone in thirteen hours . . . If you sacrificed Wynn you might last a day.'

'Not funny, Lex,' Bara seethed.

She kicked the console, tears in her eyes. 'You know, I almost thought we were going to make it.'

'You did good, Bara,' Wynn said.

'Not good enough,' she replied bitterly.

Wynn watched the swirling clouds outside, listened to the constant wail of the wind about the hull. The ship jostled from tiny impacts, rocking him in his seat. There was nowhere to go, and yet he wasn't ready to give in. As he stared into the eye of an approaching storm an idea began to form in his head. 'Do we still have coms?'

Bara stared at him. 'What?'

'Communication. Do we still have it?'

She checked the console. 'Yes, why?'

'We can't run, we can't fight, we can't hide, but we can talk.'

'Wynn, what do you mean?'

'We contact the *Fenrir* and tell them we surrender.'

THE CLOUD WATCHER

Gofal gazed into the vast storm that battered the little ship. It had taken all his energy to remain attached during their escape from Melchior. He had found refuge just behind the bridge, tucked beneath the sensor pod for protection. Even so, he was badly damaged from the EMP and in need of power. He had tried to tap into the ship's supplies but his host was as drained as he was.

His predicament was poor, his chances of survival slim. But he looked out at the balletic movement of the gas clouds about him and he could not help but feel awe. If he was to die today, he was glad he had seen this with his own eyes.

Gofal checked the ship's status once more, already knowing they were doomed. They would not make it through the Ouranos Cloud. He had come so close to completing his mission, only to fail at this last hurdle. He had survived the destruction of the *Obsidian*, he had tracked this survivor, he had confirmed his identity, he had endured an EMP blast, he had escaped the fall of Melchior, he had . . . but it was no good berating himself. He had done his best, that was all that really mattered.

He turned back to the view. He knew exactly how this storm front was formed, he could predict its movement with a certain level of accuracy. He knew everything about it, he could taste it and see into its molecular composition, but none of that detracted from its artistic splendor. At least he would have something beautiful to watch until his death. He thought about all the things that had befallen him and he realized how lucky he was.

SURRENDER

'A signal?' Orcades checked.

'Yes, sir,' the communications officer replied. 'The transmission is coming from inside the Ouranos Cloud.'

Orcades smiled. 'Well then, let's hear it.'

A static-filled voice came from the console. '. . . merchant ship *Lexica* to the arkship *Fenrir*. I'm the one you're hunting . . . I'm the survivor from the *Obsidian*. I want to negotiate terms for my surrender. Respond.'

Orcades' eyes widened. He could hardly believe what he was hearing. 'Negotiate?' he said to himself, laughing. 'The audacity of the man . . .'

He paced the flight deck, listening to the repeating message, then stopped at the windows and gazed at the violent clouds ahead. *Could he really have survived?* Orcades smiled again, almost admiring the gall of his prey, then he returned to the communications console.

'Open a channel,' he said quietly. The officer obeyed, nodding when the task was complete. Orcades straightened. '*Lexica* . . . this is the *Fenrir*. Who am I talking to?'

There was short pause, then the distorted voice returned. 'I've already told you who I am.'

'Your name, sir.'

'You've chased me from the *Obsidian*. You've done everything you can to destroy me, but I'm still here. You know who I am. But you, I don't know you.'

'Heir Valtais Orcades Draig.'

The channel cracked with static.

'I believe you wished to discuss your surrender,' Orcades continued. 'But tell me, sir . . . why do you wish to surrender? Out of fuel, perhaps? Air running low? What purpose does it serve you to give in now?'

'Survival,' the voice replied. 'You're right, we're in bad shape here. You're the better of two options. And I want to negotiate safe passage for my companion, in return for my surrender.'

'Why do you suppose I would want your surrender?' Orcades mused. 'Your signal has been very useful, I have you locked on our scanners now. What's stopping me from destroying you where you stand?'

'You've thought me dead twice now, and you've been wrong both times. Could you be sure of destroying me a third time? Or would there always be a doubt in your mind? Could you sleep at night, certain of my death? Or would part of you wonder if I was still out here, plotting my revenge? My surrender is your only certainty, Draig. You can see me die with your own eyes.'

Orcades nodded. 'You make a good point . . . but I sleep well at night. Very well. And I do not need your surrender, sir.'

Orcades pressed a button on the console and the channel broke off. He straightened his jacket, then he traversed the semi-circle of consoles to the weapons section. 'You have a lock on that signal?' he asked the officer at the console.

'Yes, sir,' the officer replied happily. 'Target acquired and locked.'

'Very good,' Orcades said, making sure his voice carried across the flight deck. 'Please, fire.'

EAVESDROPPING

Derward Tarkkail had been sleeping. It had begun as a simple meditation to help calm his thoughts, but exhaustion gnawed at his eyes, and he didn't have the will to fight it.

He forced his eyes open, uncertain where he was, just for a second. Then he saw the bridge of the *Leughadair* and everything came back to his mind. He had escaped the terrible destruction of Melchior. He had followed Bara's ship through the debris field, making sure he was undetected, just a shadow in amongst the wreckage. His ship was in blackout mode and gave off no signals that could be tracked with a standard scan.

But then Bara had made a mistake: she had powered up her systems and the arkship *Fenrir* had spotted her. Bara had set course for the Ouranos Cloud, and Derward had followed, watching with relief and awe as she outmaneuvered a volley of missiles from the *Fenrir*.

Derward stretched in his seat, listening to the crackle of the coms channel. He'd managed to tap into the

Fenrir's internal chatter and had learned a great deal from the formal chain of orders passed throughout the ship. It seemed like the newly-appointed Commodore was no longer in charge; orders were coming directly from Orcades Draig now. And Reader Durante was missing, presumed to be off-ship. Derward wondered where he might be. They had both been trained in the same stealth techniques. Durante would not be found by the *Fenrir*, unless he wanted to be.

He listened as the arkship prepared to leave; they presumed their last attack on Bara's ship was a success. *Lexica* was destroyed and now the *Fenrir* was getting ready to depart. Good, that would make Derward's job easier. He would wait until the *Fenrir* was underway before he rendezvoused with *Lexica*, he would have time to decide how much was wise to tell her and Wynn.

'. . . is the merchant ship *Lexica* to the arkship *Fenrir*. I'm the one you're hunting . . . I'm the survivor from the *Obsidian*. I want to negotiate terms for my surrender. Respond.'

Derward bolted upright, hardly able to believe what he was hearing. He checked the signal's source: it was definitely coming from *Lexica*. If they were willing to give away their location they must be in worse shape that Derward supposed.

He powered up the ship, doing his best to conceal his new trajectory from the *Fenrir*. 'I'm just an asteroid,

I'm just and asteroid,' he muttered as he worked.

'. . . signal has been very useful, I have you locked on our scanners now.' He recognized that voice immediately: Orcades Draig.

Derward calculated the distance between him and *Lexica*. This would be tight.

Wynn's voice broke through the static. 'My surrender is your only certainty, Draig. You can see me die with your own eyes.' He sounded more confident now, in charge in spite of his predicament. But Wynn had miscalculated. Derward surmised what was about to happen. He plotted his course and rested his hand on the drive button, waiting.

'. . . I sleep well at night. Very well. And I do not need your surrender, sir.' Orcades again.

Derward cursed, knowing what would happen next. Even so, the sight of the missile launches on his console made his stomach turn. He hit the drive button and felt the G-force ram him into his seat.

THE VISITOR

'What happened?' Bara asked, leaning closer to Wynn.

'They cut the channel,' Wynn said with a feeling of finality. 'I don't think they're interested in my surrender. I'm sorry, Bara.'

'I'm picking up a missile launch signal from the *Fenrir*, inbound to our location,' Lexica said.

Bara closed her eyes. 'Suggestions?'

'None,' Lexica replied.

'How long have we got?'

'Eighteen seconds. Would you like a countdown?'

'No, thank you, Lex.' Bara glanced at Wynn, her lip quivering. 'This is it.'

Wynn nodded, feeling defeated. He stared out of the window at the distant shape of the arkship *Fenrir* and the approaching point of light. He was going to die, never knowing who he really was. All his questions would remain unanswered. *Would it be painless?* he wondered.

Then he saw a blur of movement, something approaching rapidly from the port side. Suddenly he could no longer see the arkship, or the missile. A new shape had blocked the view.

'What was—' he managed to say before the blast threw him backwards. The ship rocked violently, spinning away from a huge explosion. Alarms sounded across the console as Bara regained control.

'Lex, shut off the alarms,' she shouted. 'Are we silent?'

'No external signals,' Lexica confirmed.

'Good.' Bara let the ship drift, the source of the explosion rising and setting in the bridge windows. 'Now, what the hell just happened?'

'Something obstructed the missile's path,' Lexica replied. 'The missile detonated on impact with the object.'

'An object? What sort of object?'

'Hard to tell. It appeared to be an asteroid but it was moving very quickly, and seemed to adjust its course. That could have been caused by the storm current, or—'

'Or it was a ship,' Wynn deduced.

The fiery debris came into view once more, it's mass expanding.

'The arkship *Fenrir* is moving away.' Lexica said.

'They think they destroyed us,' Bara mused.

'Well, they destroyed something,' Wynn replied. 'Could it have been a drone?'

Bara shook her head. 'Too big for a drone. If it wasn't an asteroid it was almost certainly a ship. Could have been under computer guidance.'

'I am picking up another object on an intercept trajectory,' Lexica informed them. 'It is much smaller.'

'A lifeboat?' Bara asked.

'The size and configuration does match some standard single-person lifeboats. It is moving with the debris field, but making minor adjustments to its path to bring it in line with us.'

Wynn stared at Bara, uncertain what this meant. He was still getting used to the idea that he was alive.

It took fifteen minutes for the other craft to get close enough for them to spot it out of the window.

'It is a lifeboat, I think,' Bara laughed. 'I've never seen one so compact. Someone survived that blast.'

'And they look like they want to dock.' Wynn replied. 'Should we let them?'

Bara shrugged. 'No fuel, not much air . . . I don't think we have much choice. Besides, I want to see who saved us, don't you?'

'Yes,' Wynn replied. In spite of their situation he felt a flurry of excitement as the lifeboat approached.

Gradually, the two ships adjusted their positions until they moved as one. The lifeboat inched closer and closer to Lexica's docking ring and, with a barely audible thud, it made contact.

'Shall we see who's come for dinner?' Bara grinned as she unbuckled her harness and floated towards the door.

Wynn laughed, joining her as they moved through the ship. Without gravity, he was soon completely disorientated, but Bara knew her way, leading them towards the docking hatch. As they approached, the mechanism was already beginning to turn.

'Here we go,' Bara mumbled, her grin disappearing.

The circular door hissed, then began to rotate, slicing into the hull to reveal a darkened void beyond. A hand reached out from the lifeboat and found Bara's. She helped the figure, pulling him into the light.

Wynn smiled with relief at the sight of a familiar face out here in the middle of the Ouranos Cloud.

'Derward?' Bara laughed. 'How the hell did you find us?'

'I'd say it was nice to see you,' Derward said wearily, 'but given the circumstances . . .'

'It's still good,' Bara laughed, comforting the visitor with her arm.

'What's our situation?' Derward asked as he rested against the wall.

Bara's smile faded. 'Grim. The *Fenrir's* leaving, but we don't have much of anything.'

Derward nodded knowingly as he returned to the lifeboat's hatch. He opened a control panel and worked through a series of functions. 'I'm transferring my lifeboat's fuel and air to your ship. It's not much but it'll be enough to get us clear of the cloud.'

Wynn laughed with relief. 'You're the best thing

that's happened all day.'

'It's been a very bad day then,' Derward quipped.

The ship began to hum as the fuel transfer took place.

Derward checked the readings, satisfied. 'There. You have it all now, but we should conserve the air. I didn't have a huge supply, and there's three of us in here now.'

Bara nodded in agreement. 'Let's go to the bridge. We'll seal off the rest of the ship.'

Derward smiled, then turned to Wynn. 'And it's good to see you still in one piece. I overheard your barter with Draig. Held your own quite well.'

'He tried to kill us!' Wynn scoffed.

'And he failed.' Derward reminded him.

'Thanks to you. If you hadn't put your ship in the way of that missile . . . well, I'm very glad you did, Derward.'

'I'm sorry about the *Leughadair*, I know what she meant to you,' Bara said quietly.

Derward dismissed her remark with a wave of his hand. 'A ship's a ship. It's what's inside that matters.'

'Don't let Lex hear you say that. He's likely to throw you off.'

'Noted,' Derward chuckled. 'I'll be discreet.'

They climbed the last flight of stairs towards the bridge when the deck shifted under them. The hull vibrated as power throbbed through the ship.

'What's happening?' Wynn asked, struggling to

keep himself upright.

'We're moving!' Bara exclaimed, already pulling herself up towards the bridge hatch. She pressed the door control, but nothing happened. She tried again, frustrated, then activated her wrist communicator. 'Lex, what's happening?'

The ship did not respond.

'Lex? Why are we moving?'

Wynn nudged past her and tried the door for himself. When it didn't budge he peered into the thin window recessed in the door to see into the bridge. The space was dark, just the pale light of the console to see by, but he could make out a figure moving on the bridge. He squinted, uncertain of what he had seen, but as he checked again he was sure there was someone sat in Bara's seat.

No, not someone. It was a machine. A bot with a pair of blue glowing eyes.

RHAPSODY

Gofal turned to look at the sliver of window in the bridge hatch and saw the face of his prey staring back at him. He took a moment to study him, to try to understand the emotions he saw there. The man was shocked, that was obvious, but there were other feelings there as well, ones that were harder to quantify. *Was one of them recognition?* Gofal wondered. Did he look back at him and remember their life before the demise of the *Obsidian*? No, probably not, Gofal concluded. The conditioning on his memories was substantial, and the chances of him remembering something was slim. This last thought filled Gofal with a sense of loss that he couldn't quite comprehend.

He turned back to the console and the view. This ship had enough power to get them to their destination now, thanks to the arrival of the lifeboat. A fortuitous turn of events, one that had taken him by surprise, but he had been quick to take advantage of. The ship's on-board intelligence had proven difficult to circumvent, but now that Gofal had full control it was a simple task to keep the Lexica personality suppressed. He was in command now.

Gofal checked his course, making sure his corrections did not rouse the attention of the retreating arkship, then he rested in the chair, his work complete, for now.

On the other side of the door the three people were getting agitated. They had made several brute-force attempts to override the door software, and one actual brute-force attempt to prize the door open. All had failed, but he was concerned for their own safety. He had not come all this way to see his prey delivered in a less-than satisfactory condition.

Perhaps some music might help?

He rifled through his archive and found something he particularly liked, a piece of music from long before the Fracture. He had always found it calming, and he was sure they would too. Gofal tapped into the ship-wide com system and fed the music through it.

ARRIVAL

'How did it get on board?' Wynn said, catching his breath. The door wouldn't move, no matter how hard he tried.

'I'm more concerned about where it's taking us,' Derward replied, wringing his hands together.

'Sol! If it's harmed Lex I'll rip it apart,' Bara muttered from the open panel.

'It's just a ship, Bara,' Derward replied.

She twisted round to glare at him. 'He's not just a ship!'

Derward retreated from her, his hands held up defensively.

Bara gave in, kicking the console cover. 'We can't just wait here till it takes us wherever it's planning on taking us! We have to do something.'

'I'm open to suggestions,' Derward replied.

Bara pressed her head to the window, staring at the intruder. 'When I get in there I'm gonna unscrew your head and fill it full of waste oil, do you hear me?'

She hammered on the door, appeasing her frustration.

'We're wasting air,' Derward noted. 'We should stay calm.'

Slowly, Bara turned to face him. 'Calm? This is me being calm, Derward, trust me.'

Before Derward could reply the com system crackled, then a piece of music began to play. It started with a single instrument, a melancholic tone that grew more complex, with other instruments joining it until the sound filled their ears.

'What is it trying to do?' Bara shouted.

'It's antagonizing us,' Derward said.

The music played on, the tempo increasing, the tone becoming more optimistic and frantic, and a memory sparked in Wynn.

'Gershwin,' he muttered.

Derward looked at him, confused. 'What?'

'Gershwin. The word just came into my mind,' Wynn explained, talking loudly over the sound. 'I think I know this.'

'And how does that help us?' Bara inquired angrily.

'It doesn't' Wynn replied, dismissing it. 'Do you have any weapons on board?'

She shook her head. 'Nothing that will cut through that door. You don't think I've thought of that?'

'What about the com system? Can we talk to it?'

Bara thought for a moment, her eyes darting from side to side. After a few seconds, her face lit up with an idea. 'If I trigger an evac situation the ship goes into safety mode and I'll get access to the coms, but I don't see how that will help us.'

'If you can stop this damned music I'd be very grateful,' Derward moaned.

'I want to talk to it,' Wynn said to Bara.

Bara muttered to herself, unconvinced, then returned to the exposed panel and began to work.

'There,' she said eventually. 'I've convinced the system that there's a fire in the drive section.'

A loud alarm sounded, killing the music.

'Is this meant to be better?' Derward asked.

Wynn ignored him and stood next to Bara at the panel. 'Can I talk to it?'

She nodded and pressed a series of commands into the panel. The alarm stopped abruptly.

'Okay, channel should be open,' Bara said softly.

Wynn nodded, composing himself, thinking what to say. 'Intruder, where are you taking us?'

The bot did not reply.

Wynn tried again. 'Are we your prisoners? What's our destination?'

The bot glanced at the door, then turned slowly back to the bridge consoles.

'I demand you answer me!' Wynn shouted in frustration.

The bot turned its head once more and a deep calming voice resonated from the com system. 'I will answer. What would you like to know?'

Wynn, startled by the bot's response, thought for a moment. 'Answer my questions.'

'I cannot say where I am taking you, not yet, but you are not prisoners.'

'Then why won't you let us onto the bridge?'

'It is critical that you reach your destination unharmed. Given my previous encounters with you I anticipated some level of resistance to this. So, you see, you are locked out of the ship's system for your own protection. Would you like some more music?'

'No!' Derward shouted from behind Wynn.

'No,' Wynn copied, more softly. 'We just want to talk. Can we come on the bridge and talk?'

The bot cocked its head to one side. 'I am sorry, but I suspect you're trying to trick me. I was not born yesterday.'

Wynn smiled to himself. 'Do you have a name?'

The bot did not reply.

'Why are you hunting us?'

'*You*,' the bot replied. 'I was hunting *you*.'

'Why me?' Wynn asked, suppressing a shiver.

At first the bot said nothing, then, 'Please, make yourself comfortable. We will arrive at our destination soon.'

Wynn peered through the window. 'Is that all you'll tell me?'

'For now, yes.'

As he stared at the bot Wynn felt his frustrations

ebb away. There was something about that odd voice of his, something familiar. He leaned against the door, letting his back slide down until he was resting on the floor. He glanced at Bara and Derward. 'Any ideas?'

Derward joined him on the floor, cross-legged, back straight. 'Why don't we see where it's taking us?'

'That's it?' Bara asked as she paced the floor of the small space. 'We're just going to let him take my ship and deliver us to who-knows-where?'

She stared at them both on the floor and, with an exasperated sigh, joined them. 'This is a mistake,' she added.

'Probably,' Derward said with a sly grin, then he closed his eyes and took a deep breath.

'What are you doing?' Bara asked, sounding disgusted.

'Meditating,' Derward replied without looking at her. 'Is that okay with you?'

Bara rolled her eyes, ignoring him. Instead she looked at Wynn, her face softening with a tiny smile. 'Thank you,' she said at last in a whisper.

'For what?' Wynn asked, keeping his voice quiet.

'For what you tried to do back there,' Bara explained. 'For trying to save me. Trading yourself for me. That was . . . kind.'

Wynn shrugged uncomfortably. 'Seemed like a good idea at the time.'

She shuffled next to him, leaning against the wall

with her legs stretched out in front of her. He could feel the warmth of her arm against his own. They settled into a comfortable silence and, after a while, Bara's head lolled onto his shoulder as she slept. Wynn let his own eyes rest, and he drifted in and out of sleep as he listened to the sounds of the ship's drive system.

'Attention.'

Wynn awoke with a jolt.

'Attention, we have reached our destination. Please prepare to disembark.' It was the hunter bot speaking through the ship's com system.

Wynn stood up and peered through the window. He could just make out a portion of the view from the bridge. A huge ship approached, too close to see it all, slowing as it came alongside. They felt the vibration of contact as the two ships docked.

Derward looked at the ship, then turned to the others. 'Shall we?' he said, gesturing towards the lower decks.

Wynn and Bara followed him as they returned to the docking ring. On the opposite side to Derward's lifeboat was another docking port. They watched as the lights to the hatch cycled from red to green and, with a gentle hiss, the door began to rotate. As they waited Wynn heard something moving behind them. He turned to see the hunter bot approaching. It stopped behind them, bowing reverently.

'My name is Gofal,' he said. 'Please, follow me.' The

bot bent over and walked through the constricting hatch.

'We could leave, get to the bridge, take the ship back,' Bara suggested to Wynn in a low voice.

'I have disabled your ship,' Gofal shouted thought the hatch. 'I will release it soon. Please, this way. They are waiting for you.'

'They?' Wynn mused to himself. He looked at Bara, then Derward and, with a resigned shrug, he entered the docking hatch. A breeze of fresh air greeted him as he stepped out into a much larger space. Gofal waited for him there, surrounded by a troupe of at least twenty guards. Each was dressed in a polished golden armor that fitted closely to their body. Over their right shoulder was a red cape that hung to the floor, and about their waist was a gun.

Behind him he sensed Bara and Derward coming through the hatch. They stopped at his shoulder, and he heard Bara let out a small gasp at the sight of the guards.

One of the company – an older woman with a stony face – stepped towards Wynn.

'We could not have hoped for this,' she said, her voice faltering. She halted in front of him and lowered herself onto her right knee. The rest of the guards followed her lead and, one by one, they all kneeled in front of Wynn, their heads bowed respectfully.

Wynn stared at them, lost for words.

'You are confused,' Gofal said, 'that is to be expected. Please, come this way, and you will have answers.'

KNOWING

Gofal led Wynn and the others to an ornate room many levels above. It was a round space, dominated by a vast circular table at its center. Around the edges was a view of space projected onto the high walls, the shifting image leading the eye towards the ornately carved ceiling high above.

'Where are we now?' he asked the bot.

Gofal held out a chair for Wynn, waiting until he was seated. 'All of your questions will be answered shortly. The process will not be easy for you, but I will be here throughout.'

'The process?' Wynn asked as Bara and Derward sat beside him. Gofal said nothing. He walked to the edge of the room and waited, his blue eyes fixed on the gigantic doors at the other end of the space. After a moment they opened, and two guards entered. A third figure appeared, an older man with dark skin and a bald head. Wynn stared at the man as he came towards the table, his polished grey and red uniform catching the glittering lights. He stopped at the other side of the table, an odd expression on his face, and Wynn suddenly realized he had seen this face before.

'You were there,' he gasped. 'I . . . I saw you, when I was in the lifeboat, on the *Obsidian*.'

The man said nothing. He glanced to Gofal who walked to his side and, with a gesture from the stranger, began to speak.

'Welcome,' Gofal said. 'You are on board the *Caerleon*, the last arkship loyal to the Royal House of Kenric. This is Lord Chamberlain Cam Tanis, second-in-command to the late Prince Thyred. He is responsible for your memory block.'

'You did this to me?' Wynn blurted. 'Why? What are you hiding?'

Tanis raised a hand, silencing him.

Gofal continued. 'It was necessary, for your own protection during the attack on the *Obsidian*. We were afraid you would be captured and your identity revealed. We could not afford to lose you. But you are safe here and the memory block will be removed now. You will have access to all of your memories once more. This will, no doubt be a painful and disorientating process.'

'How? How can you remove it?'

'It is a simple audio primer, triggered by the sound of the Lord Chamberlain's voice. When you are ready he will speak to you.'

Wynn realized he was trembling. He turned to Bara

and she took his hand, her face full of warmth.

'Whoever I am,' he said to her, 'whoever I turn out to be, it won't change anything between us, will it? Promise me that.'

'I promise,' she replied, squeezing his hand.

'I'm afraid,' he confessed.

'This is what you want,' Derward said. 'This is what you need. Let it happen.'

Wynn nodded, steeling himself, then he stood to face the Lord Chamberlain. 'I'm ready.'

The Lord Chamberlain Tanis smiled, his dark eyes glistening, and he opened his mouth to speak.

'Welcome home, Hal.'

Wynn felt a jolt deep inside his mind, and a flood of images erupted, vivid recollections with a clarity that took his breath away: he could no longer tell what he was seeing and what he was remembering. He fell back into the chair, aware of Bara and Derward's concerned faces watching over him. His mind reeled: it was an explosion of memories, attacking him out of sequence, a cascade of joy and grief, of childhood adventures, of family occasions, of duty and training and education. He knew this ship, he knew this man in front of him, but most of all Wynn finally knew himself. Tears fell from his eyes as he struggled to control his emotions.

Eventually he composed himself and stood up, taking in the room with a newfound understanding.

'I know my name,' he said.

ECHO

Orcades Draig opened the door to his mother's suite and stepped over the threshold. The room was unchanged since her death, every ornament in place, the photos and art still hanging on the walls, even her collection of antiquated Earth novels was still here. Her holograph could be loaded with millions of books in an instant, she had no need to sit and read, and yet he had often seen her taking comfort in the yellowed pages of some long-forgotten text. How human.

At first, he could not see her, and he wondered if he was alone. He descended the steps that led to her garden room and found her gazing out at the view of The Infinite. Had she already been there? Or had his arrival triggered her holograph? She turned to greet him, her face weighed down by sadness.

'Mother,' Orcades said formally as he approached her. They embraced, brief and icy, then he retreated to one of the high armchairs that bracketed the windows. Slowly, she turned to the opposite chair, pausing to touch one of the flowers that grew in the stepped platform along the far wall of the garden room. She eased herself into the seat, arranged her gown, rubbed her hands together as if to remove some residue of pollen, then raised her eyes to him.

'Well?' Sinnsro asked brusquely.

Orcades gazed at her, as if seeing the holograph for the first time. It really was quite remarkable, easy to forget she wasn't real.

'Your Reader has fled,' he replied without emotion. He rubbed the side of his head, hoping to ease the numb pain that festered there. Even without Reader Durante on board, Orcades had considered it wise to continue with his course of suppressants, upping the dose to avoid any surreptitious mental attacks.

Sinnsro Draig nodded quietly. 'I have read the report. You felt it necessary to kill Commodore Thorwald?'

'Necessary?' Orcades asked, his voice rising. 'Of course it was necessary. How could it not be? He had betrayed me!'

'Under the influence of Reader Durante, or so you suppose.'

'You doubt it?'

Sinnsro frowned, her anger growing. 'I doubt a great many things, Orcades, most of all your ability to lead.'

Orcades stood, his face reddening. 'We are on the brink of a great victory, and yet you doubt me? I have all but defeated the House of Kenric, I have killed its heir. Only one Kenric arkship remains – soon even that will fall to Draig. I have achieved all of this, and yet you question my leadership?'

'You have made an enemy of the Church. Do you think that is of little consequence? Do you think you could win if they chose to turn their fleet against you?'

Orcades dismissed this with a wave of his hand. 'They have no army, just rumors and fearmongering. They weave lies to keep us in check. Has anyone ever seen this supposed fleet of theirs?'

'It exists,' Sinnsro replied emphatically, 'and you would be well advised to keep the Church as an ally. You must contact them at once, explain what has happened and beg their understanding. I have already sent a message to Librarian Horst. I only hope she is willing to hear your plea.'

Orcades' rage grew. 'You contacted them? You have no right!'

Sinnsro stood, stepping closer to face up to him. 'You forget yourself, Orcades. I am still Valtais. This is not your time. You have proven yourself unready to rule in my place. I have given you too much responsibility too soon. It is clear to me now that I must command with a stronger hand until you are mature enough to take my place.'

'No!' Orcades bellowed. He swung his arm, catching his mother's face. She stumbled to the floor, her withered hand protecting her head. She gazed up at him, simulated blood marking her lip, and Orcades saw fear and resentment filling her cool eyes.

'You dare to–'

'Be silent!' Orcades screamed, his arm raised again. 'You are not my mother.'

Sinnsro's voice trembled. 'I am, in all but body. The law of the people decrees it.'

'Then the law will change,' Orcades declared. 'You are just a simulation, and your time is at an end. From today I am Valtais, and I rule alone.'

'No . . . you cannot,' Sinnsro hissed as she climbed to her feet. 'This is our tradition, our birth right. Every Valtais is trained and advised by the ghost of the last, an unbroken line of continuity stretching back to the time of the Fracture. You cannot–'

'Do not tell me what I cannot do, woman!' Orcades said, turning away. He couldn't look at her any more. He closed his eyes, trying to ignore the pain inside his skull, then turned towards the holograph control system he knew was kept at the heart of her suite.

'What are you doing?' Sinnsro shouted as she watched her son march towards the concealed system.

Orcades ignored her, removed the panel cover and tapped in his authorization code. The system recognized his identity and the screen glowed, awaiting his command.

'Step away from there!' Sinnsro cried from behind him.

Orcades' heart pounded, and a flood of emotion

erupted inside him. Bitter tears fell from his eyes as he turned to face her. 'I must rule alone. Goodbye, mother.'

He returned to the console and accessed the personality matrix. 'Computer, purge all files of Sinnsro Draig from the holograph system.'

Behind him, he heard his mother's holograph gasp.

'Don't do this,' she pleaded, falling to his feet. 'You'll kill me.'

'My mother died a long time ago. You are just an echo.'

The computer acknowledged his request and asked for confirmation.

Orcades stared at the screen, a tremble of hesitation holding him back. This wasn't his mother, he reminded himself. This was just data on a very sophisticated holograph system, nothing more. Not flesh and blood. He could not rule in its shadow. It had to end. He tensed, resolute in his decision. 'Delete all files. Permanently.'

Sinnsro Draig screamed. Her scream distorted into a staccato digital tone that faded away to silence. Orcades gripped the sides of the console, his eyes shut, waiting for the noise to end. When he finally opened his eyes again and turned around, he was alone in his dead mother's suite. He bent down and took the ring of the Valtais from the floor where it had fallen. He held it to his finger and watched as it adjusted to fit him. He flexed his hand, studying the ring. He was Valtais now.

Orcades felt a strange sense of freedom, and an unexpected smile broke over his face. But tears still welled up in his eyes, and a dreaded knot of guilt weighed him down as he walked out of the room.

CHANGE

Wynn pulled at the collar of his jacket. It was rigid and formal, the material itching his skin. He wanted to take it off, to throw away this stupid uniform and return to his dirty overalls, to find Bara and escape on *Lexica*. He looked out of the windows, to the stars, and felt lost.

He'd been on board the *Caerleon* for three weeks, and was gradually acclimatizing to his new role and position, but it had not been easy.

He turned his back on the view and took in the splendor of the Grand Hall. It was a vaulted space, with stone columns that were covered in intricate carvings that told the story of the Kenric family all the way back to the time of the Fracture. In between the columns were vast tapestries that added slices of color to the cream stone. The floor was made of polished tiles, laid in a precise interlocking pattern that led the eye from the far end to the raised podium and the impressive windows.

At the entrance to the hall stood Gofal, waiting steadfastly. Wynn smiled at the sight of his old friend and companion, his shattered arm repaired. They had been inseparable since he was a young boy, and it seemed odd now to recall his fear at the sight of those glowing blue eyes after the fall of the *Obsidian*.

So much had changed.

The huge doors opened and he saw a distant figure enter the hall. Recognizing the visitor, Wynn ran to greet her.

'Bara,' he laughed as they embraced. 'I've missed you.'

She smiled, her eyes glancing away. 'It's not easy to get an audience with the prince.'

Wynn sighed, feeling awkward. 'I'm the same person, really.'

'No, you're not,' Bara said with a regretful look. 'I'm not even sure what I should call you any more.'

'I'm still Wynn,' he replied. 'It's from my middle name, Aldwyn. It was my nickname when I was growing up. A few friends still use it.'

'Prince Halstead Aldwyn Kenric,' Bara said slowly, as if she was trying to remember it properly. 'I'm not sure I should use a nickname.' She was teasing, he was sure, but it still gnawed at him. Wynn shook his head dismissively and walked back towards the grand windows that stretched from the shining floor to the ornate ceiling. 'I'm the same person you knew.'

Bara walked with him, taking in the view outside. 'But you have duties now, responsibilities. You have a people to lead.'

'I'm not a leader.'

Bara smiled, comforting him. 'Well, you're all they've got.'

A pang of grief took him by surprise. He remembered the father he now knew was dead. He had been stern, cold and remote, a difficult man to get close to. But he had been Wynn's father, and he had died on the *Obsidian*. Now, whether he liked it or not, the heavy mantle of leadership fell on Wynn's young shoulders.

'Hey,' Bara said, looking him deep in his eyes. 'Are you okay?'

'I'm fine,' Wynn lied. If he said it often enough he could make it true. Outside he saw other ships; cargo carriers, merchant vessels, gas scoops, wind feeders, argo farms, a few fighters and military craft. All were refugees from the other Kenric arkships that had been taken by Draig. Only the *Caerleon* remained under the Kenric flag now.

'How are the repairs coming along?' Wynn asked, wanting to shift the attention away from him.

'Almost done, thanks. Lex is complaining I'm not doing it right, but he always does,' Bara said breezily. She hesitated, then added, 'Actually, I was finished two days ago.'

'Then you're all set to go.'

She looked at him, her face full of remorse. 'Go? Where have I left to go?'

Wynn felt a fool. 'Sorry. This is your home now.'

'Is it?' she asked.

'It can be, yes.'

She stared at him, her eyes seemed to be taking him apart. 'You're different,' she said.

'The surgery?' His facial scars were almost healed now, and his hair had been regenerated. Already the dark roots had covered his head in a short, unruly mane.

'I saw you sometimes, from a distance,' Bara admitted.

'On the *Obsidian*?'

Bara nodded. 'It's the hair . . . I remember you now, but I never paid the royal family much attention back then. And I'm sure you didn't look twice at me.'

Wynn blushed, feeling guilty. She was right; he never mixed with anyone outside of his circle of approved friends. His life before the destruction of the *Obsidian* had been very different.

'You were the prince . . . not even a real person to me. The scars might have healed, your hair might be growing back, you're Prince Halstead again . . .' She put her hand on his chest. 'But you're still Wynn to me.'

The doors to the hall opened again and a swarm of people entered. Gofal spoke to them, then marched along the length of the space to join Wynn and Bara. He stood patiently, his frame towering over them. 'Wynn, it's time,' he said quietly. 'The hall must be made ready.'

Wynn nodded, remembering. 'Right, of course.'

Bara glanced between them. 'Time for what?'

'The naming ceremony,' Gofal replied.

REUNION

'You are a hard man to find,' the Lord Chamberlain Cam Tanis said with a knowing smile.

Derward Tarkkail did not look up from his work. He continued to stack the cargo crates on the edge of the hanger bay, hoping the visitor might decide to leave him alone.

Tanis, however, persisted. 'If I was easily offended I might think you were avoiding me.'

'Me? Avoiding you, Tanis? Never,' Derward replied.

'Do you have nothing to say to me?'

Derward put down the crate he was carrying and approached the Lord Chamberlain, looking about him to see who was nearby. 'What do you want me to say?'

Tanis shrugged. 'I don't know. Maybe, just a *hello* to an old friend.'

'Hello, old friend,' Derward said with a fixed smile. He picked up the crate again and placed it with the others.

'You know, we could do this in an interrogation room,' Tanis noted. 'But it doesn't have to be so . . .

formal, does it?'

Derward sighed, his shoulders dropping as he turned back to face him. 'Okay. Ask away, Tanis.'

'Let's start with an explanation. You are no longer a Reader?'

Derward glanced about the hanger bay. It was a huge space, full of noise and activity as ships moved through the bay to deposit their cargo, but this section was empty, except for Derward and Tanis. Had the Lord Chamberlain made sure of that? Derward wondered. 'I'm a simple trader, Tanis. A merchant. Always have been.'

Tanis smiled tolerantly. 'Yes, your records concur. Never a Reader. But computer files can be changed . . . memories are harder to adjust. And I remember you, Reader Vurig.'

'Don't call me that,' Derward hissed. 'That was another life. I'm a trader now.'

'Yes, of course: a simple trader, keeping his head down, not attracting attention. But you're more than that, Derward, even now. You're a trader with links to the Church, perhaps? A man with your skills – your experience – could not fully close that door. The Church would never let you go, not completely.' Tanis stepped closer. 'Truthfully, I do not care what caused your demise, but it is good to see you again. I have often wondered what happened to you. I thought you were probably dead.'

'That life *is* dead.'

'Very well,' Tanis sighed. 'I will not attempt to resurrect it. But I think you and I can still be of use to each other.'

Derward stared at him. The man he remembered was slimmer, his stubble not so silvery, his eyes less tired, but had his character changed in the intervening years? Tanis was a man to be trusted, back then. Was he still?

'Use to each other? How so?'

Tanis sat on one of the crates and undid his tunic at the collar. 'The House of Kenric is in crisis. Derward, we are on the brink of extinction, as I'm sure you know. Every single arkship has fallen to the House of Draig. They have overwhelmed our defenses, and with every defeat Orcades Draig grows stronger. Every arkship lost becomes part of his fleet. This is the last Kenric arkship, old friend.'

'I know that, Tanis, but what can I do about it?'

'We need allies,' the Lord Chamberlain explained, his tired eyes pleading with Derward. 'The other houses stand by and watch, hoping that Draig's ambition will stop at the doorstep of Kenric. We have no one we can turn to for support. But, perhaps, the Church might be able to swing the balance of power back in our favor.'

'Then speak to your Reader,' Derward suggested angrily.

'I already have,' Tanis sighed. 'She is a traditionalist.

She will not interfere, she won't even pass on my request for a dialogue with the Scribe. I need someone who still has ties to the higher levels, someone who can relay a message to them.'

Derward shook his head, feeling trapped. 'Why should I help you?'

'Because you're a good man, Derward. You try to hide it. You pretend not to care. But if you do nothing here today, then the *Caerleon* will fall and thousands of people will die. Draig will grow in power and, eventually, even simple traders will be affected.'

Derward cursed under his breath, feeling himself being drawn back into events. 'Even if I could, what makes you think the Scribe would listen to me?'

'You and the Scribe were . . . close, if I recall.'

'Your memory is flawed,' Derward seethed, his anger growing in spite of his best efforts to tame it.

The Lord Chamberlain stepped closer, his eyes narrow. 'Damn it, Derward! You are the only one who can stop this.'

'You give me too much credit.'

'I don't think so,' Tanis said as he grasped Derward's shoulder. 'I remember you, Derward, and I know what you're capable of.'

NAMING

When the vast doors opened for Wynn to enter the Grand Hall, the space was unrecognizable from his last visit with Bara just a few hours earlier. The once-empty floor was now filled with seated spectators, who rose at the sound of his approach, their heads turning in unison. Bara sat on the front row, her seat reserved for her by Wynn. She watched her friend approaching, noticing how much taller he appeared now, how much older. The pristine royal tunic suited him, she noted with a smile.

Wynn followed the Lord Chamberlain towards the raised podium, the congregation staring at him with a sense of awe and wonder. His eyes caught Bara's. Blood flushed his cheeks and he managed a brief smile before he climbed the steps and stood alongside Tanis. Bara realized she was grinning at him, her heart pounding in her chest as she was drawn into the emotion coming from the crowd about her.

The audience returned to their seats, Bara too, and an expectant hush filled the air.

'Welcome,' Tanis began, speaking at the dais. 'We gather here today, at a turning point in our history. We have suffered much, we have lost friends . . . family. Our collective future – the days ahead we had planned and hoped for – have been ripped from us, by the brutal hand of our enemy.' Tanis paused, letting his words echo around the chamber, the audience hanging on his every breath.

As he spoke Bara couldn't help but picture her own family, lost in the destruction of Melchior, and she was overcome with emotion. She lowered her head, closing her eyes as she composed herself.

'That future we hoped for is gone, 'Tanis continued. 'But those dreams are not dead. In the past few weeks we have suffered as one, we have all lost a part of our family. But we are Kenric, and we endure.'

A ripple of agreement cascaded through the audience.

'And today, I stand here, your Lord Chamberlain, your Regent, your servant, humbled by the strength and bravery you have displayed in the face of such adversity. For we are Kenric, and we endure.'

Some of the crowd, including a woman sat beside Bara, repeated his last sentence, a faint muttering of solidarity.

'We have been through the darkest of nights . . . together, suffering, hoping and praying for the light of tomorrow. But, by the blessing of the Infinite Gods, our prayers have been answered, and a new light shines on our House.'

The congregation grew more and more animated as a ripple of excitement flowed between them.

'Today, I stand before you, my Kenric brothers and sisters, and my heart is filled with hope once more.' The Lord Chamberlain's voice grew to be heard over the crowd. 'We are not defeated, we are not broken, we are not leaderless. For we are Kenric, and we endure!'

The chant grew until every soul in the room cried out the Lord Chamberlain's sentence: 'We are Kenric, and we endure.' Bara joined them, her heart lifted by the audience's shared emotion. She no longer felt outside, a stranger without a home. In that moment, she was one with the crowd. She was Kenric.

Over and over again, the phrase rung out, getting louder, until the Lord Chamberlain raised his hand and the room became silent once more.

'My friends, my kinsmen,' Tanis said quietly, 'our prayers have been answered. Our Prince has been returned to us!'

A deafening cheer erupted, and Bara felt her neck tingle with the energy in the room. She glanced at Wynn and realized his eyes were on her. He looked nervous, uncomfortable in front of this mass of people, but she smiled at him and his features softened, reassured by her attention.

'My people, it is my greatest honor to present to

you that which we feared we had lost forever: the heir to the House of Kenric, our beloved leader, Prince Halstead.'

The audience rose as one, cheering and clapping as Tanis stepped down from the podium and gestured for Wynn to take his place. The rapture lasted over a minute. Bara, swept along in the moment, felt she was watching a god rather than her friend. This wasn't Wynn, this was a prince with his face. It was as if everything was changing.

Wynn – Prince Halstead – stood in front of the crowd, looking uneasy in the glare of their attention. He waited for their excitement to lessen, smiling patiently. Eventually the cheering and applause ended and the crowd took to their seats again, their eyes watching him, waiting to hear him speak. Bara realized she was clutching her hands together, willing him on.

Wynn took a breath, his fingers gripping the podium as he smiled nervously. Bara had helped him to memorize the speech he was required to deliver, but now that he stood before those expectant faces he appeared to have forgotten what he had to say.

'My friends,' he began, 'it is good to be back with you.'

This wasn't his rehearsed speech, but the audience cheered and applauded, unaware of Wynn's change of plan. Even so, Wynn smiled with relief, and Bara felt her own nerves ease. He continued, his voice finding strength. 'I must thank my Lord Chamberlain for leading you during this difficult time. His loyalty and guidance have ensured the survival of the House of Kenric against extreme adversity and opposition.'

A swell of respectful applause brought the Lord Chamberlain to his feet. He bowed politely, his eyes glassy, then he returned to his seat.

'It was not my desire to lead you, not yet,' Wynn continued as the crowd became silent. 'My term as your prince lay in the distant future. But my father, Prince Thyred Halstead Kenric the third, is dead, and his duties now fall upon my shoulders. I confess, I am not ready, and I will need your support to see me through the coming trials.'

Once more the audience responded with warmth and applause.

'Only together – you and I – can we prevail. There are dangers ahead, and I will need each and every one of you to guide my hand.'

The cheering seemed to grow with every new sentence. This was better than the planned speech, Bara thought to herself. He was a natural speaker.

'And in return,' Wynn continued, 'I will carry out my duties as your prince with every fiber of my body. I will not waiver, I will not rest until the House of Kenric, our people, our arkships, our legacy is restored.'

The audience stood, and Bara joined them, chanting 'Kenric' until the Lord Chamberlain returned to the podium.

'The *Ark Royal Obsidian* has been the home of the royal household since the time of the Fracture,' Lord Chamberlain Tanis explained. 'The *Obsidian* is no more. We mourn its loss, we honor those who died, but the royal House of Kenric endures. So, from this day onwards the arkship *Caerleon* will be known as the *Ark Royal Caerleon,* the flagship of the House of Kenric.'

Once more the audience erupted as the royal crest was revealed behind the podium. Bara felt the pride amongst Wynn's people. They had someone to lead them again, someone to rally round, and their future was not so bleak any more.

As Wynn and Tanis waved to the crowd the applause died away, leaving an odd silence in its wake. At first Bara could not understand what had brought about the change, but then her eyes fell on the giant windows, and she gasped. Wynn and Tanis sensed it too, turning to look behind them at the ominous scene outside.

The dark shape of another arkship had appeared, bearing down on the *Ark Royal Caerleon*. Bara stared in disbelief at the vessel. Its form was hidden in shadow, but it had two distinctive red lights that suggested a pair of malevolent eyes, and Bara realized with despair that she had seen this arkship before.

AN AUDIENCE

Derward Tarkkail paced the antechamber floor, wishing he had kept his promise to himself. He had sworn he'd never return here, and it was a vow he'd managed to keep for more than fifteen years. Now, as he waited for an audience with the Scribe his regret grew. He wished that he was stronger, that he could turn his back on the Church and get on with his life. No regrets. But he knew he could never fully walk away.

A resonant tone caught his ear, and Derward turned to see the doors to the Scribe's library slide apart. An aide strode purposefully through the opening and, with a wave of his arm, he said, 'The Scribe will see you now.'

Derward braced himself, feeling the tingle of anticipation deep within him, and stepped towards the darkened chamber. The doors slid shut behind him, and Derward felt the temperature difference in the air, crisp against his skin.

The library stretched out in front of him, an avenue of polished stone floor bordered by walls lined with books up to the distant ceiling. This room contained the largest collection of pre-Fracture books in the entire Cluster. Derward scanned the spines as he walked the length of the library, seeing if he could spot any titles he had studied during his time here, and he realized he was smiling. *Did he miss those days?* he wondered.

Ahead, movement caught his eye; someone was waiting for him at the end of the library. Her frame was exactly as he remembered it, the same striking face, the same quizzical smile, but her robes gave her a regal quality that he had never seen before. Even so, she had barely changed in the intervening years, unlike him. Derward was tired, his body worn, his mind fatigued, so different to how he had been back then. It was as if that old life belonged to another person, Derward realized as he smiled to greet the Scribe.

'Well, this is a surprise,' she said, laughing as she pulled him into an embrace. Derward tensed, taken by surprise.

The Scribe, pushed him back, holding his shoulders to look at him. 'What? You weren't so formal the last time I saw you?'

'That was a long time ago, Scribe,' Derward muttered. 'We were different–'

'Oh, come on, Derward! Relax, will you? Yes, it was a long time ago. Yes, we've both changed, but it's good to see you. I had hoped you would be glad to see me too. And don't you dare call me Scribe.'

Derward stumbled over his words.

The Scribe closed her eyes and shook her head, disappointed. 'I think I preferred you in purple.'

She let him go and sat at a nearby table, a decorative tea set placed on its cloth-covered surface. Derward hesitated before joining her. He sat formally, keeping his eyes on the steam gently rising from the tea pot.

The Scribe reached out her hand and touched his, making him flinch.

'Tea?' she asked, pouring from the teapot before he could respond. 'I'm glad you're safe. I have heard about Melchior,' she added without looking up from the cups.

'You know?' Derward gasped.

'What would be the point in me being the Scribe if I didn't know what was going on?' She grinned mischievously. 'Biscuit?'

Derward declined the offered plate. 'Scribe, what have . . .' He faltered, seeing her scolding him with her keen eyes.

'Sorry,' Derward continued, 'Ermen, what have you heard? Was it Draig? Did they attack Melchior? I spoke to Reader Durante not long before and–'

'And he betrayed your trust and orchestrated the attack,' the Scribe interrupted. 'He seems to be working to his own interpretation of the plan, one that benefits from the destruction of Melchior.' She sighed, looking weary. 'Yes, there are many ways to slice the plan – you know this better than most, Derward . . .'

Derward Tarkkail reddened, guilt stifling his response.

'But the plan is more than just an elaborate simulation,' the Scribe continued as she blew on her tea. 'It is a starting point, an aid to enlightenment, not the end result. Reader Durante has taken it upon himself to interpret the plan without my guidance, and the people of Melchior have paid the price for that decision.'

'What of Durante?' Derward asked.

The Scribe hesitated. The high collar of her cream robe gave her a stern pose, her long neck upright, ringed by the chains of office. 'He is returned to us.'

'He's here?' Derward exclaimed.

Scribe Ermengarde Barrahaus put down her tea and crossed her hands in her lap. 'Yes, he's here. He returned to us after the destruction of Melchior. He seemed to think we'd hail him a hero, a prophet of the Infinite Gods.' She rolled her eyes in disgust. 'He was convinced he'd interpreted the plan correctly, that I was in error.'

Derward could hardly believe it. 'He questioned the Scribe?'

She held up her hands. 'He's getting help.'

'He should be killed,' Derward muttered.

'There's still time,' the Scribe agreed. 'But I don't like to rush such things. He's still being . . . debriefed.'

Derward pictured the captive Durante in the hands of the Church's inquisitors, and he almost felt sorry for him. Almost.

'But, you survived Melchior,' the Scribe noted with an optimistic tone. 'Where have you been since then?'

'You don't know?' Derward sneered.

The Scribe's eyes narrowed. Of course, she knew. But she said nothing and waited for his response.

'I have come from the arkship *Caerleon*.'

The Scribe feigned surprise. 'The last Kenric arkship. And now you are back here, on *Icarus*, back in the bosom of the Church.'

'Yes.'

'For the first time in . . . what? Ten, twelve years?'

'More than fifteen,' Derward replied.

'Fifteen? Yes, I suppose it must be.'

Derward put down his cup. 'You know how long it's been, stop playing games!'

The Scribe inhaled sharply. 'Yes, I know, Derward. And in all that time you've not once come back. You've never called. I can understand you running away from the Church. I can understand you turning your back on the other Readers, even the Scribe. But you've never once contacted me.'

'You *are* the Scribe!'

'I am now, but before that I was Ermengarde, your Ermen.'

Derward hung his head, the memories of those

last days here refusing to diminish. 'I had no choice. To return here, to contact you might have put you in danger.'

'A handy excuse.'

'The truth.'

Her jaw remained stern, her lips tight, but there was a flicker of emotion at the edge of her eyes. She stood, turning her face away from him. 'So why now? Why have you come back today?'

'I need your help,' Derward admitted.

'*My* help?'

'The Church's help. I've been sent by the Lord Chamberlain to the House of Kenric.'

'Cam Tanis?' the Scribe checked, incredulous. 'He's asking for the Church's help?'

Derward nodded. 'They fear an attack from the House of Draig any time now. They do not stand a chance against them.'

'The Church does not interfere.'

Derward laughed disdainfully. 'We both know that's not true. The Church interferes whenever and wherever it sees fit.'

'When the plan demands it,' the Scribe corrected him.

'And what does your precious plan say now? What happens to the balance of power if the House of Kenric is no more?'

Scribe Barrahaus hesitated. 'It does cause some

deviation.'

'And do you think Orcades Draig will stop at the House of Kenric? How much more deviation will the Church allow before it's forced to act?'

'We cannot be seen to take sides. We can't favor one House over another. We have influence across the Cluster. The Church keeps the families in balance.'

'Exactly!' Derward rose from his chair, becoming animated. 'That's all I'm asking you to do. Right now, the House of Draig has upset that balance, and the House of Kenric is too weak to stand up to them. All you'll be doing is redressing that situation.'

The Scribe avoided his stare. 'Orcades has a legitimate birth right. He is only claiming what is–'

'You know that's not true!' Derward interrupted. 'Orcades is out of control. His claim is tenuous.'

'But there is no other, not since the destruction of the *Obsidian*.'

Derward chuckled to himself as he slumped back in his chair. 'It seems the Scribe is not all-knowing after all.'

'What does that mean?' she asked angrily.

'It means that the rightful heir is still alive. Prince Halstead is on board the *Caerleon*.'

'But . . .' the Scribe faltered. 'You're sure?'

'I'm certain. I have been following him since Melchior, watching over him. He is back with his people, but they don't stand a chance without our help.'

The Scribe smiled, her voice soft. '*Our* help? Are you part of the Church again, Derward.'

'No. I'm not asking the Church, I'm asking you . . . I'm asking Ermen to stand with me.'

The Scribe gazed into his eyes, a melancholic smile on her beautiful face. 'You always were so overly dramatic, Derward. I'd forgotten that.'

'These are dramatic times,' he said, letting his hand touch hers. She looked down, her eyes lingering on his fingers, then she pulled away from him, straightening her spine.

'The Church does not interfere,' she repeated firmly, as if to convince herself rather than him.

'You must!'

'Sol! Derward, what you ask, it's too much. The plan will not–'

'I don't care about your plan!' Derward shouted as he marched away. 'I gave up caring about it fifteen years ago.'

'Derward, please, don't go,' she called after him.

He stopped by the doorway, looking back at the distant figure, dwarfed by the walls of books. There was so much he wanted to say, but it was too late. *It's always too late*, he told himself as he turned his back on the Scribe and marched out of the library.

TERMS

Wynn stood on the hill and stared in awe at the cobalt sky. He had never seen a place like this before, but it reminded him in parts of Melchior's great fields and parks. But this landscape did not curve round over his head, it stretched out in all directions, cutting the view in two: blue above, green below.

'Beautiful, isn't it?'

Startled, Wynn turned to see a man striding up the slope of the hill to meet him. He was of a similar age, perhaps a few years older, tall with a confident swagger to his walk. His face was long, hard lines softened by stubble and black hair that blew in the breeze. He stopped in front of Wynn, his piercing eyes studying him with a look of contempt.

'This was Earth,' he said without breaking his stare, 'from before the Fracture. When it was still a planet. Can you imagine what it must have been like?'

He turned his back on Wynn, gesturing at the distant line of hills. 'So much land . . . so much space. Ten billion people. It's hard to picture.'

'You are Orcades Draig?' Wynn asked, already knowing it must be him.

Orcades ignored the question and pointed to a distant line of grey-blue that glittered in the light. 'See that?' he asked. 'A sea. A world of water, so deep, full of life. I've seen pictures, simulations, but it still doesn't seem real. Perhaps none of this ever existed.' He turned to Wynn again, a dark smile on his face. 'Yes, I am Valtais Orcades Draig of the House of Draig. And you are Prince Halstead Kenric of the House of blah, blah, blah.' He began to laugh. 'It's all so formal, isn't it? Can we not be just two friends, meeting to talk?'

'Friends?' Wynn replied bitterly. 'You tried to kill me. You destroyed the *Obsidian*. You killed my father.'

'Mine too,' Orcades said regretfully. 'Did you know that? We're half-brothers, you and me. I'd have thought someone would have mentioned it, but I can see this is a surprise to you. Old Thyred the third, Thyred the unready they're calling him now, you know? I was his firstborn, his true heir, but he refused to acknowledge my claim.'

'You killed him for that?' Wynn said, feeling his anger grow. 'You killed all those people just for that?'

'Aren't you listening? I am the true heir to the House of Kenric!' Orcades spat. 'I could have united both houses, but Thyred would not submit. This is his doing. The blood is on his hands, not mine.'

Wynn stared at him, disgusted. He seemed to

believe every word he was saying. 'What do you want, Orcades?'

The anger ebbed away from Orcades' features and he began to smile. 'I wanted to see you,' he said with a dismissive wave. 'I wanted to look you in the eye, see who it was I'm about to kill. I wanted to make sure you had survived. And to give you the chance to surrender.'

'Surrender?'

'Of course! There is no need to kill anyone else, no need for further destruction. All you need to do is turn the *Caerleon* over to me and declare me the rightful heir to the House of Kenric. That's all I want. Then, once I'm named prince, I'll kill you. Sound fair?'

Wynn shook his head and laughed. Orcades joined in, his voice bellowing.

'You're insane,' Wynn said.

'Insane?' Orcades pondered this then shook his head. 'Halstead, I'm offering you a way out! The Kenric name will be consigned to history, but what's in a name? It's not worth fighting over, is it? Think about it! Minimal bloodshed, just one life lost, no damage to any arkship. That seems like a pretty good outcome, don't you think?'

'I tried to surrender to you before, remember?'

'Yes,' Orcades laughed. 'I fired on you, didn't I. But it's different now. You have something I want, and your surrender means I get what I want without all that noisy death and destruction.'

Wynn turned away, staring at the vastness around him. There was the sea, its surface glinting, the water breaking silently over distant rocks. His eye traced the line of blue as it cut into the green, narrowing as it zigzagged over the land towards the hills. It really was quite beautiful. He thought again of Melchior, and Bara came to mind. If he agreed to Orcades' offer she would be safe. Everyone would be safe. Everyone except for Wynn.

He turned back and squared up to Orcades. 'How can I trust you? How do I know you'll do as you say?'

Orcades Draig's eyes narrowed malevolently. 'You don't have to trust me, Halstead, you just have to surrender. I'll take it from there. I'll give you ten minutes to talk it over with your people, if I've not heard from you by then . . .' Orcades grinned. 'Well, it'll get very hot and bright over there.'

The image of Orcades Draig flickered and broke apart. Wynn took one last mournful look at the simulated landscape, then he lifted off the holograph lens and let his eyes focus on the *Caerleon's* flight deck. In front of him was the Lord Chamberlain Cam Tanis, flanked by his advisers and subordinates. Behind them was Gofal, observing passively. Finally, he saw Bara, a pensive expression on her face. He gazed into her eyes and he wished he was back on *Lexica*, just the two of them, before he knew who he really was.

'You heard all of that?' Wynn checked.

Tanis nodded grimly. 'Draig cannot be trusted. Surrender is not an option.'

'But if it saves lives,' Wynn said, feeling unconvinced.

'No,' Tanis straightened, his shoulders pushed back. 'We will not surrender. You cannot give yourself to him.'

Gofal approached, standing beside Tanis. 'Lord Chamberlain, Prince Halstead. The armament of the Draig arkship is equal to ours but I would anticipate that they have additional arkships within range.'

Wynn looked at the dark shape of the Draig arkship and made up his mind. 'No one else has to die.'

The Lord Chamberlain took his arm, speaking quietly into his ear. 'Prince Halstead, you must not do this.'

'If I am truly your prince then you will obey my command.'

Their eyes locked, then Tanis released him and lowered his head.

Wynn nodded. 'Contact the Draig arkship.'

'You can't!' Bara gasped. 'Wynn, please, don't do this.'

He couldn't look at her, he knew if he did he might buckle. He didn't want to die, he didn't feel brave, but he knew this was the best chance for everyone else to survive.

'Channel open,' one of the bridge officers announced.

Wynn composed himself and said, 'Draig, this is Prince Halstead.' He paused, sensing how odd it seemed to use that name, then added, 'We agree to your terms for surrender.'

ORDERS

'He surrendered?' Orcades Draig said to himself as he muted the communication to the *Caerleon*. 'Why would he surrender?'

'It is the preferred choice, is it not?' The voice belonged to the newly-promoted Commodore Valine, a young woman with an ambitious streak that had caught Orcades' eye.

'Preferred? Yes . . .' Orcades' mind drifted. It was so hard to focus on the details, to keep it all clear in his head. The prince had surrendered. Why would he do that? Why would he let himself be killed? He swung round to glare at his Commodore. 'Well?'

Commodore Valine didn't flinch. 'Well, what?'

'I asked you a question. Why would he do that? Why would he surrender?'

Valine eyed him with a contempt that didn't suit her rank. 'You didn't ask, but I'd imagine he is keen to minimize the death toll and the damage to his arkship. I'm sorry, Valtais, but that is what you offered him, isn't it?'

'Offered him, yes, but I never expected him to take it.' Orcades stared out of the windows at the *Caerleon*. 'He is their leader, their prince. He would never give that up, not without a fight. I looked into his eyes, I saw determination, I saw his anger. He was much like my father. But he has surrendered. That is . . . disappointing.'

The throbbing in his head grew stronger, a rhythmic beat he could no longer ignore. He punched the console next to him, startling the officer sat there. The pain eased, and his mind cleared.

'He would not surrender,' Orcades muttered, 'I see that now. He would not!'

'Sir?' Commodore Valine inquired.

Orcades laughed at her. 'Don't you see? It's a trap. He's fooling us, he's going to attack.'

'But–'

'He will not surrender, and neither will I!' Orcades took a breath, satisfied with his conclusion. 'Begin your attack, Commodore.'

'Sir, you wish me to attack the arkship *Caerleon*?' Commodore Valine checked, sounding uncertain.

'Yes!' Orcades shouted. 'Attack them, now!'

'As you wish, sir.'

Orcades eyed her intently. 'Commodore?'

Valine edged closer, awaiting his response.

'You have served me well so far, but I have been disappointed in my last two Commodores,' Orcades whispered.

Commodore Valine nodded officially. 'I understand.' She turned to face the flight deck. 'Chief of the Watch?'

A middle-aged man with a neat beard approached her. 'Commodore?'

'Power up all engines, bring our weapons online. Set Condition Red throughout the ship, and have the *Gargan* and the *Hestr* stand by.'

'Yes, Commodore,' the chief replied, then he began to carry out her orders.

Orcades watched his commodore as she walked to the operations map and opened a com channel. 'This is Commodore Valine. Valtais Orcades has authorized an attack on the arkship *Caerleon*. Prepare the ship for battle. All divisions stand by.'

She showed no doubts, carrying out his orders with conviction. Orcades liked that. She had played a pivotal role in their attack on the *Obsidian*, working covertly to undermine their defenses. Valine had taken risks to get the job done. She showed great potential, enough to get her this promotion over more experienced officers. Orcades sensed a thick seam of self-preservation running through her, an overwhelming desire to succeed. Perhaps, he hoped, this Commodore might survive longer than her predecessors.

FIGHT OR FLIGHT

'Why has he not responded?' Wynn mused as he stared at the dark shape of the arkship *Fenrir* through the flight deck windows.

'Should we resend?' the Lord Chamberlain suggested.

'Message was received,' the coms officer replied.

Bara stepped closer to Wynn's side. 'He's going to attack,' she said quietly.

'What makes you think that?' Wynn asked.

'A hunch. This doesn't feel right, does it?'

Wynn agreed. 'No, it doesn't. Lord Chamberlain?'

'We can't make any overtly hostile moves,' the Lord Chamberlain replied, 'but we can make preparations.'

'Agreed,' Wynn said, feeling a sensation of dread deep within him.

'Charge the Gilgore Grid,' Bara said as she made for the exit.

Wynn called after her. 'Where are you going?'

'To get *Lexica* ready for battle,' she replied, a hint of finality in her voice. 'The more guns out there the better.

You should get your fighters ready as well.'

'You can't go out there, not alone,' Wynn said, walking towards her.

'My prince,' the Lord Chamberlain called after Wynn. 'Your place is here, on the flight deck, commanding your people.'

Wynn hesitated, torn between his sense of duty and his desire to go with Bara. He turned and saw Gofal, observing the discussion. He had been there all his life, a constant companion, bodyguard and confidant. He was no mere hunter bot; Gofal was a trusted friend. 'Go with her,' he commanded.

'A bot?' Bara said contemptuously. 'I don't need a bot.'

'Gofal is more than that,' Wynn said, his hand touching her arm. 'Please, let him come with you. For me.'

Reluctantly, she conceded.

Wynn smiled, wanting to hold her in his arms. But he was aware of the eyes of his officers upon him, waiting for his command. He let her go, watching as Bara and Gofal left the flight deck, then turned to join Tanis at the operations map.

'Still no response,' the Lord Chamberlain said. 'Gilgore Grid is at twenty eight percent. They'll detect the radiation once it gets to eighty. We need to be ready before then.'

'How long?' Wynn checked.

'Ten minutes. I've scrambled both hanger bays. Three squadrons are tanked with feet in the seat, ready to launch on our word. All cannons are charged, ready to deploy, but we've not locked on the target yet.'

'Anything else we can do?'

'We could begin the civilian evacuation to the shelters,' the Lord Chamberlain replied.

'Do it.' Wynn checked the holograph. 'There's no cover nearby?'

'A few asteroids. Nothing of strategic value.'

'What about the cube drive?'

The Lord Chamberlain summoned one of his staff. 'CUCOM? Drive status?'

The officer reddened, speaking quickly. 'We can do a cold start in thirty minutes.'

Wynn sighed. 'You can't do it sooner?'

'I'm sorry, that's as fast as I dare go. Any faster and we risk tearing the ship apart.'

'Okay, so we stand,' Wynn said, looking back to the dark shape of the arkship *Fenrir*. 'Make all preparations.'

'New contacts!' a nervous voice shouted from the far side of the flight deck.

'Confirmed,' an officer at the operations map answered. 'Six hostile targets inbound.'

'Set Battle Condition throughout the ship,' the Lord Chamberlain announced. 'Authorization to engage the enemy is given.'

'Authorization received,' another officer barked.

'All guns, target the enemy. Load missile launchers. Scramble fighters.'

Orders and responses overlapped as the flight deck officers prepared for battle.

'GGO!' Lord Chamberlain Tanis shouted.

'Grid at sixty six percent,' the Gilgore Grid Officer responded. 'Plotting inbounds trajectory and prioritizing those locations. Anticipate eighty plus at those points before impact.'

'Not good enough,' Tanis muttered.

BATTLE PLAN

As Bara climbed into her flight chair the alarms began to sound across the hanger bay.

'The *Ark Royal Caerleon* is under attack,' Gofal noted as he strapped himself into the chair next to Bara.

'Really?' Bara replied sarcastically. She thumbed the control panel, bringing the ship's systems online.

'I can shave off thirty-six seconds from our launch, if you let me have direct interface,' Gofal offered.

'Stay away from *Lexica*,' Bara growled. 'I'll do the flying.'

Gofal did not protest. He settled into the chair and pulled the harness over his ill-fitting body.

'We're clear for launch,' Lexica announced.

'Good,' Bara replied. She pulled on the yoke and the ship lurched off its landing platform.

'Do you like poetry?' Gofal asked.

'What?' Bara replied, trying to keep her focus on the approaching hanger threshold.

'I don't like poetry, but there are many associated with the eve of great battles. Perhaps you would like me to read some to you. It might help to calm your–'

'I'm calm! Very calm!'

'You don't sound very–'

'Can you fire a gun?' Bara asked through gritted teeth.

'I can manage both of your ship's guns simultaneously.'

'Good. Do that and shut up.'

The ship cleared the hanger bay and shot into space. Already a squadron of single-person fighters and drone guns had launched, flying in formation ahead of her. The radio crackled with their chatter as Bara informed the *Caerleon*'s flight controller of their safe departure.

Gofal plugged himself into the ship's console and turned his glowing blue eyes to Bara. 'Do you have a battle plan?'

Bara laughed. 'Plan is a strong word. We're going to try to take out their grid generator.'

Gofal turned to stare out of the windows. 'Gilgore grids are typically very generalized with distribution points across the hull.'

'I'm an engineer,' Bara replied testily. 'I know what I'm looking for.'

Gofal stretched his right arm in front of him, flexing the fingers, studying the shapes his hand made against the stars outside.

Bara glared at him. 'What are you doing?'

'I don't like my arm, not since the repairs,' Gofal noted. 'It's different.' He compared it to his other arm, placing them side my side.

'Can you please just focus on your job?' Bara asked.

'I am. Both guns are primed and standing by. I have targets locked but they are not in range yet.'

'Well, you're distracting me!'

Gofal lowered his arms. 'Sorry.'

Bara brooded, watching the small dots of light ahead take on the slender shape of missiles hurtling towards the *Caerleon*. She brought the engines up to full power and throttled the ship towards the *Fenrir*.

'Missiles in range,' Gofal announced. 'Weapons free.'

The windows caught the flashes of the gun turrets mounted above and below the rear of the bridge, followed quickly by bursts of light far in front of them. Bara glanced at the console holograph and saw that Gofal had taken out three of the incoming missiles already.

'Weapons lock,' Lexica announced. 'Evasive action.'

'I've got it,' Bara pulled on the control yoke handles as a new flashing icon appeared on the holograph.

'*I've* got it,' Gofal echoed, activating the ship's guns again. A few seconds later Bara spotted an eruption of light ahead, and the holograph icon died.

She turned to look at Gofal. 'You're good.'

'I was better with my old arm,' he replied.

FIRST STRIKE

'Turn us to face the missiles,' Tanis cried over the chaos. 'Give them the smallest target possible, and keep our engines hidden.

'First wave impact in ten seconds!' an officer shouted.

Wynn checked the operations map. Many of the missiles had been taken out by the waves of fighters, or by the arkship's own defenses, but a handful had made it through.

'Grid is at eighty six percent,' Tanis shouted to Wynn. 'Brace yourself.'

The room began to shake, setting off alarms and causing the lights to flicker. Wynn felt eight impacts, the last one the closest to the flight deck. He checked the holograph: they had fared better than some other parts of the arkship.

'What about our missiles?' Wynn asked Tanis.

'Their grid is at full power, we wouldn't make a dent.'

'And our guns?'

Tanis shook his head. 'We're out of range here.'

'Then take us in.'

The Lord Chamberlain stared at him as if he was mad.

'We're a sitting target here,' Wynn explained. 'They'll pick us off before we have time to get the cube drive online. At least if we get in close we can control which part of us they're hitting, and we can do some damage to them as well.'

Tanis took a deep breath. 'It's a risky move, Prince Halstead.'

'I know it's risky, and it scares me to death. You have far more combat experience than I do. You know how quickly they'll pick off our defense system from here. You know how soon they'll launch their boarding party. You're able to calculate the chances of us holding out until our cube drive is ready. Moving us closer might be crazy, I don't know. So, you tell me, Cam. What should we do?'

The Lord Chamberlain stared into Wynn's eyes, then he glanced out of the windows at the battle, and a devilish smile grew on his face.

'Bring us about,' he shouted. 'Full power to the engines. Take us in.'

SIGNS

'Clever,' Commodore Valine mused. The *Ark Royal Caerleon* had grown from a distant shape to almost fill the windows of the flight deck. She could make out details on the other ship's surface; hanger bays, the scars in the hull from their attack, she even saw the light from some of the windows.

Orcades Draig stared at the approaching arkship in disbelief. 'What do they think they're doing?'

'They're hoping for a tactical advantage. We can't use our missiles at this range, the shockwaves could damage us.'

'But neither can they.'

'They would never have made it past our grid anyway. Now it's down to our gunners, and our pilots.'

'He makes no sense,' Orcades muttered. 'He has no experience in battle.' He turned to Valine. 'Prepare boarding rams.'

Commodore Valine almost laughed, checking herself at the last moment. 'Sir, we must break the ship first, then land our troops. It is not time.'

'They are in range, are they not?'

'Yes,' she replied.

'Then it is time.'

Valine faltered. 'Are those your orders?'

Orcades reddened. 'Of course they are! I want to see him, I want to look him in the eye and show him that I have beaten him.'

'Of course,' Valine smiled, then turned to one of her subordinates. 'Prepare the rams, but hold the troops back until we have a firm tether.'

She walked away to compose herself, suppressing her anger at the ignorance of the Valtais. Many troops would die because of this. She didn't particularly care about them as individuals but the infantry was a finite resource and not to be wasted. Orcades was a fool. She didn't know him well but she had been around him long enough to notice the recent change in his behavior. He had all the traits of a gravel head. He was hiding it well, but Valine had spent her youth around addicts and knew the signs well. Orcades Draig was addicted to some form of narcotic, his decision-making was flawed. If things went wrong Draig would look for someone to blame, and that someone would be her.

Valine cursed. She would have to tread carefully if she was to come out of this alive.

RAMMING

Bara pushed *Lexica* into a nosedive towards the surface of the *Fenrir*, turning the ship as it fell to keep its belly gun pointed at the hull. At the last second, she pulled the control yoke towards her and the ship lifted from its dive. She felt the pull of gravity increasing, pressing her into her seat, blurring the edge of her vision, as the ship gained height. Beside her, Gofal continued to fire the ship's weapons, picking targets with consummate skill. Bara couldn't help but be impressed.

'There,' she said, pointing to a faceted tower ahead on the surface of the *Fenrir*. 'That's a Gilgore substation.'

'Consider it history,' Gofal replied, making Bara laugh.

'If we can knock out enough of them maybe it'll destabilize the grid,' Bara said and she pulled the ship into a dangerously-close skim of the *Fenrir*'s hull. They blew through the debris cloud from the destroyed Gilgore substation tower and thundered towards the next target.

'I've noticed your heart rate rising,' Gofal said conversationally. 'Perhaps some music might–'

'No!' Bara replied sharply, then added, 'thank you,' in a softer tone.

Ahead, another tower fell to Gofal's strafing. Bara turned the ship, scanning for the next target, avoiding the attention of an enemy drone fighter. Something shot out of the arkship's hull and flew past *Lexica*. Bara yanked the control and the ship fell into a spin.

'What was that?' Bara asked as she levelled the vessel. She could see it now: an extending cylinder that was aimed at the nearby *Caerleon*.

'A believe it's a boarding ram,' Gofal said.

Bara gasped. 'Being fired at a moving target?'

'It would seem so. Eyes ahead, lady.'

Bara glanced from the extending conduit and saw another tube emerging ahead. Bara responded and the ship dipped violently to the left before levelling off again, avoiding the obstacle.

'Thanks,' she said breathlessly as she navigated towards the next target.

CONTACT

'Boarding rams, incoming!'

Wynn looked up from the operations map and saw a tube-like projectile rushing towards the *Caerleon*. The arkship rocked from the impact, then steadied itself.

'Can those things latch on at this speed?' Wynn asked the Lord Chamberlain.

Tanis stared in disbelief. 'I don't know. I've never see it tried before.'

Another tube fired towards them, followed by a third. The ship swayed, their progress slowed.

'Contact!' an officer shouted.

'Hull breech on level thirty-two,' another reported.

'Increase power to the engines,' Tanis ordered. 'Pull us away.'

The flight deck vibrated, then, with a jolt, the arkship broke free of the cable.

'We're clear,' an officer reported.

'Put some distance between us and the *Fenrir*,' Tanis shouted.

'More contacts.'

The ship slowed again, snagged on the lines.

'Hull breech on levels fifteen, thirteen and three.'

The arkship juddered as more and more boarding rams slammed into the hull.

'All fighters, target those rams. We need to break free!'

ATTACK RUN

Bara heard the Lord Chamberlain's urgent call for help and began to turn *Lexica* away from the *Fenrir*. As the ship was buffeted by explosions she glanced at Gofal. 'You know what to do?'

'Already in hand,' Gofal said.

Ahead, Bara saw the great mass of the *Ark Royal Caerleon* swing into view. In between it and the *Fenrir* were a dozen barely-visible cables. As they approached Gofal trained both guns on the first tether, ripping it in two. As the chain of explosions dissipated Bara saw bodies adrift in the maelstrom.

'They have boarding parties in the tubes,' Bara said, feeling sick.

'This is war,' Gofal replied unsympathetically.

'I know,' Bara replied, trying not to think about it as they approached the next line. As Gofal trained the weapons on it they were buffeted by a barrage of fire.

'The *Fenrir* is targeting us,' Gofal noted.

Bara threw the ship into a series of deft maneuvers. As she did the *Weapons Lock* warning beeped intermittently.

Volley after volley of explosions rocked the ship as she flew closer and closer to the *Fenrir*.

'Take out those damned guns!' Bara shouted.

'I'm trying,' Gofal replied, 'but at this speed those damned guns go by very quickly.'

'Would you like me to slow down?'

'No.'

The bridge lit up with a blinding flash as a deafening rumble shook *Lexica*. Smoke filled the cabin as the power flickered, plunging them into darkness.

'Lex, are we hit?' Bara asked.

The ship didn't respond.

'I've lost contact with *Lexica*,' Gofal said. 'The ship is dead.'

DESPERATION

'There's too many lines,' Tanis shouted over the noise. 'We can't break free.'

'What about our fighters?' Wynn asked. 'They've cut through some of the rams.'

'We've lost contact with most of our ships. The *Fenrir* is picking them off.'

'*Lexica*?' Wynn asked, dreading the answer.

'I'm sorry.' The Lord Chamberlain hesitated, then added. 'We don't have long. We've had a report of a boarding party on level forty-one already. We need to prepare for surrender.'

'No, we've tried that already.' Thinking quickly, Wynn added, 'Clear the areas around the boarding rams and rig them for detonation.'

The Lord Chamberlain gasped. 'Blow the ship?'

'If we can't break the rams then we'll break their hold on us.'

'We could lose half the *Caerleon*!'

'Better than all of it,' Wynn shouted. 'Can you do it or not?'

Tanis nodded grimly.

'How long till the cube drive is ready?'

The Lord Chamberlain checked his console. 'Six minutes. By time we get those charges set we should be ready to go,' Tanis said, 'providing we don't blow ourselves up in the process.'

BOARDING

'I do not recommend this,' Commodore Valine said to Orcades Draig as he approached the boarding ram airlock.

'Yes, you have already said,' Orcades replied testily. 'Your caution is noted, Valine, but the enemy is caught. They're not going anywhere, and their engines have already powered down.'

'Which could mean they're powering up their cube drive.'

'They couldn't use it this close to us,' Orcades mocked. 'The shockwave would destroy us both.'

Valine sighed. 'They have little to lose.'

'He wouldn't kill thousands of innocent people just out of spite. No, they're trapped, caught and awaiting our merciful blow to end their suffering.'

Orcades stood in front of the airlock, flanked by a troupe of assault soldiers. The controls on the door chimed and the heavy circular hatch began to rotate.

Valine felt the breeze rush past her as the pressure equalized. She looked out of the window next to the airlock and saw the boarding ram connected to the distant hull of the *Caerleon*. The tether swayed gently as the two massive vessels drifted closer. She glanced along the ship and saw dozens of other lines, all pointing towards the captured arkship.

As she retreated to the back of the chamber the airlock came to a halt. The first platoon entered the circular corridor, adjusting to the variable gravity there, and disappeared along its length. The lead soldier's voice boomed out of a com speaker above them.

'Seal is good. Hull cutter has broken through. No resistance.'

'None?' Orcades checked.

'Seems deserted.'

Satisfied, he nodded for the next platoon to enter, then he turned to join them.

Valine watched, only half listening.

'Still no resistance, moving on,' the solider said over the com as he entered the *Caerleon*.

Suddenly, Valine's body bristled. 'No!' she cried, running towards the airlock. 'Get out of there!'

Orcades turned back to face her, just as the far end of the tube erupted in a yellow light. A blast of heat slammed into her as Orcades was thrown along the boarding ram. He tumbled towards the airlock, flames licking the edges of the tube. His hands grabbed at the hatch, just as the fire around him disappeared. The air rushed out of the tube, and Valine's ears popped as the pressure fell.

Valine hung onto the airlock door and stretched out her arm towards her Valtais. She shouted at him, but her voice was lost in the torrent of noise as the atmosphere was ripped away into the cold void of space. Orcades fought against the wind trying to drag him down the tunnel, and edged closer to the door, just as it began to close. His fingers touched Valine's and she grabbed his arm, pulling him through the airlock. The heavy door slammed shut, sealing the room. Orcades lay on the floor, gasping for breath as the atmosphere returned to normal about him.

'What . . . what happened?' he asked Valine.

'They blew up their own hull,' she replied. 'The boarding rams have been torn away from the *Caerleon*.'

Orcades stood unsteadily and gazed out of the airlock window. The tube hung in space as the bodies of his soldiers drifted out of the ruptured end. He shuddered and turned to find Valine.

'No prisoners,' Orcades said, his throat rasping. 'We will destroy that arkship, and everyone on board.'

Valine nodded, activating her wrist com to speak to the flight deck. 'Call in reinforcements.'

DEPARTURE

'All explosives detonated!' a flight deck officer cried as the *Ark Royal Caerleon* buckled and shuddered.

Wynn held on to the operations table as the floor listed, determined to throw him off balance. Out of the window he could see the afterglow of the explosions ripping through their hull.

The Lord Chamberlain activated an external camera feed. As the smoke and debris cleared he gasped, seeing the huge holes torn into the *Caerleon's* hull. 'My Gods! Half the ship is gone.'

'Not quite,' Wynn replied. 'Are we free?'

'All rams disengaged,' someone shouted excitedly thought the smoke.

'Then get us clear, far enough away to use the cube drive.'

Slowly, the ship began to turn towards empty space.

'Recall all fighters,' The Lord Chamberlain ordered.

'What about Bara?' Wynn pleaded.

'Nothing. We can't wait any longer.'

The ship began to accelerate, clearing the debris field.

'Cube drive is almost ready,' Tanis said quietly.

'Still no sign?' Wynn asked, feeling desperate.

'We have to go.'

'I can't just leave her!'

'Sir,' Tanis said in a whisper, 'there are thousands of people on board, thousands of lives at stake. There's no word from *Lexica*. We can't wait any longer.'

Tears filled his eyes as Wynn nodded for Tanis to carry on.

'All hands, stand by for cube drive,' Tanis shouted.

'New contacts incoming,' a voice announced.

The operations map flashed as two signals blipped into existence and, for a moment, Wynn's heart lifted, hoping this was *Lexica*.

'New signals identified: Arkship *Gargan* . . .' an officer reported, '. . . and the arkship *Hestr* . . . both Draig.'

RESURRECTION

Bara stared out of the window at the burning *Ark Royal Caerleon*. The dying explosions lit up *Lexica's* darkened bridge, casting moving shadows over the ceiling. The ship drifted, buoyed by the shifting eddies of the battle, as fragments of debris smashed into the ship.

'I can't believe they did that,' Bara whispered.

Gofal glanced up. 'A desperate attempt to escape. It might have worked, if not for those two.' He gestured to the dark shapes blotting out the stars: two newly arrived arkships had blocked the *Caerleon's* retreat.

'We have to help them,' Bara muttered in frustration.

'I don't see how,' Gofal replied.

'If you could get the ship's systems back online we might be able to do something! Anything!'

'Your ship's personality is fried. It's blocking my control of its systems, and you won't allow me to delete it.'

Bara hit the console, her frustration overwhelming her. 'Is that the only way?'

'The only quick way.'

She sighed, feeling like she was sentencing an old friend to death. 'Do it.'

The bridge became silent as Gofal interfaced with the ship. Bara stared out at the arkships exchanging fire. *Was Wynn safe?* she wondered.

'Purge complete,' Gofal announced. 'The Lexica personality has been removed. I have control.'

The lights flickered on as the ship came back to life.

'We are in bad shape,' Gofal continued. 'No coms, the starboard stabilizer is malfunctioning, air scrubbers are down . . . we should return to the *Caerleon*.'

'We still have weapons?' Bara checked.

'Yes . . .'

'Then we fight on,' she replied steadfastly. 'Find me some more Gilgore towers to blow up.'

LAST COMMAND

'We can't take much more!' Lord Chamberlain Tanis cried over the chaos.

'Sir!' an officer shouted. 'The *Fenrir*, its grid is buckling!'

Tanis and Wynn ran to the officer's console to see for themselves. A holograph display identified a portion of the enemy arkship's hull where its Gilgore grid had failed.

'One of our ships is taking out the grid's towers,' the officer explained.

'Which ship?' Wynn asked.

'I think it's *Lexica*, sir, but its coms are down.'

She's still alive! Wynn thought, a relieved smile breaking over his face.

'Target firepower on that part of the hull,' Tanis barked as he returned to the operations map. 'Hit them with everything we have.'

Wynn joined him there, watching the holograph as the surface of the *Fenrir* erupted in fire, ripping into the heart of the enemy arkship. Cheers erupted on the flight deck as a sense of hope filled the air, but the moment was short-lived as the *Caerleon* shook from a renewed onslaught.

'They're still firing?' Tanis checked.

'Not the Fenrir,' Wynn replied, scanning the map. 'It's the other Draig arkships.'

The operations map glowed red with a multitude of impact points as the other two Draig vessels came to their sister ship's defense, firing on the *Caerleon*, tearing into her hull. Their weapons sliced into the ship, focusing all of their firepower onto the same section of the hull until, with a cascade of violent tremors, part of the drive section split from the rest of the *Caerloen*.

As the vibrations subsided an officer shouted, 'The cube drive is destroyed. We can't escape.'

'They're cutting us to pieces,' Wynn said. 'Sound the evacuation.'

Tanis obeyed. 'We must get you to safety as well. There's little time.'

Wynn took in the flight deck and the bombardment outside. He stared at the *Fenrir*, and he felt his anger overwhelm him. 'Continue with the evacuation. I'm not leaving.'

'What?' Tanis gasped.

'Turn the ship towards the *Fenrir* and give me any thrust we have left.'

'You want to ram them?'

Wynn smiled. Perhaps, he thought, his sacrifice

might give Bara and the others time to escape.

Tanis shook his head. 'You're insane,' he said, then he began to laugh. 'I must be insane too.'

As the flight deck emptied the Lord Chamberlain gave out his last orders, and the giant arkship turned to face its enemy. He pointed to the console in front of Wynn. 'That button will give you everything we have left. It's rigged for rapid acceleration. A single burst of power. It won't be a comfy ride.'

'For any of us,' Wynn replied. 'You really should leave.'

Tanis shook his head.

'I could order you.'

'Do not make me disobey you, my prince.'

Wynn smiled sadly, and he held out his hand. 'Together?'

The Lord Chamberlain joined him, and their hands hovered over the thrust button. 'Together,' he replied.

Wynn felt a wave of sadness overwhelm him. He had been through so much to get to this point. He had lost everything, only to regain it all again. Now, he would lose it forever. But it wasn't his title, or his people, or his arkship that came to mind. All he could picture was Bara's face. He looked out to the stars and he thought of her as his hand descended towards the button.

'Wait,' Tanis said, his fingers tensing.

'What is it?' Wynn asked. He followed the Lord Chamberlain's stare, out beyond the windows.

Something huge had just appeared in between the *Caerleon* and the *Fenrir*. The flight deck rocked as another giant shape burst into view, followed by another and then another. Wynn blinked, trying to comprehend what he was seeing. These were giant ships of sinuous curves, their mass overwhelming the other arkships. Their golden hulls glistened in the light of The Infinite, throwing off reflections that dazzled the eye.

The com system bristled with static, then a hard, male voice broke through. '. . . This is the blessed arkship *Spero* of the Church of The Infinite. We are on a sacred pilgrimage to bring the light of the Infinite Gods to this part of the Cluster. Her divine spirit the Scribe has observed your dispute and it displeases her. She commands you to identify yourselves.'

Wynn stared at Tanis, wide eyed with disbelief, and then they both started to laugh. The attacking Draig arkships stopped firing, and a strange serene quiet fell over the flight deck.

'I think we might just live after all,' the Lord Chamberlain grinned as he picked up the com. 'This is the *Ark Royal Caerleon*, flagship of the House of Kenric, home to the rightful heir, Prince Halstead. The people of Kenric request sanctuary from the Church of The Infinite.' He put down the com and smiled at Wynn. 'Let's see what they say to that.'

The com system hissed and crackled, then the

clipped voice returned. '*Ark Royal Caerleon*, this is the blessed arkship *Spero*. Your request for sanctuary has been heard by the Scribe. She requests an audience with Prince Halstead.'

Relief broke over the Lord Chamberlain's face, and he slumped against the operations map. 'We did it,' he muttered, wiping his eyes. 'We did it.'

DEFEAT

'Identify yourself, or face the wrath of the Church of The Infinite.'

Orcades Draig gazed at the fleet of arkships surrounding the *Caerleon*, great golden structures that took his breath away. So, it was true after all; the Church *did* have a fleet.

Valine stood next to him, watching the giant ships drifting past the flight deck windows. 'I've never seen anything like it,' she muttered.

Her voice seemed to break his fascination, and Orcades found his anger growing. 'How dare they stop me!' he shouted.

'They are the Church,' Valine said. 'They outnumber us.'

'I will not be defeated!' As he watched those strange ships he felt his headache worsen. Were they trying to manipulate him, across such a distance? Uncertainty took hold, and Orcades found his thoughts clouded with indecision. He turned to Valine and whispered, 'What should we do?'

'Retreat. It is the only victory we have left.'

Orcades pondered this and nodded. 'A victory, yes. Retreat, that is the way forward.'

Valine turned to carry out his orders, leaving him alone at the windows. He watched as one of the Church's arkships glided by, its movements graceful and purposeful. He forced himself to remember every contour as he vowed to destroy them one day.

The *Fenrir* turned away from the guarded *Caerleon*, building speed as it retreated. In the distance, Orcades could see the *Hestr* and the *Gargan* drifting away, becoming distant flecks of light before their cube drives stole them from his view. As the *Fenrir* also prepared to leave Orcades Draig saluted the *Caerleon*, hoping that Prince Halstead had survived this attack.

'See you soon,' Orcades muttered as the cube drive took him to safety.

SURVIVORS

'They're leaving?' Bara said, as the vast shape of the *Fenrir* blinked away. 'What's going on?'

'Without coms it's hard to know,' Gofal observed, 'but those new arrivals fit the description of Church arkships.'

'The Church? What are they doing so far from The Infinite?'

Gofal didn't answer. After a moment, he asked, 'Do you need weapons?'

Bara stared at his smooth face. 'What do you mean?'

'If you no longer need the ship's guns I can take them offline and patch the coms system through their omniflex relay.'

'We could communicate again?'

Gofal nodded, his blue eyes dimming to approximate a blink. 'But no more shooting.'

'Then do it!' Bara enthused.

The bot fell silent as he accessed the ship's systems. The com sparked into life and a dozen voices burst into the bridge.

'. . . stand by for docking.'

'*Ark Royal Caerleon* to the *Spero*, we have multiple lifeboats awaiting retrieval, any assistance you can . . .'

'Hanger bay six is destroyed, wait for a clear pad, *Avonis Three* . . .'

'. . . require immediate assistance, I have casualties here!'

'No sign of Draig activity.'

'. . .all Kenric ships report in.'

Bara laughed with relief, picked up the com and found a clear channel. 'This is Captain Sēbarā Delaterre of the merchant vessel *Lexica*, registration MC-89409-LX, out of the *Ark Royal Caerleon*, request permission to dock.'

A voice broke through the silence. 'Bara?' She recognized it immediately and tears filled her eyes.

'Wynn!'

'We're still here,' Wynn replied. 'It's good to hear your voice. Are you okay? Do you need help?'

'We're fine,' she laughed, overwhelmed with emotion. 'We're coming home.'

ICARUS

The light of The Infinite was painfully bright, bleaching the color out of the polished stone walls of the chamber. This whole space hurt Wynn's eyes, forcing them into narrow lines, and he wondered how the people who lived here coped with such brightness. Wearing eye shades was frowned upon, as was shielding the windows. The Infinite was a sacred thing, they said, not to be blocked. But he'd discovered there were many places without a direct view into space where most people preferred to be. Outer chambers were kept for special occasions, like today.

Wynn blinked, finding the overexposed shapes of Bara and Gofal as they entered the room. He smiled at her, walking to meet her in an embrace.

'I'm sorry I couldn't see you sooner. Did you sleep?' he asked, still holding her.

'Slept, eaten, slept some more,' Bara laughed. 'They like to look after you here.'

He turned to Gofal and took his hand. 'Good to see you again, old friend.'

'And you, Wynn,' he replied. He took in the space and said, 'I had heard of Icarus, but I never expected I would see it for myself. It is majestic.'

Wynn smiled. 'I thought you'd like it.'

'So much art to ponder,' Gofal said as he gestured to one of the carved statues that lined the edge of the chamber.

'Never mind art,' Bara replied, her eyes widening, 'have you seen the dock? It's big enough to take an arkship.'

'Yes, I saw it,' Wynn replied, glad to have his friends close to him again.

The door to the chamber opened again, and Wynn felt a tremble of anticipation, knowing who would be coming: Tanis was bringing the Scribe to meet them. Wynn straightened, surprised to see the shadow of three figures enter. Tanis led the group, smiling with the flair of a diplomat. He had led the negotiations with the Church which had allowed the *Caerleon* to be towed to The Infinite and find a berth at Icarus. He had arranged rations for the survivors, medical attention for the wounded, and services for the dead. All this in the twelve hours since the battle. Had he slept? And what had Tanis agreed with the Church in return for their assistance?

The Lord Chamberlain greeted them warmly and turned to introduce the Scribe.

She was taller than Wynn expected, and beautiful too,

a natural grace in the way she approached them. She held out her hand to Wynn and he kissed it, as Tanis had told him to. She greeted Bara and Gofal, keeping her features set, then she stepped aside to reveal the third person who had entered the room.

'I believe you already know Derward Tarkkail,' the Scribe said.

Wynn and Bara exchanged a look of surprise as they greeted their missing friend.

'I thought you had been lost in the battle,' Wynn said.

'He left before it began,' the Lord Chamberlain admitted, 'at my request.'

Tanis did not elaborate further, but the Scribe said, 'You can thank Derward – and your Lord Chamberlain – for bringing your plight to our attention.'

Wynn stared at Derward. 'I didn't know you held such sway within the Church.'

'Neither did I,' he replied, his cheeks flushed slightly. 'I really didn't do anything. It's the Scribe you should thank.'

'And I do,' Wynn said, trying his best to be statesmanlike as he spoke to her. 'The entire House of Kenric is in your debt.'

'A debt I am sure you will repay in kind one day,' she said coolly. Glancing to the windows, she added, 'The Infinite Gods will guide you to that destiny.'

The Scribe led them down to a lower level of the

chamber, a smaller space with a long table stretched in front of the windows. As Wynn approached he saw the tendrils of The Infinite reflected in the dark mirror-like surface of the table, their slow movements hypnotizing him.

'What do you know of The Infinite?' the Scribe asked as they sat down.

Wynn hesitated, uncertain of the right answer.

'You over-think things, Prince Halstead,' she said with a coy smile. 'Do I make you nervous?'

'A little,' he confessed.

'That is as it should be,' the Scribe replied. She nodded to an aide who had remained unseen at the edge of the room, and dark, red-colored drinks were placed in front of Wynn, Bara and Tanis.

'The Infinite is all that remains of a great star,' the Scribe explained. 'Our sun, the giver of life to humanity. Long ago The Sun was torn apart in the Fracture. The shockwave pulled every planet apart as well. This you all know. You live in the aftermath of that terrible day. The Church exists to try to decipher that catastrophe, and to make contact with the Gods that reside inside The Infinite. This you also know. Everyone knows of the Church and its sacred work.' She paused, taking a drink from her glass. When she spoke again her voice was hushed, reverential.

'What most do not know is that the Church works towards the day of Restoration, when the Cluster shall be reformed and the solar system as it was shall be made whole once more. There will be planets again. The Sun will shine on us all. This is the will of the Infinite Gods. We built this station for the single goal of furthering that plan. Thousands of minds, billions of pieces of data, have come together to generate a mathematically accurate model of the future of the Cluster. We test new theories, run simulations of every hypothesis, hoping to find the single combination of events that will unlock the future and restore the past. We are close to a perfect equation. And in every new simulation that we follow your name appears, Prince Halstead. Your influence – in time – will bring us closer to the Restoration.' She smiled, her eyes piecing him. 'Questions?'

'I'm not sure I understand,' Wynn confessed.

'You are important, Prince Halstead. The House of Kenric's destiny is entangled with the Restoration.'

'What does this mean for Wynn?' Bara asked, her hand touching his arm. 'Are you saying you want him to work for the Church?'

The Scribe laughed. 'We all work for the Church, one way or another.' She glanced at Derward. 'But I'm not asking you to do anything for me, not yet. All I'm saying is that you have the support of the Church. We will – discreetly – help you and your people. You will stay here under our protection while you rebuild your fleet. Then, when the time is right, you will return out there and go about your business. Your destiny is still your own.' The Scribe smiled knowingly.

'I want revenge,' Wynn whispered, his thoughts consumed with Orcades Draig. 'I want him to pay for the *Obsidian*, for Melchior, for the *Caerleon*. He has to answer for the lives he's taken.'

Tanis and Bara nodded their agreement, but the Scribe rolled her eyes, disappointment written across her face.

'That's up to you,' she replied. 'You're free to go back out there, blow him up, kill a few thousand more people, I won't stop you.'

The Lord Chamberlain leaned across the table. 'You're offering an alternative?'

'Enlightenment, nothing more, nothing less. Stay here, learn, heal your wounds, grow, then decide on your course of action.' The Scribe emptied her glass and stood to leave. 'There's no rush. I'm sure we'll talk more.'

As the room became still, Wynn eyed his companions: Derward, Tanis, Gofal and, finally, Bara.

'I swear to you,' Wynn said, taking Bara's hand. 'I swear to you all, I will repay my debt to you.'

'There is no debt,' Bara replied.

Wynn shook his head. 'You've all sacrificed so much for Kenric . . . for me. I won't forget that, I promise. We'll stay here, we'll take what the Church is willing to give, but when the day comes I swear to you I will make things right once more. Draig will . . .' He felt Bara squeeze his hand, and his words faded from his lips.

'Whatever the future holds, we'll face it together,' she said.

He looked into her comforting eyes and it was as if Wynn had finally found himself again. He raised his glass and smiled. 'Together.'

AUTHOR'S NOTES

Thank you for buying and reading *Arkship Obsidian*, I really hope you enjoyed it.

I have to mention a few people who have helped to make this book a reality: Barry Hutchison, Nick Cook, Jonathan Mayhew, Mark Robertson, Tommy Donbavand and Chris Chatterton. A huge thank you to my ARC team and other early readers for their insightful feedback, especially B Allen Thobois. Finally, a big hug to my family who support me every day through the ups and downs of the writing rollercoaster ride!

I had so much fun writing *Arkship Obsidian*, and I'm looking forward to finishing the next book in the series. There's lots more to tell about Prince Halstead, and I hope you'll join me for the next installment. In the meantime, you can help me by spreading the word about the Arkship Saga. If you've enjoyed this book it'd be really helpful if you left a review on Amazon. Or maybe you could tell your friends about it on Facebook, Twitter, Instagram, Snapchat, Goodreads, or even in real life! (Do people still do real life?)

Book two is called ***Arkship Vengeance*** and is out now. If you want to know more about it, and get to read the first few chapters then sign up to my mailing list newsletter! You'll get regular updates on my writing, sneak peeks of cover art, free stories plus lots more.

Thanks again, I hope you'll stick with me as we explore more of the Cluster.

Best wishes,
Niel

Look out for the next book in the Arkship Saga!
The story continues in
Arkship Vengeance – out now

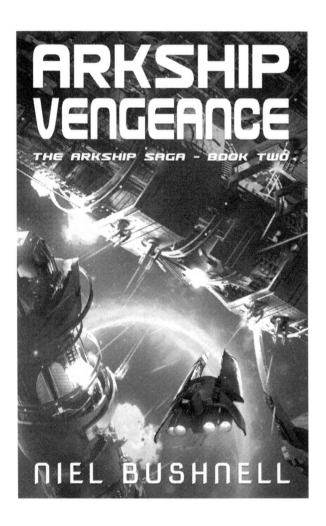

Read the first chapter from book 2:
Arkship Vengeance

THE STRANGER

'What will you name her?'

Owen Sinclair smiled at his newborn daughter as he held her in his broad arms. He watched the rise and fall of her tiny chest as she slept, marveling at the miniature perfection of her features. She had been worth the wait, worth the heartache and uncertainty. He was a father now, and he was determined to revel in every moment of it. 'What's that?' he asked, finally registering the voice beside him.

Reader Aronson waited patiently. 'Have you chosen a name?'

'Yes,' Owen said, his gaze resting on Kina.

'Ealasaid,' Kina added quietly. 'After my mother.'

Owen nodded, reaching out to hold his wife's hand.

'A fine name,' Reader Aronson said approvingly as he held his hand over the baby's head. 'I bless this child, Ealasaid, and open the door to the Church of the Infinite, so that she may walk amongst the Infinite Gods.

May their reflections shine upon her, and guide her to their wisdom.'

'May their reflections shine upon us all,' Owen said, his head bowed.

The Reader lowered his hand, his face growing solemn. 'A child is untouched by fractures, innocent and pure in the eyes of the Infinite Gods. It is your job to protect and guide Ealasaid through the early years of life. This is not a task to be burdened alone. Will you allow the Church to share your burden?'

'I will,' Kina confirmed.

'I will,' Owen replied. They knew their rehearsed responses. A Reader's blessing of a newly-born child was an expected ritual, but formal ceremonies like this made Owen feel uncomfortable. He wasn't sure what he believed in, not any more, but it gave Kina comfort, and that was all that really mattered to him. Sometimes he wished he shared her convictions. They made life seem simpler, more reassuring, somehow.

Reader Aronson smiled. 'Let no man break this holy bond between child, parents and the Church. May all the days of Ealasaid's life be bathed by the reflections of the Infinite Gods.'

Owen opened his mouth, ready with his expected reply, but before he could speak the arkship rocked to one side. The floor tilted, and he fell onto Kina's bed, bracing himself to protect his daughter. An alarm sounded from the corridor beyond the hospital room as equipment began to tumble across the floor. He looked up into his wife's eyes and saw the same expression of terror he knew was on his own face.

'They've found us,' he gasped.

Reader Aronson helped Owen to his feet. 'We don't know that yet. It could be an asteroid strike, or a grav line malfunction, or–'

'Attention! Attention!' The artificial voice filled the room, booming from hidden speakers in every part of the hospital. 'The *Braal Castle* is under attack. All flight crew personnel to their stations. Civilians: remain where you are and await further instructions.'

As the floor corrected itself Kina tensed upright in the bed, pulling at the monitors and tubes attached to her arms. 'We can't stay here.'

Owen handed the baby to her with a regretful smile. 'Where else can we go?' He walked towards the corridor, watching as the hospital staff hurried by. He looked back at Kina and said, 'You're safe here.'

'Don't you dare leave me, Owen!' she cried.

'I'm just going to see.'

'See what?' Reader Aronson asked.

'There's a window, in the reception area. Maybe I can see what's–'

The room vibrated, and the lights flickered. Along the corridor he heard screams. Owen held the doorframe, waiting for the movement to subside as the unsettling grind of metal filled his ears. Finally, there was silence, and the lights returned. His daughter was still sleeping, as if nothing was wrong.

Owen looked at the Reader. 'You'll stay with her?'

He nodded, closing his wrinkled eyes. 'I'm not going anywhere.'

'Owen!' Kina protested. 'Don't!'

'I'll be quick,' he said, not waiting for a reply. He ran to the corridor and stumbled towards the reception area. Around him, he saw stunned patients being herded back into their rooms by members of the hospital staff.

'There's no need to panic,' a porter shouted as he waved his arms above his head. The corridor shook again, and the porter lost his balance and fell to the floor. Owen helped him to his feet, noticing blood on the man's forehead.

'You're hurt,' Owen said.

'Right . . .' the man replied, sounding stunned. 'I'll . . . I'll get it looked at.'

Owen let go, hesitating to watch the stranger stumble away. As the vibration from another impact coursed through his feet, Owen ran along the corridor. Opposite the entrance to the hospital was a line of narrow windows that stretched up to the top of the atrium, breaking the view beyond into vertical slices. He moved closer, pushing his face close to the glass so that his breath condensed into a hazy patch on the cold surface. Outside, he could see the vastness of space, the grey-black void broken by explosions of color. A dark shape caught his eye, and he moved along the wall to see it more clearly. He felt a knot of anxiety deep in his stomach as he confirmed his worst fears.

'The *Fenrir*.'

The voice startled him, and Owen turned to see the porter again, standing next to him at the windows.

'What?' he managed to reply, feeling like he was wading through a nightmare.

'The arkship *Fenrir*,' the man said. A blood-stained badge on his white uniform displayed the name F G Wilson, Porter.

'The *Fenrir*?' Owen repeated slowly. 'Then it's Draig?'

Wilson nodded grimly. He held a length of paper towel to his cut, the blood slowly expanding into the material. 'We're the last. It was only a matter of time.'

Owen turned to face the windows again. He could see the insignificant dots of fighters on their attack runs, gliding over the vast bulk of the *Fenrir*.

'I . . . I should get back to my wife,' Owen mumbled.

'Do that,' Wilson agreed. 'Do that while you can. Gods bless us.'

Owen returned along the corridor, staggering against the shifting floor. Around him he could feel the terrible impacts of missiles, and his mind began to shut out the unthinkable reality of his situation.

'What about my girl?' he muttered to himself. 'What

about Ealasaid?'

Ahead, he saw the dark rectangle that was the door to his family. Reader Aronson appeared there, glancing both ways along the corridor. He saw Owen, and his stern expression softened. 'Thank the gods,' he said as he guided Owen into the room.

Kina, still holding their sleeping child, burst into tears at the sight of him. 'I didn't think you were coming back,' she confessed.

'Sorry, sorry,' Owen replied, distracted by his thoughts.

'What did you see?' the Reader asked impatiently.

'An . . . arkship.'

'Which one?'

'It was . . . it was huge. Our ships don't stand a chance.'

Reader Aronson grabbed Owen by the shoulders. 'Which arkship? Is it Draig? Was it the *Fenrir*?'

Owen nodded, unable to look him in the eyes.

The Reader gasped, then let go. He retreated until his back hit the wall, an ashen expression on his face as his eyes darted quickly.

'I'm sorry,' Owen managed. He turned to comfort his wife, joining her at the edge of the bed. Ealasaid looked so peaceful, oblivious to the events unfolding around her. Her beautiful face brought tears to his eyes.

Kina's hand wiped his cheek, her eyes reassuring him.

'We stay together, no matter what.'

Owen nodded, kissing her hand. 'No matter what.'

A new alarm sounded, low pitched and insistent.

'They're docking,' Reader Aronson noted, his voice a bitter whisper.

Owen stared at him. The Reader was old, but there was still some fight in him, surely. 'You could run . . .'

Reader Aronson shook his head. His face contorted in anger, then he found a determined smile. 'No . . . no. This is the will of the Infinite Gods. Soon I will be with them. There is nowhere left to run.'

'Take off your robes,' Kina pleaded. 'You can disappear.'

Aronson looked down at his purple garb. His gnarled hands lifted the golden loop of The Infinite that hung around his neck. He studied it, then let it fall to his chest again. 'I will not hide. I am a Reader of the Church of the Infinite. I will meet my fate with a smile. We have a plan, you see? And this is just another step, another part of the plan.' His voice faltered, choked with emotion. 'I am sorry. I will leave you to your new family.'

'Where will you go?' Kina asked.

'To meet our visitors.'

Owen held the Reader's arm. 'Stay here.'

'I will not hide.'

'Not to hide, to be amongst friends. To share in our new joy . . . while we can.'

Reader Aronson's eyes fell on the sleeping form of Ealasaid, and the tension eased from his face. 'You honor me.'

Kina smiled as the Reader drew up a chair and took his place at the end of the bed.

Owen held his wife as she caressed their daughter. He listened in silence; the docking alarm ended as a deep vibration rocked through the arkship *Braal Castle*. This was his home, this was the only place he had ever known. Now, all the dreams he had made of their future together, watching their child grow, were in tatters.

For a while the hospital was silent. The alarms had died, the rumble of battle ended. There was just the pathetic sound of distant tears echoing along the corridor. The attack had been swift and efficient. After the fall of the other Sinclair arkships, the Earl must have known better than to put up much of a fight. At least this way most of them might live, Owen supposed.

He flinched at the sound of gunfire coming their way.

'We have to hide,' Kina pleaded, trying to climb out of bed.

The Reader stood, resting his hand on her shoulder. 'Offer no resistance. You and your child will be safe. They will not harm you.'

'How can you be sure?'

'It is their way: spare the women and children,'

Reader Aronson replied wearily. He glanced over to Owen. 'At least they no longer execute the men. They need healthy bodies, people willing to work.'

'I'll fight them,' Owen said defiantly.

Reader Aronson shook his head, a far-away look in his eyes. 'No, son, you will not. You are a father now. Your family comes first.'

'But we are Sinclair!'

'The House of Sinclair just died!' he barked. He let his anger fade, then added, 'Can't you see? You have no house to fight for any more. That was the old life. Now, the world has turned, and a new life awaits you and your family. I am sorry, but that is the way of things.' Reader Aronson straightened, inhaling sharply. 'Now, I must prepare. It will not be long.'

A high-pitched whine approached, and Owen spotted a number of tiny drones as they buzzed past the door. One of the devices stopped at the opening and scanned the room. First it focused on the walls and geometry of the space, then it locked on to the people, tracking each in turn with its numerous sensors. Finally, it focused on the Reader, paying close attention to him, then it retreated from the room, making a series of quiet beeps.

'They know I am here. They will be coming,' Reader Aronson said.

Kina's eyes pleaded with her husband. 'What should we do?'

Owen hesitated, hearing the noise of voices coming along the corridor. He looked to the door and saw soldiers dressed in black marching through the hospital. One entered the space, a gun outstretched in front of him, then a second and a third appeared. Soon the little room was filled with soldiers, weapons ready.

'We have him here,' one of the soldiers said into his com. 'Standing by.'

Footsteps echoed through the space, getting louder, getting closer. The soldiers stiffened, stepping aside so that the approaching figure could be seen in the doorway. He was a young man, probably in his early twenties, Owen guessed. His face was lean, pale skin taut over chiseled cheeks, dark hair making lines away from his face. His mouth was tense, as if he was carved from rock, but his eyes seemed to shift quickly, their movements hidden by rapid blinks. He wore a high-collared coat that covered his body down to his booted calves. The material was the color of blood, but a fine embroidered pattern covered the garment, reminding Owen of exposed veins. The polished buttons caught the hard light of the room, throwing off tight mirror-like reflections of the frozen scene. The man removed his gloves and handed them to one of the soldiers. A nebulous smile broke his frozen expression as he stepped towards the Reader.

'You know me?' the man asked. His voice was soft, almost soothing.

'Yes.'

'Then you know I am protected.' He tapped the side of his head, the movement sharp and aggressive.

'I am no threat to you.'

'No, you are not.'

He turned to look at Owen and Kina. Finally, he saw the sleeping baby.

'Congratulations,' he said. 'Girl or boy?'

Owen hesitated.

'It is not a difficult question,' the man said with a grin.

'A . . . a girl.' Owen replied.

'Wonderful. You must have a name. I presume that is why the Reader is here.'

Owen tensed.

The man insisted. 'Her name.'

'Ealasaid.'

'Owen, don't . . .' Kina whispered.

The stranger laughed. 'I had heard you Sinclair's were a hospitable bunch. Is this how you treat guests? After all, I am your friend.' He looked again to the sleeping child. 'May I hold her?'

Kina tensed, tears falling from her face. 'No, I won't let you.'

Reader Aronson stepped towards the man. 'Your quarrel is not with them.'

Immediately the soldiers held the Reader, forcing him to his knees.

The stranger smiled, waiting as Kina sobbed. 'I just want to hold her.'

Kina shook her head, trying to control her terrified sobs.

At a glance from their leader the soldiers trained their weapons on Kina and the baby.

Owen felt hands on his shoulders even before he could react.

'Please,' the man soothed, 'I am asking nicely, am I not?'

He stepped closer, watching, waiting. All the while tiny red dots danced over Owen's beautiful child.

'Give her to him,' Owen said to Kina.

At first Kina resisted, but with a heartfelt sob, she released her newborn.

The man took the child in his arms, gazing down with serene happiness on his face. 'She really is quite beautiful, isn't she? You must be very proud. I have no child of my own, not yet.' He looked into Owen's eyes. 'I envy you, Sir.'

'Please, don't hurt her,' Kina muttered.

'A happy day,' the man continued. 'A glorious day! Your daughter has been born into a new age, where she will want for nothing. She has been freed from a life of mediocrity. I welcome her – I welcome you all! – into the House of Draig.'

Startled by the raised voice, Ealasaid awoke and began to cry.

'She'll be a fighter,' he laughed as he handed the baby back to the protection of her mother.

The man turned swiftly to face the Reader. 'You're right, I have no quarrel with these good people. I am their leader now, their beloved Valtais, Orcades Draig of the House of Draig. They are under my protection now. As for you, Reader . . . what is your name?'

'Reader Viktor Aronson.'

'Well, as for you, Reader Aronson, there is no place for you or your religion in my House. I do not offer you my protection. You will not receive my love.'

'I do not seek it.'

Orcades leaned close to his ear. 'All I have to offer you is my sword.'

In a single swift movement, he threw back his coat, drew his blade and thrust it into the Reader's chest.

Owen cried out in shock as the tip of the weapon protruded from the Reader's back.

Reader Aronson's body became still, held up by Orcades' blade, then he let the weapon fall, and the old man's lifeless body dropped to the floor. His open eyes caught Owen's, unflinching as blood pooled around the Reader, soaking into his robes.

Ealasaid's cries grew louder, an inconsolable wail that filled the room.

Orcades Draig squatted beside the body, watching as it made tiny involuntary movements. He put his hand to the staring eyes and closed them. Satisfied, he stood, smiling at Kina and Owen. 'Welcome to the House of Draig.'

Keep reading Arkship Vengeance
Order the next book in the Arkship Saga now!

36636085R00218

Printed in Poland
by Amazon Fulfillment
Poland Sp. z o.o., Wrocław